Praise for Bare-Naked Lola...

Bare-Naked Lola

A LOLA CRUZ MYSTERY

Bare-Naked Lola

A LOLA CRUZ MYSTERY

Melissa Bourbon Ramirez

Entangled Publishing, LLC
2614 South Timberline Road
Suite 109
Fort Collins, CO 80525
Visit our website at www.entangledpublishing.com.

Edited by Libby Murphy
Cover design by Heather Howland

Ebook ISBN   978-1-62061-005-3
Print ISBN   978-1-62061-004-6

Manufactured in the United States of America

First Edition May 2012

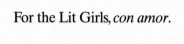

For the Lit Girls, *con amor*.

Chapter One

Abundantly flowing locks, perfectly tanned bodies, and perky breasts with enticingly rounded cleavage—these were not the things I'd expected to see walking into the Camacho & Associates private investigation office on a Wednesday morning. *Pero, Dios mío*, that's exactly what I *did* see. Two women lounging at the conference table, each exhibiting their own take on "aloof," stopped me dead with their blinding beauty. I was afraid I'd be scarred for life.

I could hate them on the spot, except, super-detective that I am, I knew they had to be clients. And clients meant that I remained employed as a detective. Hating them for their otherworldly beauty? Not allowed.

Manny Camacho, owner of the small investigative firm in Sacramento, ex-cop, and super-P.I., stood in the doorway of his office quietly talking with yet another attractive woman. It might as well have been the Miss America pageant—there was no escaping them. This one was older than the others by a good fifteen years or so, but she had the body of a twenty-year-old. She had a long neck, nary a wrinkle in sight, and a tall, gazellelike body. Her hair shone like black velvet and was pulled back into a severe bun. Her angular face and chiseled cheekbones intensified her exotic appearance.

Dancer. Had to be.

Reilly Fuller, part-time clerk for the agency, scowled from her desk.

"*¿Qué pasó?*" I asked, stopping to get the 4-1-1.

Her Spanish was limited—and often amounted to adding a strategic *O* to the end of a word—but she understood me and liked to use what she knew.

"*No se*," she said, sounding very disgruntled that she didn't know anything.

Reilly made a strangled noise that left me wondering if all the colorful dye she used on her hair had finally done some deeper damage, perhaps affecting her vocal cords. Reilly *lived* for gossip, though at the moment she was oddly silent.

I heard the *zip-zip* of the surveillance camera bracketed to the wall in the top corner of the room. Ah, so that was the source of Reilly's grief. Neil, a caveman detective who could scarcely string words together in a sentence, but who was a master of technology—and Reilly's bed buddy—was in his lair watching the Barbie show.

"Remember our motto," I said, patting my thigh and speaking softly so only she could hear. "More to love."

She blinked heavily and patted down her green color-washed hair. "Right. More to love, and Neil does love this," she said, doing a subtle chair shimmy. I swallowed my laugh. Reilly was a JLO wannabe—only not Latina, *pero* more full-figured, and monolingual.

But otherwise, hey, they were like twins.

I noticed Sadie, fellow detective and my own personal nemesis, fidgeting uncomfortably at the table, client intake form clasped in a brown folder in front of her. Her spiky, red-tipped blond hair seemed to inch up every time one of the two women at the table moved the slightest muscle.

I'd recently surmised that Sadie and Manny had an on-again/off-again thing that defied explanation. Sadie wasn't the lovable type. Neither was Manny, for that matter. He was tall and dark; she was petite and fair. He was bitter coffee and clipped sentences; she was Spicy Hot V8 with attitude and too much lime. He was *un poquito* intense and brooding, and she was, well, a shrew. What kept bringing them back together was a mystery to me, but some things were just better left unsolved.

From my vantage point at Reilly's desk, I took a closer gander at the two women at the table. They seemed familiar somehow. I searched the recesses of my brain for answers. Were they in a breast-enhancement ad? Poster girls for plastic surgery? As much as I wanted to pull the information out of my mind, I couldn't quite manage it.

Manny walked to the table, his barely perceptible limp altering his gait just enough to make a girl curious about what had caused it. I was plenty curious, but I had no idea. War wound from his time on the police force was my guess. His gaze caught mine. "Dolores."

He flicked his cleft chin toward the table and I threw up my hand in an all-encompassing greeting. "Hello."

It was my afternoon to man the agency so the other detectives—Manny, Sadie, and Neil—could be in the field.

We rotated, though with my junior detective status, the ink on my California private investigator's license barely dry, I usually pulled bonus shifts for more pay. My docket wasn't as full as any of the three senior associates, though after my recent successes in solving several local crimes I was hoping *that* would change. I'd worked my behind off. Time to reap the benefits.

The exotic gazelle girl whispered into Manny's ear. His arms were crossed over his chest and his biceps bulged under his black T-shirt. There was something peculiar about the way he was acting. He was almost, er, pleasantly attentive. Very unlike him. He subscribed to the same school of communication Neil Lashby did: cut to the chase. *Punto.*

"Dolores," he barked.

I jumped. Busted for staring. Damn, not a good P.I. move. "Yes?"

He crooked a finger. *"Ven aquí."*

Apparently his pleasant attentiveness didn't extend to me. His words hadn't sounded like a friendly "come here." I ran through all the things Manny could have a beef with me about. My outfit topped the list. October usually had decent weather, but Sacramento was in the midst of an Indian summer and the air was heavy with uncommon humidity. I'd caught a glimpse of my reflection in the glass as I'd entered the agency: my salmon-colored blouse clung to me like plastic wrap. In the right situation—say in the privacy of Jack Callaghan's bedroom—this could be a good thing. At work? Not so much.

But I held my chin high and walked over to Manny and the gazelle. "Yes?"

"Turn around."

"*¿Cómo?*" My astonishment at the order pinballed through my mind and I slipped out of my dominant English and into my native Spanish.

"*Por favor*," he added as an afterthought. Speaking Spanish and being detectives were probably the only two things Manny and I had in common. He was my mentor and damn good at his job. I worked hard to impress him and still stay true to myself—not always easy, since I was Dolores Cruz to him (and to *mi familia*), but Lola Cruz to my friends. In my mind, I was a combination, but I didn't think anyone really knew both sides of me.

Except maybe Jack Callaghan. He'd gotten a few glimpses of both Dolores and Lola. And he seemed to like them both.

"It's about our new case," he said. "Turn around."

I heard the faint *zip* of the surveillance camera and I knew my Neanderthal coworker wasn't missing a single beat from the lair, his personal high-tech office, just waiting to see what I'd do. A solid but basic roundhouse kick, perhaps? Or maybe I'd go airborne kicking both legs, one at a time, with a double whammy. Not a bad idea. I weighed my options, in case it came to that. Which it just might.

In the end, I did neither. If it was for a case, I could only assume Manny had a reason for wanting to check out my backside. I just wasn't convinced it was a *good* reason. My black capris were probably just as clingy as my blouse, but I couldn't help that and I was not going to let sticky skin stop me from doing my job. Sucking in a bolstering breath and straightening my spine, I turned around in a slow circle, hands on hips. I turned to Manny and the gazelle again and waited. She was so familiar, but where did I know her from?

Her back was as straight as a two-by-four. She had one arm across her chest, the other bent at the elbow, her fingers tapping her puckered lips. "Good bones. Nice shape. Could be taller, but I guess she'll do," she finally said, dropping both arms to her sides.

What was I, a horse?

"Don't you want to check my teeth?" I asked as Sadie snickered and the Stepford women at the table shifted positions and eyeballed me.

The gazelle didn't crack a smile, and neither did Manny. Instead, he gestured with his hand. "Dolores Cruz, meet our new client, Victoria Wolfe."

I grudgingly held out my hand. Victoria shook it with a firm but bony grip. "Pleasure," she said just as a man materialized from inside Manny's office.

"She'll more than do," he said.

Sadie's snicker turned into a disbelieving gasp.

"*Con permiso*," I said under my breath. "What, exactly, are you talking about?" But then realization hit me and I gasped. Him, I recognized. Lance Wolfe, owner of the Courtside Dancers, Sacramento's answer to the Laker Girls. Now I knew where I recognized Victoria from! She and Lance, along with the Courtside Dancers, cheerleaders for the Sacramento Royals basketball team, had done a reality TV show: *Living the Royal Life*. Their high-profile effort to combat the drug, sex, and steroid scandals that had plagued the basketball team for a few years. They were local celebrities, probably recognized everywhere they went. I hadn't been a fan, but my cousin Chely had never missed an episode.

Victoria's face had hardened when the man stepped out

of the shadows. Now she gave me another once-over. "Yes, she'll more than do. You were right," she said to Manny. "She's curvy but athletic. Fit."

That's how Manny had described me? Oh no. The heat of embarrassment crept up my neck.

"She definitely has presence," Victoria continued. "How about energy?"

"I can answer that," Lance said. He sounded calm, and to look at him, you'd think he was Mr. Businessman, all buttoned-up in his periwinkle blue shirt with thin white stripes, his brown hair brushed to the right and neatly gelled into place. But I knew from local sports lore that he was a hothead on the court. He walked around me like he had his detective radar out and was gauging my effectiveness. "She's got it in spades. If anyone can get to the bottom of this stupid mess, it's this girl."

Manny's eyes bored into me. "I agree. She's got it."

¡Híjole! That was as close to a compliment as Manny ever came. I had *it*, whatever *it* was. But really, it didn't matter as long as I had active cases to investigate.

I waved a hand in front of them. Despite the praise, they still had *huevos*, talking about me as if I were the lone artificial plant in Camacho's lobby entrance. "Excuse me," I said again. "What am I perfect for?" I asked, although knowing that Lance Wolfe was involved could only mean one thing.

"Do you dance?" Victoria was clearly used to being in charge, asking her own questions rather than answering someone else's.

"If she doesn't," Lance said, "she can learn."

"She can't learn to dance in a day," Victoria snapped.

"No, she has to be able to dance or it won't work."

Her husband threw up his hands. "Fine," he said, then turned to me. "Well?"

What he didn't say was that I better not disappoint him.

I twined two of my fingers together. "Me and salsa dancing, we're like this." Throw some Juanes on the iPod and I'd dance circles around Victoria, the twig. "And I can do a mean *merengue*."

Victoria clapped three times, *muy rapido*. "Jennifer. Selma."

They rose in unison like perfect specimen robots.

Victoria directed, telling the women where to stand. "Do the beginning of the new routine," she ordered. Jennifer, a tall, languid beauty, glided, while Selma, who was a bit shorter and seemed more eager to please, hurried into position. Once Jennifer was ready, Victoria clapped and counted. "And one, and two, and three, and four…"

The two women launched into a professional cheerleading routine, stepping wide with their legs, dipping their torsos, moving their arms in exact rhythm. *¡Ay, caramba!* They were like sex puppets tied together with invisible string.

After a series of risque moves, they stopped abruptly, both ending with their right feet extended, toes arched and knees bent in a hip jazz dance stance.

Victoria rolled her hand at me. "Okay, your turn."

¿Está loca? Where was the salsa music? Where were Ricky Martin and Menudo? *¡Ay, ay, ay!*

Sadie inhaled sharply, then broke into a coughing spasm. *Pobracita*. She'd swallowed her laughter and now had thrown herself into a tizzy.

I knew exactly what she was feeling, but I glared at her

for a beat before turning my stare to Victoria. "You want *me* to do *that*?"

Manny took a step forward. "Dolores," he said, pronouncing my name with a perfect Spanish accent. *Do-LOR-es.* It echoed in my mind. I was smart. Educated. A licensed P.I. Did he understand what he was asking me to do?

From his steady gaze, it was clear that he did. I shook my insecurities away—after all, I'd solved two murder cases in the recent past; surely I could pull off a few dance moves—and mimicked the jazz pose Jennifer and Selma Stepford had ended with. So what if I had to pretend to be a dancing sexpot? It was for a good cause. I hoped.

Victoria was a client, and this was a case I was potentially going to be working. *If*—and it seemed like a pretty big if to me—I could pull this off.

I got in line with the two cheerleaders, watched carefully, and copied their every move, exaggerating my steps like they did, spinning around, and feeling utterly ridiculous and on display. Dance lessons had not been part of my childhood, and as a teenager, I'd taken up kung fu. While other girls my age had been spinning in pirouettes or planning for prom, I'd been stalking Jack Callaghan and learning the Eighteen Arms of Wushu, determined to master each and every one of the main weapons in Chinese martial arts.

I was still working through them.

The mini routine ended in the same extended-toe, bent-knee position, and I tried to recapture my breath while I held the pose. Damn. Wielding a chain whip and a battle-ax was easier.

Lance lowered his chin in approval and Victoria clapped her hands three times, good hard claps that seemed incapable of coming from her petite body. "Bravo. You did fine," she said, but her lips pursed together. Except for her furtive glances at Manny, I got the impression she didn't really want to be here.

"Thanks. Now, can you please tell me what this is about?" I filled a paper cup with water from the cooler, downed it, refilled it, and waited.

This time Lance spoke up. His voice boomed, taking on the tenor of a game show announcer. "How would *you* like to be a Courtside Dancer for the Sacramento Royals?"

I choked on the water I'd just sipped, coughing my way back to life as I peered at the women standing next to me, then at the camera in the corner. A thought ricocheted throughout my brain. Was it Neil watching from the lair? Was I secretly being taped for a reprise of *Living the Royal Life*? Or maybe I was being hazed. Maybe this wasn't about a case at all.

Except Manny wasn't fraternity material and practical jokes weren't his style. No, this had to be real.

Despite being "perfect" and getting a "bravo" from Victoria on my routine, I suddenly felt frumpy and ten pounds overweight. The size eight—occasionally size ten— hips that were so fantastic this morning when I pulled on my pants now felt *way* too curvy.

I poked a finger in my ear, wiggling it around, glancing at Reilly. Was she as shocked by this dog and pony show as I was?

She was riveted, like she was watching a *telenova* in living color. I bet she'd loved *Living the Royal Life*. Sadie, on the other hand, studied her fingernails, although I could practically see the steam billowing from her ears. She was not so entranced by the celebrity in the room.

I sputtered. "I'm sorry, did you say a Courtside Dancer? So this *is* an undercover assignment?"

"That's right," Victoria said. "My husband has just hired this agency"—she paused and laid a delicate hand on Manny's arm—"and you going undercover was your boss's idea, actually. Which means you'll have to train as one of our dancers. It's every girl's dream," she added, as if that was supposed to mean it should be my dream, too, and I should suddenly feel like Cinderella.

I bit back telling her that my dream had always been to be a private investigator, brought home by the undercover surveillance I'd done of one Jack Callaghan and Greta Pritchard doing the mamba in his car when we'd been teenagers. I'd always wanted Jack to do that with me. It hadn't happened yet, but when it did...*ooh-la-la*.

Cheerleading? Not even close to one of my dreams.

When I want something, I get it. When I need something, I get it. I'm a doer, not a cheerer of other doers.

"I'm sorry. What did you say your name was?" Since we hadn't actually been introduced. The two women glided back to their chairs and I fought the vertigo that settled over me. I'd become Alice in Wonderland and this was the rabbit hole.

"Victoria Wolfe," she purred. "Director of the Courtside Dancers."

The man stepped forward, right hand extended. "And I'm Lance Wolfe. Victoria's husband and"—he paused, then continued with emphasis—"co-owner of the Royals."

The smile that had been lacing Manny's lips vanished. Because he hadn't known the woman he was flirting with was married—and that Lance was her husband? Certainly not. Manny was too smart not to have known that. Because Victoria had removed her hand from his arm? Or because Lance held on to mine, clasping it so that he had me in a hand lock?

Hard to say, but the fact was that Victoria and Lance *were* married and she'd been making a subtle move on Macho Camacho. *¡Ay, dios!,* She was brazen, a *puta,* as my mother would say. Judging from his grip on my hands, Lance was a player, too.

They seemed perfect for each other. Manny needed to steer clear.

"This is Jennifer, and that's Selma. They're two of our dancers," Lance continued, waving toward the women grinning engagingly at Manny.

I pulled my hand free as the women acknowledged me. Did they speak? Or formulate thoughts of their own?

I sank down onto a chair. The intake form in front of Sadie had her scratchy writing all over it but I couldn't read it upside down. Sadie's nostrils flared and her fingers curved into claws. She was about a second away from blowing a gasket.

"So why do you need someone undercover?" I asked.

Victoria sat at the head of the conference table—in Manny's usual spot. The whir of the surveillance camera told me Neil had noticed that intrusion. Reilly's quiet gasp told me she'd noticed, too. Sadie started and raised her lip like a tiger on the prowl, nostrils flaring, ready to pounce to protect her territory. Which, in this case, was Manny. I waited for her typical caustic remark, but it didn't come. Another shock.

Manny stood back, arms crossed over his muscled chest,

rocking back on his alligator skin cowboy boots, the lines of his jaw hard and set. He watched Victoria and Lance with sudden intensity, like he was trying to figure them out, but he let her remain in his chair. *Híjole*. This day was going to be off the Richter scale.

"One of our dancers suddenly left us. Just quit the squad without a word. No notice, no nothing," Victoria began. "The ladies here"—she gestured toward the dancers—"have all received mysterious, somewhat threatening letters." She pushed a small stack of envelopes toward me. "The girls think Rochelle leaving and the letters are related. They came to me—"

Lance cleared his throat again.

"—to *us*," Victoria added. "We've tried to find out who's behind them, but—"

"No luck," Lance interrupted. "So I said we needed to hire someone to stop whoever's messing with our girls. Their work is starting to suffer."

"Okay," I said, as if I understood what he meant, but all I could come up with was that the dancers' feet were tangling during a grapevine or they were dropping their pompoms mid-cheer.

Victoria grimaced.

I was an expert at reading facial expressions. Twenty-nine years living with Magdalena Falcón Cruz had its perks. "You'd rather handle it yourself?" I asked her.

"Of course. The girls are a tight group. These letters have rattled them, understandably, but my job is to keep them focused on *their* job. An outsider poking around is going to mean disruption—"

"But we can't afford to lose another girl," Lance said.

So I knew why they hadn't called the police. I had a bit of experience with the local police department in my previous cases. An image of Detective Seavers—not my biggest fan—and his comb-over popped into my head. Him lumbering around a bunch of nubile cheerleaders at a basketball game would be *muy* disruptive.

"The letters are anonymous," Victoria continued. She brushed a hand over her taut hair before continuing. "Jennifer and Selma have each received one. No one seems to know who's writing them or what they're about."

She shifted in her chair, stretching her long neck to gaze up at Manny. He met her eyes, tilting his head slightly. I watched in utter amazement as his expression seemed to soften almost imperceptibly. Victoria was striking, in a scary dancer kind of way, and I'd bet a year's worth of lunches at Szechwan House, my all-time favorite restaurant (sacrilege if my family ever found that out, considering they owned Abuelita's), that Manny was wishing she wasn't married.

But as far as I knew, right now he was dating Tomb Raider Girl, aka Isabel. Surely he wouldn't dump his model girlfriend for a married woman? Or maybe her marriage didn't matter. I didn't actually know what direction Manny's moral compass pointed to on adultery.

I'd always thought he'd keep business and pleasure separate, but then again, I knew something had gone on between him and Sadie. I just didn't know what.

I slouched in my chair, feeling like I was slipping farther down the rabbit hole, but then the attack from Sadie finally came, setting everything right again. "I'm the undercover expert," she said, nearly spitting her words across the table. "If Dolores isn't up for the assignment, I can certainly take it."

The surveillance camera *zipped*, as if in laughter, and I knew Neil had caught the double entendre. He knew something had gone on between the boss and Sadie, too. He probably knew what, for that matter.

Victoria frowned. "The Courtside Dancers have a certain, er, image. No." The force of her shaking head threatened to undo her bun. "You're not right for the team."

Sadie balked, but then she started to get up. "I can do the routine."

"No." My voice was firm. I might not want to be ogled by sports fans or dance in an arena, but there was no way Sadie was taking an assignment from me. "It's my case."

I doubted anyone else noticed, but she shot daggers at me, which I boldly dodged with imaginary shields. She could thank me later when she realized how I'd saved her from her own desperate humiliation.

Victoria's lips curved up like the cat that swallowed the canary, only it felt like I was the canary. She motioned toward me but spoke to Manny. "She needs coaching."

I cringed, indignant. Sure, I may waffle between size 8 and 10, but I was in prime physical shape. A black belt in kung fu. A yogi wannabe. A salsa fanatic.

"She'll do whatever it takes," Sadie said, her voice dripping with disdain.

So apparently she didn't like my boundary lines. Which was ridiculous, since I didn't even know what my boundaries were and I hadn't done anything during my career, so far, that I regretted.

"What do the letters say?" I asked, getting back to the case. I reached inside my purse for my handy latex gloves, but Manny had his on before I'd even found mine. Super detective. He was my role model.

He snapped the latex at the wrists before picking up the first envelope. He carefully pulled out the paper inside, flipped it open, and examined it. It was thin and I could see it only contained two typed lines.

"They're all the same?" Manny asked as he slid the letter over to me.

"Not identical, but all similar," Victoria said.

With my gloves on, I picked up the letter and silently read: "*I know what you're doing. Stop while you still can.*"

"Stop what?" I asked.

Silencio.

Sadie turned to the dancers. "*None* of you knows what it's about? Not even an inkling of an idea?"

The women shook their heads in unison.

"No idea," Jennifer finally said.

Ha! So one of them could speak!

If I were going undercover, I might as well take the lead in the investigation right now. Show Sadie what I was made of. I'd spent the last couple of years proving myself worthy of being a lead detective. Now I felt like puffing out my chest, preening. I was beginning to really walk the walk.

"When did the letters start?" I asked Jennifer and Selma.

Selma threw back her slim shoulders, but her voice was soft and tentative. "I got the first one about two weeks ago, but Jennifer got one before that—"

"They started about three weeks ago," Victoria interrupted. "Rochelle was the first." She darted a glance at her dancers. "She was seeing one of the players."

Muy interesante. "And you think it's related?"

Selma pulled at the neckline of her tank top, shifting

in her chair. "The letters keep coming, so it can't be about Rochelle and Michael."

Lance shook his head, disgusted. "*Everyone* knows about them?" he said to Victoria with a hiss.

Más silencio.

Jennifer and Selma shot a quick glance at each other before dropping their gazes.

Victoria leveled her steely eyes at her husband. "Yes, Lance, everyone knows. Even Michael's wife. There are no secrets with the team."

I reached across the table, laid a flattened hand on the file folder Sadie had been guarding, and drew it toward me. "You're Jennifer—?"

"Wallace," the tall blonde said. "I'm the team captain."

I wrote this down on a blank sheet of paper inside the folder.

Victoria cleared her throat, taking over. "The letters have been arriving at every home game, like I said. Jen's received three. Selma one. Carrie, another dancer, received two letters. Some of the rest of the girls have gotten one."

I jotted this down, shifting my attention from Victoria to Lance to Jennifer to Selma. "So you want us to find out who's writing the notes—"

"That's why we're here," Lance said, coming to stand behind Victoria.

"—and what happened to Rochelle?" I finished.

"Rochelle is gone. I don't want her back." Victoria shook her head, and I could almost picture her stomping her foot with finality. "You don't shirk your responsibilities. You don't quit a team that depends on you. You don't break the rules. No, Rochelle is out."

"It's not like she's the only one," Selma muttered under her breath. I made a mental note to ask her about that at some point.

"Just find out who's sending the letters and why," Lance said. "And stop them. That's it."

I knew my mission, but my nerves were on high alert in the pit of my stomach. Every eye was on me. This was my first undercover case. I couldn't blow it. I quickly opened the other plain white envelopes and found Victoria had been correct. They were all basically the same. Typed and printed on ordinary printer paper. There was no blackmail attempt in any of them.

So if blackmail wasn't the letter writer's motive, what was? The most obvious conclusion I could draw was that it was some unbalanced person who wasn't targeting anyone in particular. Unless Rochelle and her affair had been the main target and the rest of the letters were just a distraction. But then why hadn't they stopped since Rochelle was gone?

"Have the letters been read by all of you?" Manny asked Jennifer and Selma, snapping off his gloves.

"Passed around," Jennifer said. "They've had us pretty freaked."

His lips drew into a thin line. A thousand fingerprints had already contaminated the evidence. There'd be no discovery there, even if we did alert the police. Which, considering no crime had been committed—that we knew of—seemed premature, and against our client's wishes.

"Next time one of you gets a letter," Manny said, "try not to touch it. Getting decent prints could help."

They nodded in perfect Stepford unison. No more muttering under their breath. No more thinking the letters didn't mean anything. Maybe they didn't, but until we proved that, it was better to assume that they did.

"When do I start?" I asked, getting back to business. Going undercover was expected as a detective. And I was down with it. So far I hadn't come across anything I wasn't willing to do, even being a Courtside Dancer. Beautiful people didn't scare me and I had a job to do. So what if, at five-foot-six and three-quarters, I was a couple of inches shorter than the women here before me? So what if, as a dark-haired Latina (with a nice shock of highlighted hair framing her face), I stuck out like a thorny cactus in a field of wildflowers?

So what?

Híjole. Nerves rattled my gut. I sure hoped I'd be able to pull it off.

A thread of silent communication passed between Victoria and Lance. After however many years of marriage, I guess you could read your partner's mind. Jack and I had been seeing each other for a few months now—give or take twelve years or so. But the time in high school—and all the years he'd spent in San Luis Obispo with Sarah, his ex— meant we didn't have that kind of connection. I envied them.

Victoria broke her gaze away from Lance and sighed, deep and put-upon. "You'll come to practice this afternoon." She glanced at her watch. "One-thirty. We have a game Friday night. I'll work with you until you're ready, if it takes a twenty-four-seven schedule."

I pressed my hands flat on the table and clamped my teeth down on the inside of my cheek. "*This* Friday?" I choked out. *¡Ay, caramba!* There was no way I could be ready to perform in front of a huge crowd in a few days' time. Which meant that my public humiliation on Friday would be seen far and wide. Damn. Maybe I should have considered letting Sadie take the case, after all. Sexy and curvy were overrated. I mean, I had to work double hard to be taken seriously in a male-heavy profession. After Friday, would Manny or Neil be able to look at me the same, or would they always see a cheerleader?

I wasn't sure I actually wanted to know the answer to that.

Victoria seemed to zero in on my doubt. She threw up her hands and turned back to Lance. "See? She can't do it."

Manny stiffened. "Yes, she can," he said as I forced a smile and replied, "I'll be there."

I could do this. I'd imagine I was salsa dancing. Only without Jack Callaghan as my partner, and without salsa music. And on the sidelines of a basketball court with zillions of people watching. But otherwise, it would be practically the same thing.

"I'll make sure you're ready. I'm never wrong about people."

"Mrs. Wolfe." I stood to face her as she rose. "There is one problem. If I'm going undercover, none of the other dancers can know who I am or why I'm there. How are you going to explain a new person on the team? I didn't go through tryouts. The season's well under way." Not to mention the fact that I'd grown up in Sacramento, often worked at my family's *muy* popular Mexican restaurant, and had been on the news recently thanks to a stolen-identity case where I was the victim. I wasn't a local celebrity, but I was familiar to some people.

She waved her hand. "Not to worry. Rochelle's gone,

remember? You'll take her spot."

Victoria made it sound so simple, but somehow I doubted the dancers would buy it. I sidled up to Jennifer and Selma as they gathered their purses and bags, making my first attempt at camaraderie. No dice. They didn't flash a single pearly white.

Victoria turned to Manny. "You'll be in touch, I assume?"

"*Por supuesto*," he muttered, his lips curving up.

Sadie and I both stared at him. I checked my watch to be sure it was still ticking, then I pinched myself. And grimaced from the pain. Nope, this was not a dream.

I was pretty sure Victoria didn't know he'd said *of course*, but she'd gotten *something* from his tone. She batted her eyes, just once, then glided away after her husband and the dancers.

Manny walked them to the door, the surveillance camera *zipping* along as it recorded their departure. A moment later, Manny sauntered into his office, the almost nonexistent grin still lingering. He closed the door behind him without another glance at me or Sadie.

"*Son locos*," I muttered as Sadie shoved back her chair and marched out. I waved at the boxy camera in the corner. "Did you get all that? Enjoy the entertainment?"

As if in response, the camera *zipped* up and down. Yep, in his lair, Neil was laughing his ass off.

Chapter Two

After spending the next ten minutes writing down information on one of the whiteboards that hung around the conference room, I dubbed the case *Operation: Dance*. I finished by putting the lines of the mysterious letters the dancers had received across the top of the board, then I stood back to think.

Being a detective was like being a scientist. Manny had taught me to come up with a hypothesis and then work to prove or disprove it. Most of the time that was easier said than done. Still, I studied the facts, such as they were.

- *Victoria Wolfe: director of Courtside Dancers*
- *Lance Wolfe: co-owner of the Royals basketball team and married to Victoria*
- *Rochelle Dupre: former dancer; had been having an affair with a player*
- *Selma Mann: current dancer — one letter*
- *Jennifer Wallace: current dancer — two letters*

- Letters began arriving three weeks ago
- Thin and fit is out as a body type; sexy curves are the preferred for Courtside Dancers

I stood back to survey my progress. No great stroke of brilliance surfaced in my mind.

After another minute of perusal, I capped the dry-erase marker and wiped away the last bullet. My curves weren't pertinent to anyone but me. And maybe to Jack Callaghan.

Definitely to Jack Callaghan.

Except that Jack's ex-girlfriend was holed up at his sister Brooke's house and he was helping her—and not nearly as indignant about Brooke helping his ex as he should be. And what were they helping her with, anyway? So Jack had no claim on my hips, boobs, or any other curvature right now.

I'd been as patient as I could be, *pero* enough was enough. If he wanted to see any of my curves again, he had to make some choices. *Muy difícil* choices, *pero* choices. My disastrous relationship with Sergio had early destroyed my faith in love, but Jack—Jack showing up again after so many years of being gone—he had restored it.

My mind drifted back to when Jack had told me the truth about Sarah. I'd solved a case and when the dust had settled, he'd taken me to meet her. We'd sat in his sporty silver Volvo in front of his sister's house.

"You ever see the movie *Fatal Attraction*?" he'd asked me.

I darted my eyes toward him. Did a double-take. "As in Glenn Close psycho rabbit killer *Fatal Attraction*?"

He tapped the tip of his index finger to his nose. "That's the one."

My eyes narrowed. "Yeah, great movie."

If you like demented, obsessed, murderous adultery cinema.

"Remember how Alex—"

I arched a questioning brow.

"—Alex is the character Glenn Close plays," he clarified.

"Oh. Right." Jack had a keen knack for movie trivia, it seemed.

"Remember when Alex spies on Michael Douglas's family?" Jack asked.

"Vaguely," I said, suddenly connecting the acting dots between Michael Douglas and Kevin Bacon. My brother Antonio was the master at the game, but I did pretty well. My mind wandered. Michael Douglas to Glenn Close. Hadn't she been in some pseudo-romance movie with Christopher Walken? I was positive she had been. I couldn't name the movie, but I went to see Christopher anyway.

I kept at it. Self-preservation, I think. It was better than facing whatever Jack was trying to tell me about his ex.

Jack took my hand and gave it a squeeze. He was saying something about Glenn Close and a gleam she had in her eyes, but I was trying to connect the dots between Christopher Walken and Kevin Bacon.

Until I realized he'd stopped talking. And was watching me.

"Six degrees to Kevin Bacon," I explained, feeling a bit sheepish at being such a chicken.

"Ahh," he said, as if playing the game in my mind was a perfectly normal thing to do. "Starting with whom?"

"Michael Douglas."

"And you got to—"

"Glenn Close, then Christopher Walken."

He tapped one finger against the steering wheel, thinking. "Yep, that'll work. Walken was in *True Romance*. It's an early Tarantino flick," he explained when I raised my eyebrows. "It's sort of a classic. Brad Pitt was in it."

He was?

"And Pitt was in—"

"Brad Pitt was in *Sleepers*!" I said, feeling like I was the big winner on *Who Wants to be a Millionaire?*.

"…with Kevin Bacon," Jack finished.

We high fived, and then I suddenly registered what Jack had been saying before I got sidetracked. I turned to him. "Glenn Close had a gleam in her eyes?"

Bless his heart, Jack caught right back up to speed. "She did."

"And?"

"And…" He hesitated, gripping the steering wheel of the parked car before turning to me again. "Lola, I've seen that in Sarah's eyes."

I stared at him, shoving my hair out of my face. *¡Dios mío!* "Seriously? You're comparing your ex-girlfriend to a murderer?"

"Crazy, huh?"

"The idea, or Sarah?" I said, completely backtracking on my plan to introduce myself to the woman and tell her to back the hell off. Kung fu wouldn't do squat against crazy.

But then I had a flashback of Jack knocking on Sergio's door, coming to my rescue then—even though I hadn't needed it. I was Xena: Warrior Princess, not a damsel in distress. But he'd come, risking his life for me. Now it was my turn to face Sarah.

"Don't worry," I said. "I don't have any rabbits."

He laughed. "Well, that's a relief."

"It is, actually." I was dead serious. "If I *had* a rabbit, and Sarah was off her meds and got all *loca* on said rabbit, I'd have to open a can of whoop-ass on her."

His right eyebrow quirked up. "Whoop-ass, eh?"

"That's right. No holding back. Mess with my rabbit" — or with my Jack — "and you'll pay." As it was, I was pretty ticked at Brooke for harboring Sarah. I knew she wasn't really on my side, but was she against me? "That's how I roll."

He barely managed to hold in his laughter as he said, "You harbor cans of whoop-ass. That's good to know. I might borrow some. I'm going to have a chat with Brooke after—"

"After Sarah's gone home?"

His lips thinned. "Right."

I threw open the car door. No more stalling. "You can have all the whoop-ass you want," I said, marching up the walkway to Brooke's front door.

He got out of the Volvo, slammed the driver's door, and raced after me. I turned and waited. Even in the dark, I could see that his blue eyes had turned smoky gray. I wasn't sure if he believed everything could really work out for us. If you counted the years since high school, and the interruptions thanks to Sarah, time was not on our side.

Just as we stepped onto the stoop, the front door was flung open. I stumbled backward a step, registering the radiant face of a gorgeous blond-haired woman as I regained my balance. *Híjole! This* was Sarah? She was a living, breathing, walking Barbie.

She, with her flawless skin and perfect 36-24-36 proportions, would have been a perfect fit on the Courtside Dancers.

She gazed at Jack, grinning from ear to ear. Then, as she slowly registered that someone was standing next to him, her body tensed. She moved her gaze to me.

"Sarah," Jack said cautiously, barely masking the anger I sensed brewing under the surface. It was as if he were trying to calm a feral cat. Or a rabid dog. He slipped his arm around my shoulder. "I want you to meet someone."

Her expression turned wary, but I put out my hand and she reluctantly gripped it.

"Hi, Sarah," I said. The annoying cheerleader voice that surfaced when I was nervous came out in force. "My name is Lola. Lola Cruz." I felt like James Bond. I wondered if she could make me a martini—shaken, not stirred.

"Lola," she repeated in a dazed voice.

"Right. I'm a friend of Jack's." A *good* friend. As if he'd heard my thoughts and was offering reassurance, Jack squeezed my shoulder. "It's a—" I hesitated, but forced myself to continue. "It's a pleasure to meet you."

The Glenn Close craziness Jack had described a few minutes ago passed over her face and her grip on my hand tightened.

"Um, Sarah?" I said, pulling back, trying to pry my hand free.

She held tight.

Jack wrapped one hand around her wrist and the other around mine. "Babe," he said.

Sarah and I both turned to him. "Yes?" she said, at the same time I said, "Hmmm?"

The faint indentation of his Adam's apple slid in his

throat as he swallowed. So *she* was babe. My heart pounded. I was ready to take this girl down. And maybe him, too.

"Sarah." Jack spoke with clear intention this time, his voice calm but strained. "Babe, let go of Lola's hand."

I yanked, and at the same time, she released her death hold on me. Jack had said he could calm Sarah down when nobody else could. Had I just witnessed him in action? Was that all it took? A strategic "babe" and a placating voice?

"Jack's told me a lot about you," I said, but I was thinking that he hadn't told me nearly enough. He hadn't said a word about how gorgeous she was. And he'd seriously downplayed the *locura*.

"Yeah." Her beauty turned menacing as she snarled. "He's mentioned you, too. Lola this and Lola that. But I thought he said you were dead."

I tried to ignore the chill that swept up my spine. She sounded decidedly disappointed that I wasn't six feet under.

"I thought she *was* dead," Jack said, "but thank God she's not."

We'd come here thinking that if Sarah saw Jack and me together she'd realize whatever they'd once had was over. But from the possessive glint in her eyes, I got the impression the plan hadn't worked.

Brooke appeared behind her houseguest. She shrugged at her brother over Sarah's shoulder, her expression grim. So at least she didn't seem to *want* Sarah around. That was some consolation.

"How long are you here for?" I asked Sarah, hoping she'd show us her packed suitcase and her bus ticket out of town.

"Oh, I'm here to stay," she said slowly. Very slowly.

All of Jack's muscles seemed to contract at once. "To stay," he repeated. Not a question but a disbelieving statement.

"I'll be sure to send the Welcome Wagon," I said, biting back the urge to ask what mental institution she'd be checked into. Her proclamation felt like the final nail in Jack's and my relationship coffin. I wanted her gone. G-O-N-E. But since *she* wasn't going, *I* would.

I lifted my hand in a quick wave to Brooke, turned on my wedge heels, and, knowing full-well that they were all three watching me, I held my head up high and sauntered back to the Volvo.

"Don't need your help," she said to my back. I could hear the Billy Idol sneer in her tone.

A muffled ringing coming from my purse brought me out of the memory. I dug inside and pulled out my cell phone. "Hello?"

"Hey, Cruz."

Speak of the devil. "Hey, Callaghan."

"You free for lunch?"

"I don't know, Jack." I was a one-man woman, and I expected Jack to be a one-woman man. Sarah was making that difficult. Her parents had taken her back to San Luis Obispo, but two weeks later she was back in Sacramento.

He hesitated, only briefly, but long enough for me to pick up on it. "I'm working on it, Lola."

Uh-huh. My mother had always called Jack *un mujeriego*. He'd been a player back in high school—and I'd wanted him then. He'd outgrown his ladies' man status and I wanted him more. But I needed his undivided attention and, right now, I didn't have that.

"*Lo siento*, Callaghan. Can't do lunch." I slung my purse

over my shoulder and headed out to my car. I had a legitimate excuse. I had to race home, change into sweats, and get over to dance practice.

"New case?" His voice had an enticing timber that made my knees weak. "Because there's nothing to worry about with Sarah."

The casual way he said her name irked me. I called her she-who-must-not-be-named, a la Harry Potter, in case saying her actual name gave her power or something. "New case," I confirmed.

He waited a beat before prompting me to elaborate. "And?"

I started my car and maneuvered out of Camacho's parking lot, heading toward the midtown flat I shared with my brother, conveniently located above my parents' house—where there was always a full refrigerator. Pathetic that Antonio and I lived together and in our parents' house, technically? On the one hand, yes, but since neither of us were home much and we were both saving to buy our own places, it made sense.

"Jack…," I said, stalling. I was trying to protect myself from getting hurt. I'd spent too many years with the wrong guys to forge ahead without some assurance that there was a solid future ahead with the *right* one. "It's just…it's a new case. I didn't think you'd be interested."

Lame. The guy had taken a bullet for me. I *knew* he cared, even if his life was complicated.

"I'm interested in everything about you, Cruz. You know that."

Good to hear. "It's confidential," I said, touting the unspoken P.I. code I'd made up in my mind. Like the pirate code, it was really just a set of guidelines, but at the moment, I clung to it.

He pulled out the very same bit of history I'd just thought of. "A crazy-ass woman shot me because of one of your cases and I'm still here, Cruz. You know you can trust me."

And therein lay the problem. It's not that I didn't trust Jack. I didn't trust myself around him. He made my resolve weaken, and I didn't like being weak at anything. Warrior princess. 'Nuff said.

I cruised right past McKinley Park, too distracted to revel in the beauty of the late-season blooms in the rose garden. "I have an exercise class to go to. Let's talk later," I said, shocked that the words had come from my mouth. I was a Cruz. I didn't skirt around issues. What was wrong with me?

There was a silence as he regrouped. "So not work? Kung fu? Yoga? I could use some…exercise." I sensed his grin through the line. "Another bike ride by the river, maybe?"

I flushed, remembering what had happened after the *last* bike ride we took together. We'd come close to doing the deed before my good Catholic upbringing had kicked in. I needed commitment. "None of the above."

"You're holding back, Lola. I feel that wall creeping up again."

How right he was. It took all my strength to not melt into a puddle from the sound of his voice. "I really have to go. I-I'm late, *and* I have to work at Abuelita's tonight. It's a busy day."

"What happened to Sylvia?"

"I'm filling in for her." Abuelita's was our family restaurant and Sylvia was our newest waitress, the only one my *Mafioso*-wannabe grandfather hadn't been able to scare off yet.

"Okay," he said. "We'll talk later, then. See you tonight, Cruz."

"No!" I didn't want the temptation of seeing him.

But he'd already hung up. Knots coiled in my stomach. In anticipation of seeing Jack in a few hours, or from the prospect of holding my own with eleven professional dancers?

I was no fool. Both. Definitely both.

Chapter Three

The sports arena was an enormous compound that used to be in the middle of vast fields, but houses and retail centers were sprouting up like dandelions in a neglected lawn. The complex that used to stick out of the ground like part of a lost city was now surrounded by commerce.

Following the directions Lance had given me, I parked my car, found the entrance, and tried to contain my nervous energy. Eleven perfect women were on the court in various stages of warm-ups: spread-eagle on the floor, stretching out their inner thighs; legs propped on bleachers, lengthening their hamstrings; bodies bent at the hip, hands flat on the ground. They were all *way* too flexible to be human.

"Come on," Victoria snapped when she saw me. "No time to waste."

I dropped my backpack, retied my sweatpants, and jogged to her side.

"Ladies!" Victoria waved the Courtside Dancers over and they formed a circle around us.

Taking stock, I realized I fell somewhere in the middle in height and body type. Some of the women had boobs and hips and others were straight as a board. The common denominator was the taut body factor. They were all lean, muscular, and athletic.

They might be lithe and graceful, but I could take any one of them in an alley.

Victoria cleared her throat. "This is Dolores—" She paused, realizing she'd never asked me my last name.

"Actually, I go by Lola," I said.

"Let's welcome Lola to the team," Victoria commanded in a "do it or else" voice. "She's taking Rochelle's place."

A choir of scoffs spread through the women; it was the sound of a collective cold shoulder. Nice.

I frowned, the coils in my gut winding tighter. It felt like high school all over again, the instant rivalry between the cheerleaders and the outsider. I had an urge to collect my stuff and escape to the library where I could read my favorite novel and be in my own world.

I realized immediately that in order to solve *Operation: Dance*, I'd have to make a huge effort to get to know these women. That would be no easy feat. But there was no time for schmoozing and kissing cheerleader booty at the moment. I had routines to learn.

Victoria, the slave-driving gazelle, clapped her hands and practice began. Less than an hour in, I knew I was in trouble. The routines were complicated, and the dancers' talent and commitment were evident. I'd underestimated what it took to be a Courtside Dancer and overestimated my ability and endurance.

My legs were already like boiled spaghetti; right now,

even Miley Cyrus, in her younger days, could totally take me in an alley. Wearing sweatpants had been a bad choice. Sweat dripped between my cleavage and down my back. The dance shorts or leotards most of the girls wore would have been a much better option. I took mental notes so I'd be prepared next time around.

Another half hour passed before Victoria finally let us break. Not a second too soon. My entire body felt like rubber, and I panted. I gulped from my water bottle, but the others sipped, delicately dabbing the sweat away from their foreheads and the backs of their necks. Show-offs. Seriously. Were they even human?

The girls I'd met at Camacho's managed to mask their amusement at my suffering—just barely—but the others weren't so kind. I fought hard not to scowl. "I need them," I muttered to myself.

The last two-and-a-half hours of practice felt like an eternity. Or a traditional Spanish Mass at the pink Catholic church off of Broadway, which went on forever. And a day. I was beginning to feel the crack of the invisible whip Victoria used to drive the dancers into submission. I was all over the map, my legs and arms flailing in exactly the wrong positions a good part of the time. My head went right when it was supposed to turn left. Victoria clapped. "Stay with it, Lola! Oh, good God. Right. *Right*! That's it."

I gritted my teeth through my panting.

One of the dancers turned to Selma and said in a stage whisper, "Where'd Victoria find her? What are we, a charity? She's going to make us look bad."

Selma shrugged. "She's not that bad, Carrie. She'll be fine by Friday."

"Hard to replace Rochelle," Carrie said, clearly not convinced that I'd be anywhere close to ready by Friday.

Victoria called for a break and I gulped another liter of water while straining to listen.

Carrie and Selma continued their conversation. "Have you talked to her?"

"Who?"

"Rochelle."

My ears perked.

Carrie dabbed her chest with a towel. "Larry did. Guess he saw her at some club they both go to."

"She's definitely not coming back?"

Carrie flicked her chin toward me and I quickly turned away. She dropped her voice and I heard her say, "Lance won't let her. Fraternizing with the players. I heard he really laid into the players, too."

They walked farther away from me and I pursed my lips. Being undercover with a partner would be so much more fun. Reilly as a Courtside Dancer? If only...

Not a single one of *these* dancers, including the ones I'd met at Camacho's, had welcomed me. Where was the team spirit? Where was the camaraderie?

Of course, with my red, blotched face and the sweat soaking through my shirt, I might as well have screamed, "I'm an amateur!" How could they *not* know I was just a poser? I couldn't keep up and I was having a major #fail moment. Not a good first day on the job.

After another run-through of the most difficult routine, Victoria clapped her hands together three times. "That's it for today."

Finally!

I doubled over, catching my breath, and managed to straighten as the dancers applauded. I collapsed onto a chair and watched as they chatted and trickled into the locker room.

"Great," I said. My voice echoed, the arena sounding hollow now that the eleven other dancers were gone.

Victoria came up next to me, folding her arms over her chest. "I didn't think you could do it, but you held your own."

I arched a brow at her. "Ha! I'm not even close to being in their league."

Her harsh expression softened. "They're a hard group to please. You'd be surprised if you saw yourself. You have a natural rhythm. You were right in there. By Friday you'll be perfect."

I dropped my head between my knees. "I can't feel my legs and I think I'm going to throw up."

"Tomorrow will be better. You'll see. I'll see you then at two thirty. Be ready to work. And trust me."

Trust her. Maybe after my head stopped pounding and I could stand again. But I found myself believing her. Despite the fact that I thought she was completely crazy, her compliment buzzed around in my head. I knew I had natural rhythm with salsa. That was sultry, sexy, and I felt the music in my core. But this type of dance was bold and extreme and athletic. It wasn't *me*.

Only, apparently, it was.

"I'll have your outfits by Friday's game. Size six, right?"

I shook my head. "Eight. Medium shirt."

She scanned me, arching a brow. "Are you sure?"

"I'm sure." I had been a six once upon a time—when I was, like, twelve years old.

Victoria cleared her throat. "Bra size? Thirty-four?"

"Yep."

"Cup?"

I peered at her through my lashes. My dog didn't know this much about my underclothing. This woman was Mensa good. "C."

"See you tomorrow then," she said, apparently committing my measurements to memory.

I lifted my hand in a wave. After another few minutes, I managed to haul my carcass toward the locker room to see if I could talk to Selma, all the while not sure I ever wanted to see Victoria and the rest of the Stepford dancers ever again.

• • •

The dancers still weren't in a reach-out-and-touch-the-new-girl kind of mood. I didn't learn a thing, except that, after a long, hot shower, I could feel my legs again. By the time I was coherent, I was also alone in the locker room. No Selma. So much for starting strong out of the gate.

Perfect. I changed into my restaurant uniform, which consisted of black pants and a gauzy white blouse with brightly embroidered flowers across the front, and proceeded to do a thorough search of the lockers—and found each one empty. I rummaged through the garbage cans and found used tissues, tampon casings, a Hostess Twinkies wrapper, paper towels, and a slew of other personal hygiene items. But no clues. No mysterious letters. *Nada*.

I hurried into the hallway and ran smack into a custodian and his giant yellow cleaning cart.

"*Con permiso*," he said quickly.

"No, no," I said, waving away his apology. "*Está bien*."

Was he the regular custodian? Could I get any information

from him? "*Me llamo Lola*," I said.

A deep frown pulled the skin of his face downward. "*Mucho gusto.*"

His tone didn't seem particularly pleased, though he'd given me the polite response. I tried again, asking him if he was the regular custodian here.

"*Sí,*" he said, his expression wary. Probably because I looked like a murderer in my waitress outfit.

"*Bueno,*" I said, but my teeth clenched. Only it wasn't actually good. I was getting nowhere. Which meant I had nothing to lose. I asked the only question I could think of: Did he have a letter for me?

His frown deepened and his eyes turned to slits. "I don't have any letters," he said in Spanish. "I know nothing." He shoved his cart forward, forcing me into the locker room.

Oh, he knew something, all right. With my hands on the edge of his cart, I pushed back, stopping him. "You know nothing about what?"

He clamped his mouth shut. "*Nada.*"

"*Mira,*" I said. Then I told him one of the dancers had gotten a letter but didn't know who it was from. "*¿Me puede ayudar?*"

He screwed up his face, concentrating. "I no help. I know nothing about nothing," he said, this time in broken English, then he shoved his cart forward.

I made a show of taking my hands off his cart and sidestepping out of his way. If this man was anything like my grandparents, the fact that he'd spoken in English meant what he'd said was final. I knew better than to push.

"*Gracias,*" I said. More flies with honey and all that, but inside my head I added, *Thanks for nothing.*

Chapter Four

In the kitchen at Abuelita's, my father worked the stove. Sauces simmered. Meats sautéed. One by one, he constructed burritos, enchiladas, gorditas, and tacos. "*Hola, mi'ja*," he said as I came in.

"*Hola, Papi.*"

The knife my brother, Antonio, had been using to mince green onions stopped its rapid chopping. He scowled the second he saw me. "You're late."

I was so not in the mood for him playing boss. I was tired, starving, sore, and anxious about seeing Jack. I scowled back. "I have a new case at my *real* job."

"Good for you." Antonio tossed the green onions into the vat of guacamole, squeezed a lime into it, and stirred. "*Pero*, you need to be here when you're scheduled. *Somos tu familia.*"

"Yes, but the restaurant is *yours*," I said, "not mine. I'm here now." I tried to end my sentence the way my mother did, with an implied *punto*.

But my *punto* fell short because he kept pushing. "It's all of ours."

I really had to start paying more attention to *Mami* and how she made things so final with her tone.

I flicked my chin toward the swinging door that led to the dining room. "It's all good, Tonio. Sylvia's still here."

My brother grumbled, but he knew I was right. He went back into the dining room, the obligatory harassment over. Appealing to my father, I smiled sweetly, rubbing my rumbling stomach with one hand. "*¿Papá, por favor, puedo tener una enchilada?*"

His leathery face relaxed into a thousand lines, his salt-and-pepper hair aging him beyond his fifty-three years. "*Sí, pero*"—he wagged a wooden spoon at the kitchen at large—"stay behind the cooking line."

I waited while my father crafted two cheese enchiladas, filling them with minced onions, a mix of shredded cheese, and sliced black olives. He topped them with a ladleful of red chili sauce and slid the plate across the stainless steel warming shelf.

I covered the plate with a paper towel, popped it in the microwave for a few seconds, then lopped a dollop of sour cream and a healthy spoonful of chunky guacamole onto the enchiladas. I returned the plate to the warming shelf. "*¿Arroz y frijoles, por favor?*"

My father took the plate, heaped on rice and beans, and handed it to me just as Antonio came back into the kitchen, his arms weighted down with dirty plates.

I took a bite, muttering a blissful, "*Gracias.*"

"*Por nada,*" Papi said.

Antonio sighed in exasperation, shaking his head.

"Hurry, would you? Chely can't make it tonight."

Oh, man. That meant I'd be filling salt and pepper shakers, refilling hot sauce bottles, and cleaning the pint-sized flower vases to get them ready for tomorrow. "Why?"

"She has cheerleading practice."

I whipped my head around. "Since when is she a cheerleader?"

"Uh, since the beginning of the school year." Antonio waved a hand in front of my face. "What's going on in there?"

I forked a piece of enchilada into my mouth. Wow, I was too out of touch with *la familia Cruz*. Then a thought struck me. I could get private cheerleading help from my fifteen-year-old cousin if Victoria couldn't get me up to speed *muy rápido*. *Pero, no*. Chely couldn't keep a secret.

"What are you mumbling about?" my brother asked.

I swallowed and took another bite. "Nothing."

"You better watch it," he said, still peering at me as if I'd done something wrong. "You're gonna pack on the pounds if you keep eating like that."

"More to love," I said, my mouth full of enchilada. I swallowed and readied the next forkful. "Busy day. Lot of running around," I said.

He grabbed the plates my father slid onto the warming shelf, backed out the swinging door to the dining room, and left me to finish my dinner.

When I was done, I stopped in front of the mirror by the In door, ran my tongue over my teeth and my fingers through my hair, pulling it into a bulky ponytail. Streaks of copper shot through the dark brown like shards of light. I liked the effect, even if my grandmother constantly reminded me that it was unnatural and indecent to have dyed hair.

Of course she didn't believe in painted fingernails, either, something I'd embraced at ten years old. The fact that nail polish was forbidden but earrings on infants were commonplace was something she could never give me a satisfactory explanation for. If I ever have a daughter, I know my grandmother will be the first in line to make her scream by piercing her tiny lobes.

With a half-apron tied around my waist, I tucked my order book into the pocket and pushed out the swinging door into the dining room. Antonio was right. It was a busy night. Three-fourths of the tables were occupied with diners and I got right to work filling baskets with chips, spooning homemade salsa into *molcojetes*, delivering water, and bussing tables. Sylvia waved as she grabbed her purse and ran out the front door.

"Where's she going?" I asked Antonio as he headed toward the kitchen to pick up an order. Sylvia had been taming my brother's philandering ways ever since they'd started dating a few months ago, so I knew he'd have the scoop.

"Meeting with the social worker. She's supposed to get her son back next week."

I felt a surge of joy for Sylvia and I suddenly didn't mind pulling the shift at Abuelita's; Sylvia had spent too long thinking that her infant son was dead and now she was getting him back. That was more important than my aching thighs.

I worked steadily for the next hour and a half. Finally, there was a lull and I leaned against the hostess counter, running through one of the dance routines I'd learned in my mind. My eyes opened at the *ding* of the bell above the door. And blinked when they registered Jack coming into the restaurant. He had his laptop tucked under his arm and his ever-present journalist's notepad clutched in his hand. God, he made my insides turn to goo. Tousled brown hair, dark skin, the faintest hint of a dimple gracing his cheek, and eyes just for me.

My gaze had started to travel down his body, but it screeched to a stop at his torso. Oh no, not eyes just for me. He had eyes for Sarah, too. Or some crazy sense of responsibility toward her that he couldn't explain to me for some reason. Which made him honorable. Damn it, this was too complicated.

"Working hard?" Jack's question interrupted the reality check I was giving myself.

I brought my gaze back to his face. "Always." Absently running my hand over my hair, I fed the ponytail through my fingers. Then I took a slow yoga *Ujjayi* breath to get some balance in my thoughts. "Do you want a table?"

A slow smile spread onto his lips. "In your section."

I frowned. If he kept looking at me like that, I might have to kick him out. "My section is the whole restaurant. This way." I led him to what was fast becoming "his table" and pulled out the chair that faced the wall. I didn't want him spending the entire evening watching me. We'd come too close to making love too many times. He wanted it. I wanted it.

But I'd had a few too many years of crumbs in bed with Sergio, and I wasn't about to give myself to a man who wasn't fully committed to me.

No way, no how.

I was not a one-night-stand kind of girl.

He set his laptop on the chair I'd pulled out for him. "Thanks." Then he sat down on the other side of the table, facing the dining room. And me.

Damn. So much for *that* plan. "Do you know what you want?"

His dimple enticingly etched itself into his right cheek. "I know exactly what I want."

A slow tingle burned its way through my body. *¡Dios mío!* If I wasn't careful, Jack's charm would wear me down and my grandmother would be saying rosaries to save my heathen, wanton soul. Again.

I swallowed and regrouped. "From the menu. To eat."

His smile took on a hint of wicked. This wasn't going well.

I breathed in through my nose. Constricted my throat. Out through my nose. *"For dinner,"* I added.

He picked up his menu. "Not sure yet."

I waved my order pad around. Other tables needed service. Hot food waited in the kitchen to be delivered. "Okay!" *Way too perky, Lola. Get a grip.* "I'll be back. Take your time."

We did our own seductive dance from that moment on. I took his order, and he flirted with me. I refilled his water. And he flirted some more. I brought him his food, and he tried to get me to sit with him.

"I have other customers," I said, weakening from repeated exposure to his pheromones.

"Yes, but will they tip you like I will?"

"What, are you going to give me the answers to the *Sacramento Bee*'s Sunday crossword puzzle?" He could do it, too, being one of the paper's most popular columnists.

"Not quite what I had in mind," he said.

"Oh yeah?" I grinned, *un poquito* seductively. Two could play at this game. I put my palms flat on the table and leaned toward him. "Just what *do* you have in mind?"

His eyes smoldered, turning from blue to gray, and his lips parted slightly. Just enough for me to imagine exactly what he was thinking.

"*¡Dolores! ¡Ven aquí!*" My grandfather's Marlon Brando voice swept me out of my fantasy with Jack and back into the restaurant. My grandparents held court in their booth, receiving guests, day in and day out. He was sauntering up to his regular table and seeing his wannabe mafioso face and his slick peppery hair knocked the sense right back into me. Jack and I were on hold.

"*Espera, Abuelo,*" I said over my shoulder as I straightened.

Jack blinked, the heat of attraction under control again. "Better go see what he wants before he fires you."

I laughed. "If only he would. Then I could work on my cases without splitting my time."

"Can't wait to hear all about it."

Ah, but I couldn't do that. I'd learned that revealing my undercover status to Jack was a risky business. He—and my brother, Antonio—had nearly blown my first incognito moment when I'd worn a wire to catch some flashing shoplifters at Laughlin's Market. Distance, I reminded myself. The less time I spent with him, the better. And I was still hoping I'd make some great discovery before game time and be able to avoid actually doing the cheerleading thing.

"I'm closing, Jack, then I'm going home."

He flashed that crooked grin, but something in his expression reminded me of the married mind-reading stare

Victoria and Lance Wolfe had shared at Camacho & Associates. "I could come with you," he finally said.

Yes, you could, I thought. Especially if he didn't stop making me feel like he was undressing me with his eyes. "N-no you can't."

He blinked, breaking the thread connecting us. "Her family's coming to get her."

I shifted my weight to one side and put my hand on hip, my elbow angled out. "*¿Otra vez?*"

He gave me a long, searching look, finally saying, "For good this time. And they'll keep her on her meds."

Right. And I really was Xena. "They haven't been able to do that so far."

"There's a first time for everything."

I caught—or maybe I imagined—the double entendre. "Maybe," I said, but I wasn't sure there would ever actually be a first time for Jack and me.

Chapter Five

I somehow made it through the next two days without learning a thing about the letters. Not reassuring, given my green status as a detective. I hadn't gotten paid for my last big case, since it had been personal and off the books. I had to prove myself with this one.

Victoria, it turned out, was more like a bullfighter than a dance team director. She grabbed *el toro* by the horns—the bull in this case being me—and did what needed to be done. If I didn't know she was determined to make sure I didn't tarnish the reputation of the Courtside Dancers, I'd think she'd made it her personal mission to torture me. And leave me absolutely no time to investigate.

My attempts to chitchat with the other women on the team had gotten me polite dismissals. I still knew nothing about Rochelle Nolan, the dancer who'd had the affair and left the team. I'd yet to see a letter on the premises. And muscles ached in parts of my body I hadn't even known existed. If I made it through the Royals's game that night it would be a miracle.

Arriving two hours before the game, my new super-sized duffel-bag-on-wheels in tow, I made my way through the lower level of the arena and into the locker room, a huge area with two enormous mirrors adhered to the walls. The stereo blared Gloria Gaynor's "I Will Survive" and someone screamed, "Downtime disco!"

Whatever *that* meant.

A refrigerator stocked with drinks sat in one corner, while salad, bread, Rice Krispies Treats, chicken, rice pilaf, steamed and fresh vegetables, cookies, and PowerBars weighed down the king-size buffet table.

I perused the room, awed by the transformations taking place. The women were going from stunning to spectacular. I pulled my bag up next to Jennifer, the dancer who'd been the least unfriendly. "Hi."

She lowered her chin. Not bad as far as greetings from this bunch went. She hung her outfits for the evening on a portable wardrobe. I stared in amazement. There would be four changes tonight. I hadn't laid eyes on my costumes yet and had no idea if the outfits Victoria was bringing would even fit.

I gestured toward the buffet. "Does all that get eaten?"

"Pretty much. Dancing drains you." Jennifer studied me. "After three days of practicing, even *you* should know that. Energy is key."

Here was the attitude I'd been expecting. I leaned in so I could speak without anyone else hearing. "Listen, I'm here to do a job. You can make it easy or hard. That's up to you. But the easier you make it, the sooner I can get out of here."

Spider lashes curved up to her brows as her eyes grew

wide. She flicked her gaze around and then pushed her bag over to make more room for me.

About time.

She brushed her chin-length brown hair, teasing out the top layer of expensive highlights. She ran her curling iron over the ends, flipping them up. "I'll try to help," she said quietly.

I thanked her and then went to work on my own hair. I pulled up the sides, clipping them at the top with a glittery barrette, and then sprayed the long strands of highlights that framed my face and ratted out the back to create extra volume.

Jennifer examined my reflection. "I'll do your makeup."

Boo-ya. She'd come around!

She shouted over the sounds of hairdryers, the blaring music, and women chattering. "Tammy! Can I borrow your foundation?"

Tammy slinked over to us, her long, silky hair trailing behind her like a silk sheet. "It's way too dark for you, Jenn."

"It's for Lola. You have the same olive skin tone."

She gave me a once-over, then threw out a hip and perched a hand on it. "Doesn't she have her own makeup?"

Here we go again. They were talking about me like I wasn't in the room, let alone sitting right next to them.

"I didn't know we had to get made up with stage makeup. Next time I'll bring my own." I gritted my teeth and forced myself to beam at Tammy. "It's really sweet of you to share."

Tammy's scowl softened, but only microscopically. Jennifer unscrewed the lid of the foundation, took a triangular sponge out of her bag, and began dabbing my face. "Perfect."

She turned to Tammy. "I'll bring it back when I'm done."

Tammy huffed and walked away, and I saw her muttering something to another girl, peering at me out of the corner of her eye.

It was definitely like reliving junior high. I had the impression that Jennifer was the queen bee, not Tammy, but she was right up there on the food chain.

Jennifer finished the foundation and moved on to the eye shadow—deep blue on the lower lid and sparkly silver on top. She worked for a few more minutes before stepping back to admire her handiwork. I peered at the mirror and flinched at my clown reflection. "That's a bit, um, bold, no?"

"You're going to perform in front of twenty thousand people. Your face will be on the suspended monitor—"

A lump formed in my throat. Twenty thousand people. I'd realized it would be a full arena, but I hadn't actually put a number to the fans. The Royals were a hot commodity in the Sacramento sports market. They were on top of their game and the fans came out in droves to support them. And since their reality show, the Courtside Dancers had their own rabid following.

And, *ay caramba*, my brother was one of the team's biggest fans. Sweat beaded on my forehead. Staying undercover and incognito was going to be *un poquito difícil* in front of that huge audience.

Jennifer shook my shoulder. "Did you hear me, Lola?"

"I'm sorry. What?" She'd added more blush and I was sure my cheeks could be seen from Mars.

"I was with Victoria at first. I didn't want an outsider coming onto the team, you know?"

I hoped against hope that she was going to tell me

something useful. "But you changed your mind?"

"Lance made sense. Rochelle's been seeing Michael Brothers for a long time, so I don't think that's why she left. I think the letters scared her, you know, and…" Jennifer trailed off, her eyes darting around the room.

"And what?"

"Maybe you should talk to the ball boys. One of them brought the last note to me."

"Do you know which one?"

She shrugged. "No. I never really paid attention. They're all the same, you know?"

Right. Like racial profiling, for ball boys.

"What about the other letters? How were they delivered?"

"I know the ball boys have passed a few of them to the girls. A couple were left in here. Carrie found one in her bag."

My heart ratcheted up a notch. Finally, information that might actually help with the case. *Hallelujah!* I kept my voice low, masking my excitement. "Where do the ball boys hang out? Do they go into the players' locker room?"

"The players, coaches, trainer, and doctor are allowed in the locker rooms. I don't think the ball boys really have their own special place, you know?"

I tried to keep my mouth still as Jennifer traced my lips with liner. Finally she finished and I asked another question. "How long have you been a dancer?"

"This is my fourth season. I worked for a year, then we did *Living the Royal Life*. It's been craziness ever since."

"Celebrity crazy?" I asked, barely parting my lips.

Her face clouded. "We're recognized all the time. It's

not like when Arnold was in town and everyone wanted a glimpse of the Governator, but it's close, you know? Sometimes I think…"

Her hands trembled like a nervous cat that wanted nothing more than to shed its skin.

"What?" I asked.

"Sometimes I think I should just go back home, you know?" She gestured to her risque cheerleading outfit. "Sometimes this is nothing more than a costume. I'm proud of my body, but in this—"

She broke off, but she didn't have to finish her sentence for me to understand. I loved being a girl, but I was a strong girl, and the sexy cheerleader thing pushed my boundaries. "I get it. Makes you feel like just an object, right?"

"Exactly. Sometimes I just don't want people staring at me."

My gaze ran around the room. "How about them? Do they feel the same way?"

Jennifer capped the lip pencil and pulled out lipstick. "Selma does," she said softly, "but not the rest." She paused as I puckered up for the lip color. "How do you feel?"

Good question. I was a nonprofessional dancer about to spend the next three hours committing possible career suicide in front of thousands of people. Ever since this case dropped into my lap, I'd had an insatiable urge to visit St. Francis, the church on 26th Street I'd grown up attending. Light a candle and confess that I'd be shaking my bootie in the arena, say a whole bunch of Hail Marys, and be forgiven for whatever sin I might be committing in the scant clothes.

Today. I'd stop by today.

"I'll let you know," I said, picking a strand of hair from

my lips as I stood.

She took an atomizer from the bag, sprayed it into the air, and gave me a shove into the mist. The scented cloud settled around me. Sweet. Subtle. With a hint of apple and honey blossoms.

"A specially blended body mist Victoria makes for all of us," Jennifer explained.

"Makes?" I breathed in. *Delicioso*.

"Victoria and I, we both majored in chemistry. Years apart, but still."

I was pretty sure my jaw dropped open. "Chemistry? Really?"

She scoffed. "'Cheerleader' isn't synonymous with 'dumb,'" she said. She notched her head toward a few of the other dancers. "Tammy graduated at the top of her class with a degree in English, and Joy"—she pointed to a gorgeous black woman warming up in the corner—"Joy is a teacher. She does this on the side."

"Huh." Guess I'd been cheerleader profiling, figuring they'd bypassed college for a life of fame and...basketball players.

Wrong.

The chattering in the room tapered off. Someone lowered the music. I turned around in time to see Victoria gliding through the room. She wore a sparkly, formfitting strapless top and her hair was neatly slicked back just like every other time I'd seen her.

"Are you ready, ladies?" Her voice rose in controlled pep talk fashion.

A cheer erupted in the locker room and after a few more encouraging words from their leader, the dancers turned back to their spaces to finish their transformations.

Victoria floated across the room to me, giving me a once-over. "Makeup's not bad. Did you have a hand in it, Jenn?"

"A touch of eye shadow and some blush and *voilà*"— Jennifer gestured at me as if she were introducing the grand prize on a game show—"A Courtside Dancer."

"All I need is an outfit," I said, eyeing the garment bags Victoria carried. Gold zippers bisected the plastic of each one. My nerves zinged. I'd seen the other girls' costumes hanging from hooks by their mirrors. Skimpy. And that was an understatement. I was no prude, but I also wasn't an exhibitionist. Good God, I hoped my family didn't watch the game on TV tonight.

Victoria hung the outfits on a hook next to Jennifer's. "You're responsible for their cleaning," she said to me, then turned to the room and announced, "Be ready in fifteen, ladies."

And then she was gone.

I watched, slack-jawed, as the dancers scrambled around, vying for space in front of the mirrors to apply last-minute body glitter, and eventually slipped on their costumes.

Finally, after I couldn't stall any longer, I rifled through the garment bags, pulled out the first costume of the night, and held it up. *¡Dios mío!* It was tiny! Itsy bitsy, like a miniature yellow polka dot bikini. I'd said size eight but the black jazz pants would fit a ten-year-old.

This could get ugly.

"Ticktock," Jennifer said.

Right. No more stalling. I sucked in a deep breath, said a Hail Mary for my mother, and stripped down to the thong underwear I'd been told to wear. I wriggled into the first outfit of the night: black second-skin shorts and a royal-blue halter with rhinestones studded all over it. Next to go on were my black dance shoes.

I spun around, spreading my arms wide. "Well?" I asked, catching a glimpse of myself in the mirror. Holy Mary, mother of God. I couldn't have been more exposed if I'd been buck naked.

Jennifer eyed me up and down. "The boobs need work."

I cupped the front of the halter and stared at her. "What do you mean, they need work?" I demanded, suddenly protective of my *chi-chis*. I mean, hadn't Jack said recently that they were spectacular? Or had that been in a dream?

Jennifer laughed, whatever angst she had a few minutes ago about being a celebrity gone. "Relax. I only mean that we need to emphasize the cleavage. Take the top off."

I hesitated as Jennifer pulled a roll of duct tape from her duffel bag. "Um…"

"Come on, Lola."

I swallowed as I mustered up my gumption and stripped off the halter. And stood, topless, in front of her. I took back what I'd felt a moment ago. *Now* I felt utterly exposed. It was one thing to undress in a locker room as a high school girl. No choice. But here? Now? Like this? I liked my clothes, *gracias, y adiós*. I bet Xena never had to do this, and I was pretty sure this wasn't something Manny had ever done for a case.

Jennifer began sticking pieces of the tape to my body, jamming my breasts together in the middle. She didn't bat a fake eyelash. Apparently taping up another woman's *chi-chis* was no big deal in her world.

In three minutes she was done and, with the halter back on, I stared in the mirror. Boob job? *No necisito*. Duct tape really *was* a miracle worker.

Jennifer fastened a blinged-out pendent around her neck. "Don't forget the choker and the earrings," she told me.

After fishing in the bottom of the garment bag, I found them wrapped in plastic jewelry bags. The choker had an enormous Royals' emblem hanging from the center and the earrings glowed in the dark. Cheerleader bling. Nice. Taking one last appraisal in the mirror, I threw my shoulders back. I just might pull this off.

I left the dressing room, rounded the corner to the east tunnel of the arena, and found my place in line. Victoria sat at the entrance, headphones cradling her sleek head.

"What's she doing?" I asked one of the dancers behind me. Cassie, if I remembered correctly. She was the only dancer with crazy-curly, uncontrolled hair, but it worked for her. She had a super-sexy vibe, kind of like she'd just rolled out of bed.

Cassie rose to her tiptoes, then lowered back down. Over and over and over. "Coordinating our entrance with the operations crew," she said.

She'd answered me. Nice. Maybe I was making progress. If I became a familiar face, hopefully they'd all get used to me and start opening up. Then maybe I'd get somewhere in my investigation.

"Girls." Two dark-haired men greeted us as they passed. The one that spoke flashed a toothy grin, his ruddy cheeks puffing out with the stretch of his mouth.

"Hey, Larry." Jennifer gave a flirty tilt of her head. "Steve."

"Stevie," Tammy greeted. She threw her hand up to

wave at the other man.

The greetings traveled down the line. I waved when their gaze reached me.

"Ah, the new girl. I've heard about you," the one named Steve said.

"Oh?" Just what had he heard?

He engulfed my hand in his slightly pudgy one. His skin was smooth and I noted his receding hairline, firm handshake, and the warm tone to his voice. He could have been the team's personal greeter. "Very nice to meet you. Welcome to the family."

"Thank you, Mr.—"

"Steve. Just Steve."

Just Steve, who knew all the cheerleaders. "And I'm Lola."

He pushed the other man forward. "And this is my brother, Larry."

Larry barely acknowledged me before glancing down the line of dancers.

Steve gave an all-encompassing wave. "Girls. Break a leg, each and every one of you."

"Thanks, Stevie!" The women reached their hands out to Steve as the men passed by, almost as if he were a movie star.

I raised a questioning brow at Cassie.

"The team's trainer," she told me.

The way she hesitated made me think she was about to say something else. Like were they really brothers?

"Season ticket holders. They sit right next to the owner's seats," Cassie added.

So they were VIPs. Before I could find out any more, Victoria's voice drifted down the line. "Ready, ladies?"

The team let out a collective *woo-hoo*!

Victoria adjusted her headphones and held up her index finger, telling us to wait. After another few minutes she gave a succinct nod, her gaze traveling down the line, and said, "One, two, three…go!"

Adrenaline surged through my body as I jogged out onto the dimly lit court. Strobe lights and the pulsing beat of the music throbbed right along with my heart. The crowd in the arena was charged. Their energy zipped in a flurry around the court and I felt ready. As ready as I'd ever be.

We spread out, six of us on one side of the court, the other six on the opposite side. We bounced from one foot to the other, extending pointed toes as the Royals's names and numbers were called out to the cheering crowd, spotlights illuminating their lean, muscular, massive bodies. The team gathered in a circle, breaking a moment later to even more raucous cheers.

The dancers lined up and Cassie leaned in close to me. "Never seen one up close?"

I snapped my jaw back into place. "Nope."

"Check out Number Fifty-one."

I searched the back of the jerseys and saw the leopardlike body of the player Cassie was staring at. Charcoal skin. Tattoos snaking up one arm and down the other. Bald—in a sexy way. "Uh-huh."

"Gorgeous. He's a rookie. Had a slow start but now he's running circles around the others."

I was pretty sure lust had Cassie thinking that Number 51 could leap tall buildings in a single bound.

Who knew? Maybe he could.

The announcer asked the audience to rise, remove their

caps, and listen while the "Star Spangled Banner" was sung *a cappella* by a local college music major. The Royals and the opposing team lined up on the court, hands over their hearts.

"What about Twenty-Three?" I asked, noticing his heavier physique.

"Doesn't play as much 'cause he's slower." She fanned herself with her hand. "But he's hot. Hell, they're all hot. Why else would I take this gig? I'm going to get me one of them."

My eyes still searched the crowd—as if the letter writer, or a delivery boy, would be glowing red—as I talked to Cassie. "You're on the dance team to get close to the players?"

Her response? A wink.

So she wasn't one of the smarter ones.

The crowd erupted as the singer's voice stretched an octave and sang, "O'er the land of the free." Were they cheering because America was free or because she hit the note? I couldn't tell.

Jennifer turned on cue from Victoria and led us back through the tunnel.

It was a whirlwind after that. I trailed after the girls into the dressing room for a quick outfit change. I followed what Jennifer did, stripping off my halter top. The big difference? She didn't cringe at the crisscrossed duct tape across *her* chest. I shuddered at the tape across mine. But then again, after a few years, she had to be used to it.

Good God, in a million years, I'd never have imagined myself in this situation.

Jennifer slipped into a tight navy camisole, then slid a shimmering silver scarf-blouse on top of it. I followed suit, adjusting the gaping neck, then changed into the jazz pants—which were more stretchy than I'd originally thought they'd be, but I was still sure were actually made for a child.

Jennifer re-applied her lipstick and so did I. Some of the girls scarfed down food from the buffet table. I walked by and did a double take. The Rice Krispies Treats had vanished.

"They're always the first to go," Jennifer said, following my gaze.

I didn't believe in diets, and I had no problem eating dessert first. But I sure never would have pegged the cheerleaders as free-for-all eaters. "I just thought they would eat salads and fruits."

"We do. But we also like our sweets."

Or maybe they had a nasty thing called bulimia. *That* was something I didn't want to investigate.

We headed back to the tunnel and spent the next ten minutes hovering behind Victoria until a timeout was called.

One of the players, buckled over in pain, hobbled past us, the team trainer by his side. They stopped midway past the line of dancers and Carrie reached out to him. "Stevie, what happened?"

Steve breezed by, taking the player by the arm and helping him along. "Minor injury. No worries, ladies. He'll be fine."

"Is it bad?" Cassie said, and I got the impression that she wouldn't mind playing nursemaid.

I followed them with my eyes. Cassie's admission that she was on the team only to snag herself a hot ballplayer had my brain working. Rochelle seemed to have landed herself one in Michael Brothers. What if the other players didn't like the dancers breaking the rules? Or what if…I gave myself a mental head slap. *¡Por supuesto!*

It could be a player or a disgruntled wife behind the notes. Of course, that was a hypothesis—one I'd have to flesh out more.

The letter came in the third quarter. A fresh-faced ball boy jogged through the tunnel, an envelope clutched in his hand. Without a word he handed it to Geneva, a dancer who hadn't needed duct tape to prop up her cleavage, with legs about a mile long.

"Hey," I called, trying to catch the ball boy's attention, but he disappeared as play started on the court again. I scoured the perimeter of the arena, but every single person seemed focused on the game. No one was paying any attention to Geneva.

She flipped the envelope from front to back as if she were searching for some indication of who it was from. She hadn't been at the meeting at Camacho's, so she didn't know what Manny had said about not opening the envelope and minimizing touching it to preserve the fingerprints. It seemed like Victoria and Lance hadn't relayed that information, either, and being undercover meant I couldn't very well tell her.

Geneva ran her finger under the flap and pulled out a rectangular sheet of paper identical to the ones I'd seen in the conference room at Camacho's. She read the message, and with a puzzled face, flipped over the sheet.

As casually as I possibly could, I edged toward her just as she turned to Nicole, the dancer standing next to her. "I got one."

Nicole's eyes bugged and her lips parted. "Shit, really?

Says the same thing?"

I seized the opportunity to butt in. "What's wrong? What's it say?"

The message behind Geneva's scowl was clear: I better mind my own business. She crumpled the paper and tossed it to a passing waitress.

"No!" I reached for it, but the waitress scurried off to deliver a drink to one of the high-priced seats.

Damn. I'd been going for a super-smooth pluck off the waitress's tray. Utter fail. Even worse, they'd noticed.

Geneva and Nicole stared at me.

"What's wrong with you?" Nicole, the only other Hispanic dancer on the team, snarled. There was no Latina camaraderie for her. In fact, she seemed to have the most disdain for me, her expression turning to a scowl whenever I was around.

"I thought you tossed that by mistake. I can go grab it back for you." I cringed at how bad the lie was, but I had no choice but to go with it. I started to walk past them, keeping an eye on the waitress, but she disappeared into the crowd.

Victoria's voice was like a rope pulling me to a stop. "Line up," she said, followed by a quick succession of claps. "Time to wow the crowd with some Black Eyed Peas."

The music blared in the arena and Jennifer led the dancers back out. I fell into line, searching for the waitress as I left the tunnel. No luck. She was gone, and short of Dumpster diving in all of the arena's garbage bins, I doubted I'd ever find the note Geneva had crumpled and thrown away.

The clue had slipped right between my fingers.

Chapter Six

I spent the next day tracking down Rochelle Nolan, the woman who'd quit the Courtside Dancers. Finding her address—a sprawling custom home out in Granite Bay—was easy. Getting past the security guard for the gated community wasn't. I'd brought along my poor, neglected Boxer, Salsa, and poor, neglected Reilly for the company, but now I was wishing I'd come *sola*. It would have been easier to try to sweet-talk my way past the guard if I'd been by myself.

Reilly, with her newly colored orange hair (to celebrate autumn, she'd said) and slinky black leggings paired with a colorful patchwork swing blouse, filled me in on all her Neil *chisme*. She didn't leave out a single detail. Not one. By the time we reached Granite Bay, my eyes had glazed from too much information.

Salsa panted from the cargo area of the CRV as I drove, her tongue hanging out the side of her drooping mouth. What if I had to sneak in? How was I going to do that with

Reilly and Salsa in tow? *¡Ay, caramba!* What had I been thinking?

"I know, baby," I cooed, glancing at her in the rearview mirror. "I'll take you for a run later, promise."

"What now?" Reilly asked, twirling a strand of her hair.

"You and Salsa can wait here while I try to find a place to hop the fence," I suggested.

She wagged her finger at me, looking for all the world like she was going to say, "Uh-uh, no you didn't." But instead she said, "You're *loca. Loca.* First of all, I did not come all this way to the ritzy part of town only to sit in the car with your dog. No way. If this is how the other half lives, I wanna see it. Like up close and personal. And second of all, I want to see what kind of woman lands herself a professional basketball player. I mean, it didn't work out so good for Vanessa Williams, if you know what I mean, and what about Kobe Bryant? 'Course that's the Lakers, so that may be the problem, but I think they're all serial cheaters. I mean, what about Wilt Chamberlain?"

"But look at Lamar Odom—"

Reilly wagged her finger at me. "Oh no, don't even get me started on Lamar and Khloe. They're bucking the odds." She rapped her knuckles on the car's plastic interior. "Knock on wood." She kept talking, as if I hadn't interrupted.

"So if your girl...Rochelle, right?" I nodded, and she went on, working herself into a tizzy. "If your girl Rochelle landed herself one of the few monogamous players out there, I just want to take a gander at her, *entiendes*? You cannot make me stay out here. Uh-uh. No way."

"So what about climbing the fence?" I asked her, but I knew the answer. Exercise wasn't one of her favorite pastimes. Yes, she was usually game for any sidekick P.I. duty, but that didn't mean she was willing to risk her freedom by breaking into the gated community in broad daylight.

"Uh-uh, no way," she said again, and then she flashed me a flirty grin. "I save my athleticism for my teddy bear."

Salsa's floppy ears perked up, but I peered at Reilly and said, "*¿Qué dices?* No, no, no. T.M.I."

She shrugged. "I'm just saying…"

"A few months ago you were head over heels in love with Antonio. Don't you think you're moving a bit fast with Neil?"

Her mouth gaped open. "No way, *chica*! When you know, you know. Antonio was a diversion. He was eye candy. Nothing but a one-night stand—"

"But you didn't *have* a one-night stand with him!"

"Your brother is smokin' hot, Lola, but Neil? Neil is the real deal." She winked and added, "He knows just what to do."

"*¡Ay, ay, ay!*" I muttered, shaking my head. The girl had it bad. "I just don't want you to be hurt."

"Don't worry about me. I'm good. You just worry about Jack. What happened to him, anyway?" She turned in her seat, staring at me as if I were Jennifer Lopez. "Oh no! You didn't break up, did you? Oh, tell me you and Jack are together."

I patted the air with one hand. "*Cálmate.*"

She rolled down the window of my CRV, sucking in a deep breath. "I'm calm," she said, turning back to me. "Now, tell me."

Poppies growing on the side of the road gave me an idea. I turned onto Auburn Folsom Road and headed back the way we'd come, searching for a grocery store. "We're not together," I said, "but we're not *not* together."

Salsa whimpered in the back as Reilly harrumphed. My peanut gallery. "Um, what does that even mean?"

Buena pregunta. "Good question," I answered, and then debated how to answer. "I told you about the Sarah thing. She's like a disobedient child. Her family keeps coming to get her, but then she goes off her meds and sneaks away—"

"To Jack," Reilly finished.

"*Exactamente.*"

"And he takes her back, or what?"

"No." To his credit. I knew he was trying to cut ties, but the girl was crazy. "He's kicked her out."

"So what's the problem? You know he's into you."

Leave it to Reilly to cut to the chase. I gripped the steering wheel, wishing I could avoid the question. In the rearview mirror, I met Salsa's melancholy eyes. She scooted forward, resting her jowls on the backrest of the seat. Sweet girl. She thought she was human, and sometimes I wondered just how much she really understood.

"Come on. Spill it."

But I didn't have to, at least not quite yet. I spotted a Bel Air Market and whipped into the parking lot. Saved by the grocery store. The Indian summer had finally given way to cool autumn temperatures, so I cracked the window and left Salsa in the car to hold down the fort. Sixty dollars later, I owned a lovely flower arrangement, and five minutes later we were heading back to Rochelle Nolan's gated community.

"Clever," Reilly said, holding onto the flower vase.

"It's worth a shot." We'd come all this way. To go back to Sacramento with nothing to show for our time wasn't going to earn me any P.I. points at the office.

"So," Reilly said after a spell. "Nice try, but what's the answer?"

Damn. She was nothing if not dogged. "What was the question?"

"That Jack Callaghan is into you, so what's your problem? Have you, you know"—she lowered her voice, as if there were children in the car who she didn't want to hear—"done the deed?"

Any good Catholic girl would have blushed at that question. I was a very good Catholic girl. My mother would've been proud. "*Híjole*, Reilly. What kind of question is that?"

"Curious minds, and all that." She grinned like she thought she knew the answer.

Which she didn't.

"*Pues*, truth?" I finally said.

"*¡Sí, sí, sí!*" She angled herself more toward me, as if I were going to give her all the down and dirty details of Jack and me.

Only there were no down and dirty details.

"No."

There. I'd said it. If only there were a few flies in the car she could catch with her open mouth.

The flowers started lilting right. "Wait...what?"

"Reilly!"

I grabbed for the vase, but she managed to straighten it before the flowers fell out, never even blinking. The girl was single-minded. "But you were with Sergio, and—"

I threw up my hand, stopping her short. I did not need a rundown of my past sexual exploits. "*¡Cállate!* With Jack, it's different. Ever since high school, I knew—"

"Lola. This isn't high school."

Boy, did I know that. When I was a nubile sixteen-year-old, Jack was the sexiest teenager I'd ever laid eyes on. *Pero* now? At thirty-one, he was downright irresistible. How I steered clear of him on a continual basis was a mystery. "If it's going to happen, I just don't want there to be any baggage."

Reilly, the newly anointed relationship expert, scoffed. Scoffed! "There's always baggage, right? Take Neil. All his contacts, like the DMV girl, and the courthouse girl, and the Caltrans girl? Not just friends. Uh-uh. They're all *exes*. He's got loads of baggage, but he's still the right one for me." She paused, the flowers listing again, a momentary frown crossing her lips. "Pretty sure he is, anyway."

"That's my point," I said, turning onto the gated drive of Rochelle's development. "If it's going to happen, I want to know for sure. I don't want to wonder."

She shook her orange-haired head. "You never know for sure. You have to take a chance every now and then."

As I rolled down my window, I glanced at Reilly, wondering when she had become the voice of reason in my romantic life.

• • •

Reilly squealed as the security guard opened the gate and waved us through. "I can't believe it worked!"

"Yeah, easy." Some security station. Either the guard was horrible at his job, or they had loose rules about delivery people coming in and out. Either way, it didn't give me confidence that paying top dollar to live in a gated community was worth the extra money.

We wound through the rolling hills of the neighborhood, searching for the address I'd found for Rochelle. The sprawling estates with their waterfalls, fountains, cobbled driveways, and turrets made me feel like I was on a movie set rather than in a suburb of Sacramento. So this was how the rich lived.

Finally I turned onto a private cul-de-sac.

"Holy macaroni!" Reilly blurted.

She'd taken the words right out of my mouth.

I tossed a rawhide bone to Salsa, cracked the windows again, and told her to be good.

A minute later, Reilly and I stood on the driveway staring at the monstrous house with its enormous fountain, lion statues, and the soaring ceiling of the porch. I marched past the fountain, Reilly on my heels, and rang the doorbell. A tune chimed from inside. I tapped my booted foot, finally ringing the bell again when no one came.

"Darn. After all that, she's not home?" Reilly said, but the words had barely left her mouth when a figure appeared from behind the beveled glass and the door swung open.

Rochelle Nolan stood before us, a pristine white Maltese in her arms. Now that I was standing in front of her, I recognized her from past publicity shots. She was every bit as glamorous as she was supposed to be, considering she was Sacramento's version of Khloe Kardashian. The thrill of being near a celebrity went through me. My knees wobbled. Imagine what it would be like to actually meet Juanes. Or Jennifer Lopez. Or Selma Hayek.

I shut the door on those thoughts and got to work. Rochelle's stick-straight blond hair was like a perfect sheet of golden ash. It made me wish I'd taken even just a second to run my fingers through my hair instead of haphazardly clipping it up in the back with a claw. Being painted and primped for the basketball games had made me want to do pretty much nothing when I wasn't at a game. *Au naturel*, that was my new motto.

From behind me, I heard Salsa give an exploratory bark. Rochelle's dog responded instantly, straining in her arms. It yelped, and Salsa's deep, baritone bark responded back in a full-on barking frenzy. *Oh boy*.

Rochelle peered over my shoulder. "You bring your dog on your deliveries?"

"Sometimes," I said. "A girl and her best friend."

"Ah," she said, as if she knew exactly what I meant. She pointed to the flowers. "Are those for me?"

"What?" Reilly stared blankly at her.

"The flowers," I said under my breath. Reilly was a total reality-show junkie. She was starstruck.

"Oh! Yes. Sorry. Flower delivery!" She thrust the arrangement toward Rochelle, but the former dancer didn't take it.

She lifted one shoulder, showing us her yapping Maltese. "Do you mind putting it there?" she said, turning to point to a brass-rimmed glass occasional table.

Reilly hesitated, but I put my hand on her lower back and gave a shove. Getting into Rochelle's house was exactly what I wanted, and she'd invited us in.

Reilly put the flower arrangement on the table, stepping aside as Rochelle bent over them and breathed in. "No card?" she asked, straightening.

"Oh? I guess not." I forged ahead before she could

question us about who'd sent the flowers. "You were on that reality show, weren't you?" I said, infusing admiration into my voice.

It worked. She stroked her hair with her free hand, preening. "Good memory," she said. "I'll give you an autograph if you want."

I gave a thrilled smile. Rochelle Nolan's autograph was the last thing on my mind, but it was a handwriting sample. Booya! I dug my notebook out of my purse. "Very exciting! I've never met a real live celebrity before." I handed her a pen and as she scrawled her name across the page, I cleared my throat. "You're not on the Royal Courtside dance team anymore, are you?"

Her face tensed, almost imperceptibly, and she shook her head as she scrawled her name. All loops and curlicues. *Not* the note writer. Damn. "I'm not, no." She held out her left hand. Reilly and I stumbled back, nearly blinded by the sparkling rock on her ring finger. "I'm engaged—"

"To one of the players, right?" Reilly blurted. "Number Seven? But isn't he married?"

I tried to mouth *"cállate"* to Reilly, but I couldn't catch her gaze. Rochelle was going to kick us out before I could uncover anything.

Her lips froze, but she spoke through her teeth. "They're separated."

"So you haven't set a date yet?" Reilly asked.

"Reilly," I said with a hiss.

But Rochelle waved away my concern. "It's not like it's a secret. She moved out and I moved in. The divorce will be final in a few months and then Michael and I are going to Hawaii and getting married on the beach. And there won't be a thing the former Mrs. Brothers will be able to do about it."

I mustered up some sympathy, no easy task given that she was the other woman. But it was necessary. Maybe the current Mrs. Michael Brothers was behind the notes. "Has she been difficult?"

Rochelle's toy dog yipped at me, and once again I wondered if humans seriously underestimated how much dogs could understand. "Shh shh, Princess."

Rochelle stroked her Maltese, moving her fingers around the hot pink clip in Princess's hair. The high-pitched barking didn't stop.

My head started pounding and inside I was sending love to my barrel-chested, kick-ass boxer. No sissy barking allowed.

"You were saying?" I asked over Princess, amazed that Rochelle hadn't questioned who we were or why we were so curious about her boyfriend's wife. Her sheet of hair blocked her face as she cooed at Princess…who had her dark eyes trained on me. "You're a reporter, aren't you?"

Princess's bark grew sharper and more shrill. She might be miniature, but she was suddenly fierce, baring her sharp white teeth.

"No!" I waved my hands, then pointed at the arrangement of roses and gladiolas and baby's breath. "Just delivering flowers."

"Flowers from whom? There's no card. Michael doesn't send me flowers—Oh, I know," she said, a light bulb going off behind her eyes. "They're from *her*, aren't they? I'm surprised they're not black roses."

"From Mrs. Brothers? No," I said, making a split-second

decision. "I'll be honest with you…"

"Not Mrs. Brothers." She fanned her hand in front of her. "Oh, never mind." Princess's barks subsided, as if she were ready to listen to my story, too. "What. What do you want?"

"I'm a private investigator—"

Her eyebrows shot up. "You?"

I'd dressed for efficiency, in case I had to climb a fence to get near Rochelle's house. I took mental stock of my outfit. Olive green pants, flat-heeled taupe boots, a long-sleeved T-shirt, and my favorite worn jean jacket. With my hair pulled up, loose strands framing my face, I probably appeared more like I was ready to hit a casual restaurant and browse the shops at Arden Fair.

"Yes, me. I was hired by Lance and Victoria Wolfe." I watched her closely, trying to gauge her response.

"From the Royals?" Her eyes pinched as she peered at me. "Why?"

"Some of the dancers have received vaguely threatening notes."

Princess snuggled closer to her. That was one thing Salsa didn't do. She'd come stand next to me and lay her chin on my thigh, but she was too big to snuggle. If I laid down on the ground, she climbed right on top of me.

"I was there when they started. We chalked it up to a superfan. We all had plenty of those."

She moved toward the door. "I don't have anything to do with the Royals anymore. Hypocrites."

Reilly and I followed slowly, stalling for time. "Why hypocrites?"

Princess started barking again as Rochelle pulled open

the door. "How much time do you have? They kicked me off, but Michael can stay. It's not fair."

I had to agree, but double standards were everywhere. "The notes. Do you think it was about your aff—" I broke off before I offended her with the wrong word. "About your relationship with Michael?"

She shook her head. "No. Other girls got them, too."

Precisely what Jennifer had said at our first meeting.

"Do you have any other ideas about the notes?"

Again, she shook her head. "I'm done with them. They can have their stupid rules and conquests and their secret meetings and their double standards. I have Michael." And with that, she shut the door, leaving us on the porch, not a single step closer to the truth.

• • •

I sat at the conference table at Camacho & Associates, waiting for a last-minute staff meeting to start, trying not to stare at Reilly's orange hair. In the fluorescent lighting of the office, it glowed. No wonder Rochelle Nolan had been on guard. Aside from the strange flower delivery.

Neil lumbered out of his lair, head bobbing on his shoulders, no neck between. His gaze passed over Reilly and damn it if his lip didn't quirk. Guess he liked fluorescent.

"New case," he said in his caveman way.

"*Híjole,*" I muttered. When it rained, it poured. "Busy month." Everyone but me was overbooked, working two or more files. But mine was time-consuming so it all evened out.

"October. Riffraff." Neil spoke in fragments and staccato statements, leaving whoever he was talking with to fill in the blanks.

I strung his thoughts together and said, "Guess so."

I didn't have enough experience to make such a definitive claim about October so I continued my finger-strumming on the table.

At precisely three thirty the door to Manny's office opened and he sauntered out, his ever-present limp marring his swagger only slightly. "Sadie?"

Neil heaved his shoulders again and said, "Not here," just as the door to the parking lot *swoosh*ed open and Sadie breezed around the corner and into the conference room. Her long red fingernails clasped the straps of her purse, the spikes of her blond hair a lighter version of her nails.

"What's the emergency?" she demanded, not meeting Manny's gaze, yet he was the only one who'd have the answer.

Manny ignored her and got right to business. He spent the first ten minutes reviewing his active cases with us.

Next, Neil gave an overview on his cases and added a few notes to his whiteboards. "I'll be setting up sound outside an apartment I've been watching," he finished.

No response. It was the way men operated. Manny turned to Sadie.

She sliced her claws through the air. "I don't need any help. My cases are fine. I'm doing great."

Her eyes were glassy. She didn't *look* like she was doing great. The lavender smudges under her bloodshot eyes made me think she hadn't slept in twenty-four hours and was running on some thin fumes.

Manny swallowed, his Adam's apple sliding up and down his throat. His jaw pulsed as he tightened his lips. "Would you please," he said slowly and with strained control, "review your cases."

It was a demand, not a question.

Sadie rolled her eyes up to the ceiling and spewed out an exasperated sigh. "Fine. I'm *still* trying to catch a cheating husband but he's so goddamned good at losing me when I tail him." She ground one fist into the palm of the opposite hand. "Sonofabitch," she added under her breath. "I'm also working on the embezzlement case at the hair salon. It's taking way too much time. Then I have the Courtside Danc—" She broke off, tapping her nails against the table. "Oh wait, that's not mine."

Manny leveled a stern look at her but didn't bite. Instead, he used her mention of the Courtside Dancers to turn to me.

"I've been to Rochelle Nolan's house." I relayed the conversation I'd had with her, ending with, "It's possible the notes are from Michael Brothers's wife."

"*Bueno,*" he said. "*¿Y más?*"

Only that I'd lost a clue. My only consolation was that none of the recovered notes had yielded anything, so the chances were slim that the one delivered to Geneva would have been the same. But still…

"One of the girls got a letter yesterday. Same message. Delivered by a ball boy for the team. It was thrown away by a waitress before I could get it, but there's another game day after tomorrow."

I sank in my chair, sucking in a deep breath as I braced myself for the fallout, but it didn't come from Manny. Instead, it was Sadie who shook her head at me. "Good going, Nancy Drew."

I wondered if I'd ever get to the point where Sadie didn't

ruffle my feathers. I suspected that the answer was NO. "I tried to get it," I explained, "but I had to keep my cover—"

"Did you go through the trash? Come on, Dolores. You claim you want this more than anything, but any detective worth her salt will take the extra steps—"

"Enough," Manny barked. "It's done."

I breathed out, relieved that Sadie was finished with her rant, but inside I knew she was right. I should have done more to get back that note.

Manny's jaw pulsed. "Anything else?"

"It's too soon to form a hypothesis but I'm getting to know some of the women. They're not warming up easily. It's going to take some time."

"So everyone's tapped." He moved his gaze from Neil to me to Sadie. "And we have a new case."

Sadie laid her palm against her chest and said, "I'll take it."

He shook his head. "Dolores has the lightest load."

"I said I'll take it," Sadie retorted as she scooted back her chair. My mother would have been impressed by the unspoken *punto* her tone held. *I* was impressed. "She already has the cream of the crop."

That was debatable. Neither Neil nor Manny could pull off the Courtside Dancers' outfits, though they might have enjoyed the scenery. And doing a dance routine without reminding people of an elephant? Not so easy.

Sadie waited, her nostrils flaring. My heart was ricocheting around in my chest. *Let her take it*, I silently willed to Manny. I didn't want to filch another case from her and I needed to concentrate on the Courtside Dancers so I could get the hell away from duct tape, being nearly naked in front of thousands of people, and the pain of perpetual exercise.

Manny paused before saying, "It's yours then. Insurance fraud. Primarily surveillance."

Sadie waggled her head, seething. Insurance fraud was nobody's idea of fun. I bit my lower lip, holding in a snicker. She'd been duped by a master. "You've got to be kidding." She swallowed. Hard. "You can't do this. I have rights here."

I snuck a peek at Reilly, who raised her dark eyebrows at me. She was queen of office *chisme* and her gossip revealed that Manny and Sadie had done the deed once or twice. Which was intel I would have preferred not to know, but it explained the arctic temperature in the conference room. By the way she perched on the edge of her chair, I knew Reilly was as curious as I was. I suspected we were both confident that Manny and Sadie were talking about more than the case at this point.

"I never kid," Manny said, his voice calm and controlled. "You should know that by now."

Yikes. Round one to Camacho. Over and out.

Chapter Seven

"Thanks for coming on such short notice," Antonio said.

"No problem," I said, "*pero* I have to leave by five o'clock."

"Sure thing. I'll catch the end of the shift."

I did a double take. *Sure thing? I'll catch the end of the shift?* Something was up. I lowered my chin and leveled my wary eyes at him. "*¿Qué pasa, hermano?*"

He gave me his patented Cheshire cat grin, his lips disappearing under the hair of his goatee. "*Nada.* What's up with you? What'd you do yesterday?"

My stomach clenched at the question. "Oh, you know, this and that."

He lifted his chin as his eyelids lowered. "Uh-huh."

"I was working on a new case," I offered, taking the tray of silverware out to the tables.

As I laid the wrapped bundles down at each place on the first table and moved on to the next, I felt Antonio's gaze burning into me. I wheeled around to face him. "What?"

He flung his hands up, palms out, and pasted an innocent expression on his face. "Nothing."

Alarms went off in my head. Damn. Did he know I was moonlighting as a cheerleader? He was a Royals fan, but surely he would have been working during the game, not catching it on TV.

I schooled my face, making it as impassive as I could. He didn't say another word, just sauntered back to the kitchen to check on the food prep. Which left me wondering exactly what he knew…if anything.

I stared after him, exhaling the pent-up breath I'd been holding. My imagination was getting the better of me. There was no way he knew anything. Even if he'd seen the game, it wasn't like the cameramen took many close-ups of the dancers. We did our full routines during commercial breaks, and even if he saw the game, I'd been on the sidelines. I deposited the last of the silverware bundles at my grandparents' booth.

"*Mija, dame nietos*," my grandmother said, her knitting needles clicking against each other in constant rhythm.

"Give you grandchildren? Abeulita, we've been through this," I said in Spanish. "I'm not married, and I don't have any immediate prospects." Even with Jack in the picture. "*Habla con Gracie*." My sister was a happily married schoolteacher. Kids were in her immediate future.

My grandmother shook her head, as if I were a sister at the Order of the Benedictine Sisters of Guadalupe and I'd just told her I was leaving the Church. Her knitting needles clicked together faster.

My grandfather, meanwhile, stretched his arm out from the table and held the falcon on top of his cane. "Dolores, have you given up this foolishness?"

"What foolishness is that, *Abuelo*?" Their list of my follies was long and detailed. Topping it was the fact that I was a good Catholic girl who hadn't settled down to raise a passel of good Catholic babies. Being a P.I. tied with first place.

After setting my tray on their table, I crossed my arms and waited for the lecture.

"*Ah, hay mucho,*" my grandmother said. She reached out a gnarled finger and touched my arm, reciting the rosary under her breath in Spanish. Since my last case when I'd been reported as dead, she prayed for my soul daily. Multiple times. A month ago she had thought I was gone. She was still coming to terms with it, touching me and wondering if I were real.

I pulled away, scolding her. "*Abuela.*"

"*Tu trabajo.*" Grandfather paused, thinking, then stuck a finger in the air and continued in his mafioso hiss. "*Y tu novio,*" he added, referring to Jack.

It was the same conversation every time I set foot in the restaurant. Their standard complaint was that being a detective was not an appropriate job for their grand-daughter and that I needed a man. At twenty-nine, I was rapidly approaching over the hill.

"My job is fine, *gracias or preguntar.*" I ignored the rest. Whether or not Jack Callaghan was my boyfriend—and what that meant for my future—was not my grandparents' business. I was a big girl, willing to lie in whatever bed I made—with or without Jack Callaghan. Preferably with, but that wasn't happening anytime soon. I took my tray and disappeared into the kitchen.

The late-lunch/early-dinner shift passed without incident

or surprise visits from Jack. I left at five on the dot to get showered and ready for the Royals game.

Forty minutes later, my wet hair was in a towel, I'd packed folded jeans and a ruffled floral blouse into my duffel bag for after the game, and I'd pulled on a navy velour sweat suit. I put on a thin layer of makeup and was packing the whole kit-and-kaboodle into a toiletry bag when the phone rang.

It wasn't in the cradle on my dresser. Damn it. Another reason to move into my own place. Antonio never put the phone back where it belonged.

I dashed through the flat, following the ring. It wasn't by the computer in the living room. Finally, just before the fourth jingle started, I found the receiver buried between the cushions of the sofa.

"What're you doing tonight?" Jack asked across the line. He didn't sound like he knew I'd been cheering on six-foot-five basketball players the day before. I thought about just coming clean and telling him. Yes, he'd taken a bullet for me, and yes, he seemed sincere when he said he cared about all of me, including Lola Cruz, P.I. But the idea of him watching me as I jiggled and flipped and shimmied in front of thousands of people while scantily dressed sent waves of nerves on alert. In the privacy of his apartment? I was down with that, but at the Royals' arena? Um, no.

So I kept my mouth shut. Dancing for the Royals felt like a dirty little secret. I'd worked so hard in school, had earned my college degree in criminal justice, and didn't want anybody, especially Jack, to see me as *just* a body. My goal was to wrap up this case *muy pronto*, before anyone found out and saw me getting jiggy with the cheerleaders.

"Oh, I'm…um…I have plans," I said. I glanced at the clock. 5:23. I had to dry my hair and get to the arena by 6:00 for warm-ups. Friday night traffic. *¡Ay, caramba!* I had to move *muy rápido* if I was going to be on time. And seeing as I was a follow-the-rules kind of girl, I definitely did not want to be late.

"Are you sure? I have ti—"

"Sorry Jack," I blurted. "I really can't talk now. I'll call you later, okay?"

I hung up the phone before he could convince me to tell him my plans. I pushed my lingering women's lib ideals out of my mind. It was all for the job. Fifty minutes and a barely escaped collision on I-5 later, I raced through the tunnel at the arena to warm up with the dancers. Before too long, the basketball teams would be taking the floor to warm up their players.

A tall man, about six-foot-four, lean and lanky, sauntered across the court toward us as we went through one of the routines. He gave us two thumbs up before disappearing into the tunnel.

I scooted close enough to Jennifer to ask, "Who was *that*?"

"Michael Brothers," she said.

Ah. So *that* was Rochelle's ball player.

A sharp pain shot through my side and I lost my balance as Jennifer's foot plowed into me.

"Jesus, move over, Lola!" Victoria shouted from the side of the court. "Keep your head in the routine."

Processing through a potential clue and remembering dance steps was not as easy as walking and chewing gum at the same time. Victoria was right—I needed to concentrate on the dancing right now.

As Jennifer got into starting position and led us through the routine, I thought about one of Manny's mantras: *Things are rarely as easy as they appear to be.* My P.I. radar, once again, pointed in the direction of Rochelle Nolan or Mrs. Michael Brothers. Either one of them could have a grudge against Victoria or the team, Rochelle for being dismissed, and Mrs. Brothers for being replaced as Michael's wife.

The last routine finished, and I retreated into the locker room to begin my preparations for the game, beginning with makeup, which I enhanced considerably. It ended with taping my cleavage to maximum plumpness and slipping on my costume, which today consisted of shorts that barely covered more than my favorite string bikini did and a tight, glimmering royal blue iridescent shirt that tied at the breastbone.

¡Ay, ay, ay! I liked my sex appeal as much as the next girl, but this was overboard. A little cleavage and a feminine, ruffled skirt? *Sí.* A short skirt and lots of leg with a more modest top? Yes. *Pero* both? My heart pounded at how many people would be seeing me dressed in almost nothing.

I found an empty corner in the changing room. Lying flat on my back, I did fifty crunches. My abs weren't quite as defined as some of the dancers', but after the sit-ups I knew the muscles were there, even if they were buried under cheese enchiladas and breakfast burritos.

The nerves that had jumped willy-nilly in my stomach at the last game had ratcheted up again, and by the time the dance team glided onto the court, I was energized and ready. I'd rock that arena. And I'd seize any opportunity to figure out who was sending the threatening letters to my teammates.

Chapter Eight

We spaced out and did our "warming up the crowd" routine, pointing and kicking to the pounding beat of the music. The individual team members were introduced, the national anthem was sung a cappella, and the Courtside Dancers hurried back to the dressing room for the first costume change.

Game on.

When we came back to the front of the tunnel, I watched the game, paying special attention to the ball boys and the sweat moppers as they scurried around. Not a single one of them held an envelope or a guilty expression, nor did they do anything other than their job.

The team played through first quarter before we took to the floor again. I stayed in position, got every step right, and before long the first routine was over.

We went back to the dressing room for a water break. I took a deep drink, reapplied my lipstick, and sat next to Jennifer. "Tell me about the players."

"There's nothing to tell. Best to stay away from them," she said.

I gave her a sideways glance. "What do you mean?"

She studied her face in the mirror as she retied her shirt. "Victoria says it's unprofessional. We're supposed to stay away from them, especially during games."

"Why especially during games?"

Carrie, the dancer who was sitting to my left, piped up. "Look in the triangle above the bench."

"The players' bench?"

"Yup."

The players sat along the court line if they were suited up. If they were out for the game, they dressed in nice street clothes and sat out behind the players.

"When you go back out," she continued, "check out the triangle."

"Tell her why," Selma said, coming up beside me.

Carrie swung her hair behind her shoulders. "Take note and steer clear. Those are the players' wives."

They were so damned cryptic, but what they were saying registered like a neon sign. "So we can't talk to any of the players because their wives might get pissed off. Got it."

Jennifer smirked. "After you're done gawking at the wives, check out a couple rows above them."

I bit. "Okay, why?"

Carrie dropped her voice. "That's where the girlfriends sit."

I stared, the subtext of her words sinking in. Still, I asked for clarification, thinking maybe I was wrong and it wasn't quite so blatant. "So the players who have wives...those women sit in one section, and the players with girlfriends...

they sit in a different section?"

"No," Jennifer said. "What I mean is that Number Thirty-four's wife is sitting with the other wives, and his girlfriend is sitting with the girlfriends. Nice and sordid, but tidy. Almost all of them have wives *and* girlfriends."

¡Ay, caramba!

"A method to the adultery madness, so to speak," Jennifer added.

I shook my head, trying to grasp that it was just accepted that the ballplayers were unfaithful spouses. But did the wives know? I came back to thinking one or more of them might be behind the notes to the dancers.

Carrie pulled out her lipstick, carefully applying it to her plump lips. My money was on silicone. She patted my knee. "So we steer clear."

After Carrie sauntered off, Selma sat down, rolling her eyes.

"But can I talk to the players off the court?" I asked her. "I mean, how did Rochelle hook up with Michael Brothers?"

"Have you *seen* Rochelle?"

Big boobs. Blond hair. Paris Hilton's twin. "Yep."

"Guess Mike Brothers likes that."

Selma was the exact opposite. Slighter build, natural beauty, a golden all-over tan, and normal-size breasts. Even made up for the game, she was the girl next door.

"So they make the moves on the dancers if they're interested?"

Selma made a face. "Sometimes the girls will get notes from the opposing team's players, inviting us to a party or something. If you're lucky, a player from the Royals will try to hook up." She made sure Jennifer wasn't listening and lowered her voice. "If one of us goes that way, we do it at our own risk. We all signed contracts when we got this gig. We are not allowed to fraternize with the players."

"So that's why Rochelle, er, left?" She may have quit, publicly, to save face, but it seemed clear to me that Victoria had pulled a Donald Trump on her with a, "You're fired."

"Mmm-hmm."

Before I could ask her anything else, she spritzed perfume in the air, walked through the mist, and hurried back to the court for the second half of the game.

. . .

We were just heading toward the tunnel after our next routine when one of the ball boys jogged over, a white envelope clutched in his hands. He gave it to Selma. She held it with two fingers, and from the way the ball boy had been pawing it, getting fingerprints might be sketchy, but at least Selma was trying.

But then, from the corner of my eye, I saw her run a finger under the flap of the envelope. No! She'd been at Camacho & Associates when Manny had said he hoped to get fingerprints off of one of the notes. Why was she opening it?!

But I couldn't get to her in time to stop her. The envelope snapped open and she slid out the tri-folded paper, holding it by the edges.

Good girl, Selma. She was being careful, anyway. We might get prints off the note itself. She read the lines of the letter, her eyes growing wide.

I scanned the court but in the dim light it was too

difficult to tell if anyone was paying attention to her. I studied the ball boy. He slowed his pace as he walked by me. He couldn't have been more than eighteen. I crooked my finger, motioning him toward me as I jogged out of line and leaned against the wall.

"Hey," he said. The acne on his face confirmed his youth.

"Hey back." I held in a cringe at the come-hither wink he sent me. "Got one of those for me?"

The ball boy shrugged, his eyelids heavy as he considered me. "Not this time, baby."

I pouted, tilting my head to one side. "But where'd you get it?" I pointed to the rows above the players' bench. "From one of them?"

He shrugged again. "Nah. The letters are always by the clean towels. There was a note once that said for me to deliver to one of the Courtside Dancers, so now whenever there's an envelope, that's what I do."

"You deliver messages for someone but you have no idea who it is?" There had to be something in it for him.

"Pretty much."

"Do you get paid for it?"

"Sure do," he said, grinning. "Twenty bucks every time. It's always right there under the envelope."

Twenty dollars to scare the bejesus out of a dancer. Cheap labor. "And you have no idea who puts them there?"

He took a step back, wary. "I already told you, no. Why?"

Eek. Maybe I'd been too direct. *Undercover*, I reminded myself. I regrouped, giving him a flirty wink. Which, given my attire, felt altogether nasty. "Maybe someone'll give you one for me," I said coyly.

He relaxed. "Yeah. Maybe. You new here? I haven't seen

you around before."

"Just started this week." From the tunnel, the girls were intent on the game. I had a good long while to see if the ball boy knew anything that he didn't realize he knew. "How about you?"

"I've worked for the Royals since the season started." He leaned his shoulder against the wall.

I forced myself not to move away. "Bet you deliver notes to all the girls." Lame, I thought, but flirting with a teenager made me nauseous.

"Maybe I'll arrange a personal delivery." His voice rose over the cheering crowd and he edged his hand along the wall toward me.

"Oh, so you do know who—"

"From me." He stiffened beside me. "I'm right here. Why would ya want some loser who doesn't even know the players?"

Damn. "Oooh, so you know the players? Is there a party tonight?"

He leered, his eighteen-year-old, acne-scarred face making him look a touch unstable. "I'll show you a party. Real private-like."

Okay, now this was going too far. "Oh, I don't know…" I patted his hand in a gesture of dismissal, but he didn't take the hint.

"Come on, baby. Lemme show you the locker room. They don't let nobody back there anymore, but I'll give you a personal tour."

Hmm. This *was* tempting. I glanced around. We had about ten minutes before our next routine. "Can you give me the tour now?"

He seemed unsure as he glanced back toward the court, mulling it over before making up his mind. "Sure thing, baby. Hold that thought." He jogged down the court, said something to one of the moppers (who turned to gawk), then he jogged back.

He snatched my hand and pulled me into the tunnel after him. "What's your name, baby?"

What was with all the baby stuff? *He* was the baby in this equation. "Lola. What's yours?"

"Josh."

I pulled my hand free. "Well, Josh. Impress me. Why do they keep it so off-limits?"

"Scandals and stuff. Gotta protect the players." We walked side by side until he stopped short in front of the door to the locker room. "This is it."

Like any pro sports team, Royals players had had their share of accusations lobbed against them. Drugs. Gambling. Women. I hadn't been able to dig up any dirt on any of the dancers yet; the players were next in line.

"Can we go in?" I asked, wondering how I could get rid of him so I could search the lockers real quickly. Maybe I'd get lucky and find a stack of ready-to-deliver envelopes piled in a corner somewhere.

"Nah."

"Oh." I frowned. "Well, that's not much of a tour. I've never been this close to someone who actually *knows* famous basketball players."

Josh puffed up like a peacock, full of his own importance. "Well," he said, "maybe for a quick minute."

He pushed the door open, poked his head around the corner to check out the room, and, when he was sure the coast was clear, let me pass.

My heart pounded. It was only a locker room, but getting caught wasn't on my list of things to do tonight. Cubbies with the players' belongings lined the walls and a buffet spread far superior to the one in the dancers' locker room spanned two rectangular tables. Cases of bottled water were stacked in one corner, beside a soda machine, vending machine, and a closed door along another wall.

"This is it?" Despite the buffet, I expected more bells and whistles for a championship-contending basketball team.

Josh spread his arms wide as he turned around in a circle. "What d'ya mean, 'this is it?' This is the Royals' locker room. It's fan-freaking-tastic."

I walked by the cubby lockers, checking each one as surreptitiously as I could.

No envelopes.

No paper.

No writing instruments.

No big surprise.

I peeked through the window of the door next to the vending machine. Linens. "What's over there—?"

I broke off as Josh clamped a hand on my shoulder and spun me around. He crashed his mouth against mine, gripping my shoulders with his icy hands.

"Thtop!" Instincts kicked in. I hauled my knee up, slamming my foot down a split second later, landing squarely on his toes.

He screeched, pulling back. I threaded my arms in between his to knock his hands away and slapped his cheek. "What the hell are you doing, Josh?"

He held his palm to his face, hopping on one foot. "What

d'ya mean?" His eyes turned glassy. "*You* wanted to come in here."

Son of a bitch. "Right, to see the locker room. Dude, I'm way too old for you. And, uh, let me enlighten you. Girls you hook up with don't want to be groped the second you get them alone. Whatever happened to getting to know someone before exchanging spit?"

He looked me up and down, still clutching his reddened face. The cocky attitude had been replaced by eighteen-year-old confused frustration. "But you're dressed like...like..." He waved his hand up and down at my body. "Like that. And you're hot."

Pobrecito. It wasn't cool to mess with a teenager's libido. "Wanting a tour is not code for something else," I said. "Bit of advice, Josh. These dance costumes are a uniform. And even if a woman is dressed...er...suggestively, that's not a green light that she's game for a hookup."

Josh just stared at me, hurt and dumbfounded, but I didn't have time to give him any more mini lessons on how men should respect women. I resumed my quick search. I walked briskly through to the showers, glanced at the urinals and toilet stalls, and passed by another door. "What's in there?"

His shoulders slumped, his face morose, but he answered. "Doctor's room. Trainer uses it to work on the players. There's a hot tub for therapy."

I peered through the glass...and froze. We weren't alone. The trainer, Steve, was talking with someone, his back to the window, the other person out of my range of view.

I quickly retreated back to the main part of the locker room, thankful Josh and I hadn't been discovered. Victoria and Lance wanted me to investigate, but they couldn't let on they were okay with me breaking ranks—not to mention leaving the tunnel and scoping out the locker room. If I were busted, the wrath of the *real* Victoria would come hammering down on me. It would have to.

"Thanks for the tour, Josh," I said once we were back in the main corridor. "You're a great catch. Just give a girl a chance to see it."

I waved, then raced back to the tunnel.

The dancers were scattered in the opening. Selma was spooked, her black eyes like liquid pools in the midst of her creamy skin.

"Are you okay?" I asked, squeezing in between her and Cassie.

She said, "Yeah," hesitantly as Cassie whispered, "Where'd you go? Victoria'll have a conniption if she finds out you left the tunnel."

"Had to use the restroom," I said, the lie rolling off my tongue. Being a detective meant I was getting pretty good at blithe little fibs as cover stories. I'd be saying a truckload of rosaries when this case was over.

Selma clutched the envelope in her hand. I leaned closer. "Is it…?"

She fanned the envelope. "It can't be for me. *I* haven't done anything." She peered back through the tunnel as if someone back there *had* done something and she knew all about it.

"Isn't there a name on it?"

She flipped the envelope around. "Nope. Nothing."

I pried it from her fingers and scanned the letter, touching it only by the corners. *You can't hide the truth forever.*

It was definitely different than the others. "What truth? You don't know what it's talking about?"

Selma's face had paled and her voice cracked like a pubescent boy's. "I h-have n-no idea."

I didn't believe her. I was beginning to think that she had some other secrets under her sparkly sequined halter top.

A high-pitched whistle came from the stands. Selma's cheeks flared red and she turned her back on the fans.

"Do you get recognized a lot?" I asked. I got the feeling she really wished she could be in hiding rather than exposed for all to see at this game.

"All the time. Even when it's six in the morning and there's only one person in the store, someone always seems to know who I am. I wish I'd never done that reality show." She flicked her head toward the enormous scoreboard and the four gigantic TV screens mounted above the sections of stands. "Our faces get plastered up there. That's why Victoria says to never go out without makeup. Sometimes I just want to quit, you know?"

Standing on the other side of me, Cassie batted at my arm. "It's time. Let's go."

I tucked the letter behind Victoria's stool, straightened my outfit, and pumped my arms to get energized.

Jennifer skipped to her place in front of the line and counted. "One! And two! And three! And four!"

Three-and-a-half minutes later, sweat poured out of my pores and I knew why the dancers doused themselves in perfume. At the first opportunity I raced back into the dressing room and put Selma's letter into my duffel bag. Then I borrowed Jennifer's cologne, spraying into the air like I'd seen the girls do, walking through the falling mist. A few other dancers milled around the room, snacking from the buffet table before halftime. I took a stem of grapes, popping one in my mouth as I headed back toward the tunnel.

I finished my grapes, and a short while later we performed our last dance. We showered and I changed for dinner. I'd searched the crowd for Rochelle, but if she'd come to the game, she hadn't sat with the girlfriends or the wives. She was in a weird *limbo* state, existing somewhere between the two realities.

I had no chance to investigate any further. Too many people lingering postgame. Another day. With any luck, I'd have a brilliant idea by then. Or I'd find the arena empty and a slew of clues just waiting to be discovered.

I zipped up my brown platform boots and fastened the floral blouse that crossed over into a *V* at the neckline and tied at the side. I scrunched my hair in between my fingers to let it air dry the rest of the way, packed up my duffel, and wandered around the room.

More of the women smiled at me. Baby steps. If only my mother were here with a fresh batch of flour tortillas, I'd be in on the *chisme* in a second. They wouldn't be able to stop sharing the gossip with me.

The corner of a white envelope poking out of a bag caught my eye. I stopped short. Was it an old message, a new one, or something else entirely?

Nicole walked up behind me, raven hair glistening, the gap between her low-rise jeans and her half shirt equal to the dance outfit we'd just changed out of. "Can I help you with something?"

Of course it would be her bag. The one dancer who I was pretty sure had a stash of lemons in her bag—which she sucked on every time she saw me. *Pues*, maybe not the *only* one, but definitely the worst one. Swallowing, I tried to think of a plausible lie that could get her to rifle through the duffel. "I was hoping to see the earrings you wore after the last game. They were really cool."

She frowned, pulling her hair back behind her shoulders. "Which ones? I don't remember."

They *had* been cool, and I remembered thinking so. Now I racked my brain for the details, gesturing near my own ear as if I could make them materialize. "They were dangly, with a small square on top, and a bigger square under that, then a big circle. I think there were beads on them."

She snapped her fingers, her pouty red lips curving up. "Oh yeah. I dig those. I got them at this funky shop downtown."

"Do you have them with you? I'd love to see them again," I added, being sweeter than my mother's *buñuelos*.

She hesitated, and for a second I thought my buttering up was going to be a bust. But then she moved to her bag and pulled the zipper open the rest of the way. I bit my lip as the sides flapped down and the envelope slipped deeper into the duffle. I bent down to peer inside while she rifled through what seemed to be the entire beauty section of a drugstore. If she weren't a Royals dancer, Nicole could have been a traveling cosmetologist.

She took out the clothes on top, two toiletry bags, the envelope, a huge ring of keys, and finally a jewelry bag.

I tried to get a closer look at the envelope, but it was buried under the other items she'd dropped. She unfolded the trifold bag, revealing an array of enormous silver earrings, including the ones I'd mentioned. "Here they are," she said, holding them up for me to see.

The sparkling silver caught my eye. They really were fantastic. I took them and held them to my ear. She seemed to be warming up to me, so I kept chattering as I faced the mirror. "What's the name of the shop where you got them?"

"Vintage Things, off of Twenty-second Street."

Talking vintage clothing had brought out a bright side in Nicole's personality. She spent the next few minutes telling me everything about the store's eclectic fashions, right down to every single item she'd ever bought there. Pretty soon I was salivating to go on a shopping spree.

But it would have to wait. I had a case, and that took precedence over everything else. "They're cool." I gave them back and said, "Let me help you clean this up."

She tucked the earrings back into the jewelry bag while I gathered the toiletry bags and then the envelope, surreptitiously turning it over to see the back. It was smaller than the others. More like an invitation.

"I'll take that," Nicole said, pulling the envelope from my hand just like I'd slipped Selma's from her.

I summoned my acting skills again. "Is there a party? I heard there are some great ones after games sometimes."

"Don't believe everything you hear," she said, her sour mood back. She tucked the envelope into her bag, I added the clothes on top, and she zipped it up.

In the blink of an eye, she threw her bag over her boney shoulder and was out the door.

So much for building camaraderie.

• • •

The dancers had arranged to get together at a Howe 'Bout

Arden restaurant. More food. They were bottomless pits.

Trainer Steve and his brother waved to me as I wheeled my bag down the corridor. The team's leopard mascot, complete with a royal blue, gold-trimmed cape, jumped in front of me, wiggled his body, and spun around. I careened back, nearly falling on my behind. I managed to skirt around him, checking over my shoulder to make sure he wasn't following me, the rascal. He wasn't. I was in the clear.

As I rounded the corner, I ran smack into Jennifer. Not literally, but close. She leaned against the wall by the exit door, her packed duffel next to her.

"Are you coming?" I asked, stopping to talk to her.

She winked. "After a while."

My spidey senses went on alert. What was that wink about? "I'll wait with you," I said.

She sauntered down the hallway, throwing her hand up in a dismissive wave. "No, no. Don't wait for me. I'll be there," she tossed over her shoulder.

Hmm. Jennifer was up to something, and I wanted to know what. I dawdled on my way out the door. Finally, just as I was at the exit, I caught a glimpse of three Royals players heading toward her. One of them stopped while the other two kept walking my way.

"Hi," I said a few seconds later, moving out of their way.

One of them, Number 23, I think, held the door for me so I could maneuver my case through it. "Any time, baby."

I forced myself not to scowl as I moved outside, trying to see through the two enormous men, but Jennifer was gone and the other ballplayer was, too.

"How you doin'?" Number 34 asked, goggling me with dark brown eyes that matched his skin.

"Great." I gripped the handle of my case as I stepped outside, but my mind was musing over Jennifer. If I had to guess, I'd say she was breaking the rules and fraternizing with a player. But hadn't I just been warned about that very thing?

"Wanna have a private party?" the other player, I think he was Number 23, said, breaking me out of my reflections.

I tilted my head so I could see them. So tall. I much preferred the just right six-one of Jack Callaghan. "Are you married?" I asked Number 23, laughing in my head at the double entendre.

"Hell no."

Number 34 had a sneaky smirk on his lips.

Not married. Right. He might not have had a ring on, but the way he pressed his enormous thumb over his ring finger said it all. The guy was hitched and I felt sorry for his wife. And his girlfriend.

I wasn't going anywhere with them, and I was tired of playing games and getting nowhere, so I ponied up the burning question in my mind. "Do you know anything about some notes the dancers have been getting?"

"What notes?" Number 34 cracked another suggestive grin. "Come on, let's party."

"Gee. It's tempting, but no, thanks," I said. "Dinner with the girls."

They shrugged and disappeared into the night. They— and I—all knew that there was no shortage of women willing to par-tay with them, never mind a pesky wife or girlfriend.

Once they were gone and the coast was clear, I scurried back inside, dropped my duffel, and moved through the corridors, listening. What I was listening for, I didn't know, but there had to be something juicy going on behind one of these closed doors.

Didn't there?

But if there was, I couldn't find it. A steady stream of people still milled around—the cleaning crew, fans, and God knew who else. I finally gave up, gathered my belongings, and found my car. I felt like I was spinning in circles—moving a lot but getting nowhere. Some detective I was.

• • •

A short while later, I pulled into the restaurant parking lot off of Arden Way in the Arden Fair area of Sacramento and immediately spotted the rest of the dancers.

A couple of them waved as I walked up. Progress. A few minutes later, the table was ready. They turned and moved toward the entrance like a school of fish.

"Shouldn't we wait for Jennifer?" I asked, not seeing her with the group.

"Nah, she's always late," Cassie said with a wink.

A-ha! The perfect opening. "Why?"

"Boyfriend, of course."

Of course. "I saw her with one of the players. Is she—?"

But Cassie burst my bubble. "Nah. Her guy's a civilian."

"How do you know?"

"Jennifer had a few flings with players, but she's over them. Her new one? She said he's just a regular guy."

So Jennifer followed the rules, which meant no disgruntled wife. But then who was the player she'd scurried off with, and why had she gone with him? Could she be two-timing her civilian boyfriend? Could *that* have something to do with the mysterious letters?

Híjole. I had all kinds of theories, but proof of *nada.*

We filed into the bar like a line of well-dressed ants. Men and women turned to stare, recognition on their faces. Chattering came at me from all sides, and I got a taste of what it must feel like to be a celebrity on display. It was surreal. And uncomfortable. Incognito was definitely more my speed.

I searched for Selma, hoping to sit by her and find out more about Rochelle. The disgruntled Mrs. Brothers still seemed the most likely suspect at the moment, but part of me didn't really care all that much. The letters were barely threatening, and no one had been hurt. That insurance fraud case was looking better and better.

I sat next to Cassie around a long rectangular table that ran along the back wall between the bar and the restaurant. The stares and pointing continued as we ordered drinks and appetizers. And more appetizers. Chicken wings, potato skins, onion rings, artichoke dip, and chips and salsa. The list went on and on.

"Are you expecting an army to come join us?" I said after the waitress left.

Laughter burst out around the table and the girls shot knowing glances at one another. "Victoria and Jennifer."

My puzzled expression brought on more laughter. "Do they eat a lot?"

More glances. "They usually bring people with them," Cassie said. "The trainer, his brother, a few fans sometimes. Aren't you hungry?"

"Not *that* hungry."

Nicole rested her elbows on the table. "Me, too, but

dancing works up an appetite. I might as well take advantage of my metabolism while it's working with me instead of against me."

A moment later, Selma rushed in, her face flushed. She slipped into the chair next to me, out of breath but excited. "Listen, girls. I was leaving the arena and met three incredibly gorgeous guys!"

A collective roll of the eyes and an indulgent, "Selma…" floated over the table.

"No, really. Gorgeous. One of them has this goatee that you just want to squeeze and, oh my God, beautiful dark skin. One of them had a wedding ring, so I guess he's off limits. Real cute, though."

"Not necessarily off limits," Cassie said.

I stared at her, beginning to think the cheerleaders were as bad as the players, going for one-night stands and groupies who were titillated by their almost-not-there costumes and dirty dancing moves.

Selma gushed. "And the third guy. Holy shit. He could be a freaking movie star. Blue, blue eyes and a really sexy dimple." She closed her eyes for a second. The dreamy expression on her face made me think she was conjuring up an image of Adonis.

"I invited them to come along and"—she paused for effect, swinging her dark hair behind her—"they're coming!"

"I thought you had yourself a guy," one of the girls said to Selma.

"Oh, I do. I invited them for you all. You can thank me later," she said. Then she flung her head back and sunk in her chair, a satisfied lift to her lips.

The chattering continued around the table. I didn't get

any more information, but I was fitting in. Another step in the right direction. I guess this *was* better than insurance fraud.

Thirty minutes later Selma's gorgeous guys hadn't materialized. Maybe they'd stood up the poor girl. The team's trainer, Steve, and his season-ticket-holding brother ambled in, however. Selma scooted over her chair to make room for them and the small talk continued.

I focused on the conversations around me. Steve telling the girls how great they'd been. Larry, the brother, asking where Jennifer and Victoria were. Selma wiping the lipstick off her mouth while Nicole added more to hers.

A minute later, the chattering abruptly stopped. I froze, a few French fries in my mouth, gaping at the women—who were all staring at something behind me. A hand came down on my shoulder.

Selma's words came back at me and I gulped. A dimple and blue eyes. It couldn't be. But I *knew* that hand. My intestines tied themselves into inexplicable knots as I turned to look over my shoulder.

Jack.

Antonio stood behind him, a big ol' shit-eating grin on his swarthy, goateed face.

I peered around them to see who the other guy was.

Oh boy. My cousin Zac.

The guys Selma had met.

I made a series of expressions, trying to communicate to them all. *I'm undercover!* I tried to say.

"Jack," I said, sucked in by his liquid blue eyes.

The dimple Selma had admired worked its way into his cheek. "Lola," he said, looking *un poquito* hot and bothered. "Let's take a walk."

Chapter Nine

The dancers' voices came at me all at once, Selma's the loudest. "You *know* them?"

I forced a smile onto my lips. "Kind of."

Antonio's grin grew wider, if that was possible. "She better know me. I'm her brother."

Zac gave a wave. "I'm her cousin."

All the women turned their attention to Jack. Cassie hung her arm over the back of her chair. "And I guess *you* know her."

"Why yes, yes I do." He flashed a beguiling grin. "I'm her boyfriend."

I poked my finger in my ear. *¿Qué dice?*

I laughed but quickly whipped my head around so the dancers couldn't see my face and mouthed, *I'm undercover!*

He made a face at me, making it clear he already knew that. I'd wondered if Antonio had known back at the restaurant. Then I remembered Selma saying our faces were shown on the huge screens at the arena. Which meant they were probably seen at home on people's television sets, too. Oh, Lord.

Finally, I thought about the phone call with Jack earlier. He'd asked me to go with him somewhere and had started to say he had tickets—to the game, I now realized. He'd known and was giving me the chance to tell him.

I squinched my eye and flicked my chin so he'd follow me as I walked outside. I felt the weight of someone's stare on my back and glanced back at the table, keeping my smile intact. No wonder. Everyone was watching us like we were some part of a dinner theater. Oh, *bueno.* I was going to be the prime gossip tonight.

Antonio and Zac slipped into chairs at the table. We locked eyes and I shot daggers at them. God, I hoped they had sense enough to keep quiet about my being a detective.

"Hey, you," Jack said once we were outside.

I gulped down the anxiety bubbling up inside me, feeling like a big, fat liar. I hated not telling him what I was up to, but it was a toss-up if I hated that more than being caught red-handed keeping secrets. "Hey, yourself. What're you doing here?"

"Just what I was going to ask you."

"I'm working a case."

Jack shoved his hands in his pockets, his body tense. "I figured."

"I would have told you, but—"

He leaned against a brick pillar, staring off over my shoulder for a second. "But what? You don't trust me? Jesus, Lola, we're supposed to be a team."

I wanted to be, but I'd been keeping my distance, protecting my heart. "You're still dealing with Sarah—"

"I told her I'm done, that she isn't going to interfere with my life anymore." He lifted his hands and sliced his palms through the air. "She's gone."

My eyes got glassy. "*¿Verdad?*"

His eyes darkened. He'd told me that my Spanish drove him wild…in the best possible way. I could see how the one word slipped under his skin. He drew me to him. With my heels on and my head tilted back a touch, my lips met his perfectly.

"I didn't want to make a fool of myself in front of you," I said quietly.

"In front of the whole world, but not me?"

My lungs felt short of air. It sounded ridiculous when he put it that way, and I'd never been one to back away from a challenge. Hello, I was Xena, Warrior Princess. "You saw the outfits."

He spoke slowly, suddenly looking pained and frustrated. "Yes, I did." He bent, moved his mouth to my ear. "I liked what I saw. I've always liked it." And then his lips brushed my neck and a wave of goose bumps swept over my skin.

He took a deep breath and pulled back, something else simmering behind his eyes. "Your friend in there," he said. "She cornered us at the arena when I was looking for you. Finally she invited us here and promised us a *real* good time."

Indignance flared inside of me. "And you wanted that good time? Nice, Callaghan."

"I had a feeling you'd be here—"

"Working—"

"Uh-huh. And how far are you willing to go for your job, Cruz?"

Ah. Now I understood the brewing question. I'd spent months being jealous of Sarah and whatever hold she had on Jack. Now the tables had turned.

"Not *that* far. *She* might make good on that, if you're interested," I said, "but me?" I batted my eyelashes at him, my hand pressed to my chest. "I have a boyfriend."

One side of his mouth lifted. "Good to know you have limits, Lola."

• • •

Jack, Antonio, and Zac finally left, my cover was intact, and I settled back into the conversation. But Jack's statement stuck with me. How far *was* I willing to go for my job? That was the million-dollar question. I'd bared more of myself on the Royals' court than I was comfortable with. Especially given the duct-taped breasts.

I was willing to go pretty far, but I wouldn't sacrifice my relationship with Jack if it came right down to it.

Cassie had drowned her disappointment over the gorgeous guys leaving by drinking down two Long Island iced teas. "Jennifer has all the luck. Freaking guys fall all over her, you know? Anyone I meet is taken." She glared at me like it was my fault Zac was married, Antonio was smitten with Sylvia, and Jack was with me. "Why do I have all the crap luck?"

"Shut up, Cassie," Nicole snapped. "Victoria's going to be pissed if you start shooting off your mouth in public. You've had enough to drink."

Cassie flung her arms out to the side. "She's not here, is she?"

Selma picked up a chicken wing. "Yeah. Where is she? She's never this late—"

As if on cue, Victoria, pale and drawn, stumbled through the door.

I gaped. Manny was on her heels.

I jumped up, the alarms in my head going off in double-time. Something wasn't right.

Nicole was already on her feet, rushing to the dance director. "Victoria? What's wrong?"

Manny steered Victoria to the nearest chair, where she collapsed. She threw a vacant, scared gaze around the table and gave a low moan. "J-Jennifer," she finally said. "Jennifer's dead."

Chapter Ten

Dead. Surely I hadn't heard right. Dead? Jennifer?

A flood of disbelieving gasps and hysterical sobs erupted from the dancers.

"Dead!" one of the girls exclaimed. "How is that possible?"

Great question! This was a case about mysterious notes, not a murder investigation. Although maybe I was jumping to conclusions. Nobody had mentioned anything sinister.

"Dead…as in *dead*?" Selma pressed her hands against the table, her eyes wide and teary. And filled with shock.

Victoria fielded their hysteria while my gaze met Manny's.

"What happened?" I mouthed.

His face was grim, his mouth drawn in a hard line. He spoke to the group, but I knew he threw in the extra details for my benefit. "She was found in the arena parking lot. Strangled with a scarf from one of the dance costumes."

¡Ay, caramba! So it *was* murder.

Selma drew in a sharp breath, pushing the question away. The color drained from her normally rosy-cheeked face. "Strangled, as in killed? Oh God," she wailed, "then the threats are real."

Victoria stood tall, but I could see her quivering. And she'd wanted to handle things in-house. Not that having me around had stopped someone from killing a dancer. A cold chill swept over my body. I'd failed—and Jennifer had paid the ultimate price.

A rumbling started and rapidly grew louder as the women slowly realized what Selma meant. If Jennifer's death was related to the notes, then any one of them could be next.

Part of me wanted to jump up, take charge of the women, and get them to calm down so I could start grilling them for information, but I couldn't dare blow my cover. Camacho & Associates had been hired to ferret out the truth without revealing I was a detective. I had to stay in character. I flashed a reproachful look at Selma, the only one left—aside from Lance and Victoria—who knew I was a detective. She seemed to understand and quickly averted her eyes from mine.

I felt my expression turn grim as I met Manny's gaze again. He flicked his chin, almost imperceptibly, and I took his meaning. When we were done, we'd meet back at the office.

Nicole glanced at Victoria and voiced what I was sure all the dancers were thinking now. "Do you think whoever's writing the notes killed Jennifer?"

Victoria's eyes pooled. She swiped away the tears. "I think so," she finally said. Victoria shared a few other details about Jennifer. She'd been found next to her car and there was evidence of a brief struggle. Several of her acrylic nails had been broken and her blouse had been torn, but otherwise the evidence seemed minimal. Her own costume scarf, pulled tight around her neck, had been the weapon. The forensic team was already on the scene, and I assumed Manny had made contact and would hear of any developments.

My first thought was whether or not Mrs. Michael Brothers could have done it, but that didn't make sense. Killing Rochelle, yes. But Jennifer? No.

A short while later, I excused myself from the group, leaving them to grieve with one another while I hightailed it to Camacho's. Selma's terrified eyes were imprinted on my mind. The heaviness in my gut grew. Jennifer had died while I was supposed to be finding the letter-writer, who was now a potential killer. What kind of private investigator was I?

I somehow managed to push my doubt aside and focus on the situation in front of me. I had only two questions: *Why had Jennifer been killed, and would someone else be next?*

Chapter Eleven

The darkness outside pressed in on me as I drove back to Camacho's. The brightness of the office was a welcome reprieve. Manny sat at the head of the conference table, the office ablaze with fluorescent ceiling lights. "This isn't good, Lola. *¿Qué tienes?* What have you got so far?"

I grimaced. "*Nada.* Selma got a letter at the game tonight. It's not a death threat, though." I pulled a plastic baggie from my purse and slid it to Manny. "This is the one from tonight."

Manny slid the envelope from the plastic, knocked the letter free, and, using the back of a pen, unfolded the paper to read it.

I continued, frustration over my failure gnawing at my insides. "I saw the players' locker room but the trainer was treating an injured player. There's never a time when nobody's around and there doesn't seem to be a single clue in plain sight."

For a mentor, Manny was on the quiet side. He didn't offer

a pep talk. He didn't scold. All he said was, "You carrying?"

This was an area of contention between us. I didn't like guns. Most detectives didn't, actually. Too many opportunities for the weapon to be turned against you. "No."

He grimaced, shaking his head like he was disappointed, but he dropped it. We'd been round and round about my stance, and he hadn't worn me down yet. "We're meeting with the detective in charge in the morning. I'll meet you at the office, seven a.m. sharp."

"*Bueno*," I said to his back as he retreated to his office and closed the door. I turned to the whiteboards and wrote down the names of all the dancers and the number of letters they'd each received.

Jennifer 3
Tammy 2
Carrie 2
Selma 1
Vanessa 1
Geneva 1
Cassie 1
Rochelle 1
Tara 1
Nicole 2
Gina 1

I stood back and thought about what else I knew. Who had Jennifer been meeting? I thought I recognized him as Number 51. Had she been breaking her own rule and going against the contract she'd signed as a Courtside Dancer? So was there a disgruntled wife in the background?

And who was the "civilian" Cassie thought Jennifer had been seeing? Were the other dancers targets, too?

There were more questions than answers, and I went home with my head still pounding and an overwhelming feeling that I was experiencing an epic fail in my life as a detective.

. . .

The night passed slowly, the details of Jennifer's death circling in my mind while I tried to sleep. Finally, I drifted off to the comforting wheeze of Salsa's snoring, but morning came way too soon.

After a quick shower and a banana, I released my boxer to the backyard, slipped a suede jacket over my blouse, and headed out. Manny was in his office behind his desk. Another man sat in one of the wood-framed chairs opposite him. "Detective Bennett. Dolores Cruz, one of my investigators," Manny said as I walked in. "Detective Bennett is investigating Ms. Wallace's death."

I held out my hand, taking in the detective's features. He was young, probably mid-thirties, had short, dark-brown hair, and a strong, square face.

"After seeing you on the big screen last night, I almost feel like I know you." He shook my hand, lingering for an extra, uncomfortable beat and studying me with his piercing, small black eyes.

I tamped down the embarrassed heat I felt rising up my neck. "So you're a Royals fan?"

He winked. "Season tickets."

I pulled my hand free. "Great."

After the pleasantries—if you could call them that—

were over, he started tossing out questions. "What do you know about Ms. Wallace?"

My gaze met Manny's for a split second until he gave me the go-ahead to answer the detective's questions. I turned back to Bennett, perched on the edge of the chair next to his, inwardly grimacing that I had to confess I knew next to nothing. "She was the leader of the team. She was waiting to meet someone just before she was killed—"

"How do you know that?" Bennett interrupted.

"I talked to her as I was leaving the arena."

"Any idea who?"

I thought about the people I'd seen in the corridor. The place had been crawling with potential "civilians." "Not really. She did talk to one of the ballplayers. But I'm not sure which one."

My hunch that it was Number 51 was just that—a hunch. I'd tell Manny after the detective was gone, but without proof, I decided not to mention it. I couldn't, in good conscience, throw someone under the bus without evidence.

"Did she ever sleep with any of the players?"

I felt my eyes grow wide. The guy was blunt. "I didn't know her that well. You should ask the other girls."

"I'm asking you."

Huh. I didn't know what to say to that. "It's against the rules. All the girls sign a contract that says they won't fraternize with the players. She told me she was seeing someone. Not a player."

Bennett had been jotting down notes as I spoke. Now he lifted his dark eyes to me. "Did you?"

"Did I what?"

"Did you sign a contract?"

I glanced at Manny. He sat perfectly still, considering me as I spoke with the detective. "No. My contract is with Camacho & Associates. We were hired by the owners of the dance team and I'm undercover."

"Uh-huh." Bennett wrote something in his notepad. "So you're free to do what you like."

Like sleep with giant athletes? Not my cup of tea. "I'm free to investigate the case I'm working," I shot back.

He moved on, not missing a beat. "And have you seen the other girls fraternize?"

"I know Rochelle Nolan did. She left the team. So far, I haven't seen any other...*fraternizing*." And I'd been looking for it. "But I've only been with the team for two games now. I need more time."

He flashed another smile, but it lacked sincerity. "I'll give you more time, Ms. Cruz. As long as you still have a client, you'll have leeway from the department, but if Victoria and Lance Wolfe cut you loose, you'll back off. A warning: don't get in our way."

I bristled, but before I could react, Manny stood. "Thanks for your help, Bennett."

"Yep." They shook hands.

Biting my tongue, I offered my hand next. Bennett took it, holding it loosely.

"I'll be in touch," I said, wanting nothing more than to give a good shake, twist his arm until he spun around, and crank it up in the back to show him that I was a whole lot more than the skin he'd seen at the game.

But I didn't.

"Oh no, *I'll* be in touch. A pleasure to meet you, Ms. Cruz."

I gave a half nod. And no smile. He was smarmy, and

I suddenly missed Detective Seavers—who was not my biggest fan, but who didn't leave me feeling like I needed a shower.

Neil lumbered in as Manny and I headed out the door of the firm. Reilly was maneuvering herself out of her lime-green Volkswagen Beetle. So Neil went in first, then Reilly. Trying to deflect suspicion that they'd arrived at the same time. Smooth, but from the expression on Manny's face, not smooth enough. Nothing got past *el jefe*, as Reilly called our boss.

But whatever he may have suspected, he kept it to himself. Reilly had helped him keep his secret—*una poquita* Camacho who was about ten years old—so it seemed he had her back.

I drove separately, following him to Jennifer's apartment. She lived in Natomas, a suburb of Sacramento close to the arena. We followed West El Camino to the decade-old complex, a series of buildings, each two floors, eight apartments per building.

Jennifer had lived in a downstairs unit. It was a one-bedroom with a U-shaped kitchen, small living space, and back bedroom. There was hardly any furniture, dishes for two, and no pictures. *Híjole*. Had she even lived here?

Manny shadowed me as I perused the apartment, making me feel like he was babysitting me after the shoddy job I'd done on the dance team.

"I can do this," I said.

He stopped short for a beat, but then retraced his steps to the living room. I went ahead to the bedroom. If the furniture was sparse in the living room, Jennifer had made up for it in the bedroom. A queen-size four-poster bed straight out of an Ethan Allen showroom took most of the space. The matching floral bedspread and curtains complemented the dark wood. A vanity table with an oval mirror and a sheer negligee hanging from the corner completed the bedroom's plush style. I ran my fingers over it. It would be small for me, so snug on Jennifer, too, but then again, anyone wearing it wouldn't be wearing it for long.

Rifling through her belongings was more difficult than I thought it would be. I hadn't known her well, but she'd been the first dancer to let me into the group. I pushed away my sadness at her death and plowed ahead.

If Jennifer kept a journal or diary, it wasn't in the nightstand. There was an array of creams tucked into the drawer, along with sleeping pills and a bottle of pain reliever. A box of tissue discreetly hidden in a Victorian tissue holder and a wireless handset telephone sat on top of the nightstand.

I threw back the bedspread, searching for what, I didn't know. The police had come and gone, and Bennett had given Manny permission to search, but I couldn't imagine they'd left anything for us to find.

Dropping to my knees, I searched under the bed. There was a long, flat plastic box. It had already been rifled through, most likely by the police, but I pulled it out anyway. I froze at the familiar colors of the Sacramento Royals.

I moved the blouses aside and pulled out the first team jersey. Number 63, Rogers. After laying it next to me, I took out the next one. Number 11, Christof. There were five in all, two current players and three I recognized as players who'd been traded from the last two seasons.

"Manny, *ven aquí*," I called.

He ambled into the bedroom, all of four long strides, and stood beside me as I pointed to the jerseys. "Trophies," he said without even pausing.

I stared at him. He was right. That had to be it, but the idea floored me. Jennifer didn't strike me as the type to sleep around. I'd never seen her fawning over the players. *Y también*, she'd been the first one to tell me to stay away from them. Why? To protect her own territory? And who was the "civilian"? If she was into collecting the jerseys from the players she'd had flings with, the civilian boyfriend puzzle piece didn't fit.

He moved to the other side of the bed and I went to the tiny closet. I slid one of the doors over and pushed away another negligee, a black turtleneck sweater folded over a hanger, a pair of gray slacks (size four), and a red knit dress. A few pairs of shoes, each name brand, were lined up on the floor, but all in all, this wasn't much of a wardrobe and not how any normal person lived.

I moved the doors to the opposite side, pulling out photo albums and shoe boxes. I didn't know what the cops had been searching for, but they seemed to have left a lot of stuff untouched. I tackled the albums first. The top book held pictures of the Courtside Dancers.

The next book was the most interesting. Photos of the players whose jerseys she'd collected. There were none of her, but plenty of the men, each lazily sprawled on her Victorian bed, sheets rumpled, undressed, lounging as much as a six-foot-five giant could lounge.

"Risky to bring pictures like this to get professionally developed," I said to Manny.

"No risk if you develop them yourself," he said from

his crouched position on the other side of the bed. He had a smaller plastic box open and lifted out a compact photo printer and digital camera.

"So she only used it for this," I said, my hand on the second album.

Was her current fling one of the current players whose jerseys she had? I closed the albums and went on to the boxes.

The first several held shoes that had barely been worn. The next one held trinkets, presumably gifts from her lovers. There was a diamond-encrusted basketball pin, a player's bobblehead, a velvet rose, a gaudy gold jewelry box, a ceramic pillbox, a silver flask with a jersey number engraved on the front, and a slew of other tasteless items.

The last box was bigger, and I knew the second I opened it that it held the goods from Jennifer's most recent conquest. The jersey was on the bottom, neatly folded, pictures piled on top. I gathered them up and examined them one by one. She had been seeing Number 51. Rick Javorski. In my hands I held pictures of the same staged poses she'd taken of her other lovers.

It was when I came to a repeated pose, the player lounging on Jennifer's bed, that I realized these were photo sets of two different men. I looked more closely at the second man. Number 23, I think. Lance Connick. The thicker, slower player that Cassie had pointed out as *hot*.

Two at once? Jennifer got around. What was in it for her? She kept the photos and jerseys hidden. What she'd done was against the rules. She would have been kicked off the dance team if it had become known.

"Why would she do this?" I mused.

Manny didn't answer. He was rifling through the dresser drawers. Once again, it was clear that Jennifer was not a clothes horse.

"*Es muy extraño*," I muttered.

"*¿Qué?* What's strange, *poderosa*?" Manny asked.

I darted a wary glance at him. He hadn't called me one of his nicknames in a while, and I was relieved to hear it leave his lips. It meant he hadn't lost confidence in me, right? Because he wouldn't call me "strong" unless he believed it.

"She has hardly any clothes," I said. I moved so he could see in the lingerie drawer I'd gone through. "There are practically no underwear or bras," I added, in case he didn't get the significance of what I was saying.

He arched one eyebrow, like he thought women were an utter mystery. "And she should."

It wasn't a question, but I answered anyway. "I'd think so."

For a brief second, his eyes smoldered, almost like he wanted to ask, "Do you?" but then it was gone. Manny was an enigma, and one I preferred to keep at arm's length, *gracias a Dios*.

"So why didn't she?" he asked as I moved on to the next drawer. It held papers and pamphlets. I grabbed a handful and spread them out on the dresser.

Manny and I stared at the resort brochures, at each other, then back to the stack. "Huh." There wasn't a whole lot more to say.

Suddenly Jennifer's lack of clothing made sense.

"She was a nudist," I said, in case Manny didn't see the naked bodies on the glossy paper. "Ranking where she wanted to join?" I pondered aloud, thinking about the numbers jotted in the upper right corners. Two were marked by *#1*, one had *#2*, and one had *#3*.

The dent in his square chin was pronounced as he jutted his jaw out. "*Muy interesante*," he said in his low, gravelly voice.

Indeed.

I tucked the stack into my purse, and after another twenty minutes and nothing more to discover, Manny and I headed our separate ways.

Chapter Twelve

I worked the lunch shift at Abuelita's, waiting tables on autopilot. As Sylvia and I walked around each other, serving warm chips and salsa, carrying steaming plates, and refilling drinks, my mind stayed on Jennifer Wallace. I couldn't get her love life—or her *way* of life—off my mind. How many of the girls broke the rules?

"*Mija.*" My grandfather crooked his finger at me, motioning me over to his table.

"*¿Qué, Abuelo?*"

"*¿Dónde está Antonio?*"

I scanned the dining room. Wasn't Antonio here? I shrugged. "*¿No está aquí? No sé.*" Sylvia slowed as she walked behind me and I turned to her. "Antonio's not here?" I asked.

She raised her brows. "I don't know."

I wasn't sure I believed her. Damn. My job was making me cynical.

I put a hand on my hip and eyed her. "Sylvia?"

She threw up her hands, palms facing me. "I don't know anything. You have to talk to him."

Turning back to *Abuelo*, I shrugged. "There you go. We know nothing."

The rest of my shift passed without incident, and without Jack stopping by. Which made me wonder if he was more put out by my display at the game than he was letting on. Or maybe my not telling him had really crossed a line.

I chose to deal with that little worry by eating. I tossed my apron into the laundry bin in the kitchen and smiled at my father. "*Papi*, would you make me a taco salad, *por favor*?"

My father didn't understand my driving need to be a detective, but he'd never deny me food. He tossed beans, rice, lettuce, cheese, sour cream, guacamole, and salsa into a fried flour tortilla shell and slid it across the warming shelf. I perched on a stool behind the cooking line, forking the salsa-vinaigrette-covered lettuce leaves into my mouth. Halfway through the massive salad, my cell phone rang.

Having learned from past mistakes, I read the LCD readout before answering this time, but it wasn't a number I recognized. "Hello?"

"Lola? It's Selma. From the Royals?"

I started to greet her, but she cut me off, her tone urgent and scared. "I need to talk to you. Can you meet me?"

My spine instantly stiffened, and *zip*, just like that, my appetite was gone. "Sure. When?"

"It's kind of…urgent. Can you come now?" She rattled off the name of a restaurant, then *click*, she was gone.

Urgent. As in something to do with the case. It was the only thing that made sense. If only I could beam myself over there, maybe I'd finally be able to move forward with solving it.

I dumped the rest of my salad in the trash, tossed the plate in the industrial sink, and flew up the steps two at a time to the break room upstairs, then hurried back down with my purse.

"*Hasta luego, Papi,*" I called, waving to my father as I barreled through the kitchen door and into the back parking lot.

On the way, my mind ran through the possible reasons Selma would want to meet with me. She'd received a letter. She had a theory. Or, if I was really lucky, she knew something about Jennifer's death.

• • •

In ten minutes flat, I was at an eatery on the edge of downtown and midtown Sacramento. Toby's was a mom-and-pop restaurant and Selma stood out like a defiant bull in a china shop, daring the customers to recognize her and disturb her meal. I'd met her that first day when she'd come to Camacho & Associates with Jennifer, and I'd seen her at practices and the two games I'd danced at, but this was our first one-on-one meeting.

Out of her dance outfits, she was still über sexy in her thin, gauzy skirt and the plunging neckline of her red halter top. She was striking in a nontraditional way, with shiny cinnamon-colored hair and golden skin. Tanning salon—that had to be it. What surprised me most was how young she was. Without the heavy makeup, I realized that she couldn't be more than eighteen or nineteen.

"Hey," she said when I sat down opposite her. Her eyes

flittered about, repeatedly searching every area of the room. I had my back turned to the parking lot, angling myself to face her. I took out my notebook, glad that I didn't have to hide from her the fact that I was a detective.

"What's up?" Cut to the chase. I was tired of having nothing to show for my investigation.

"I didn't know who else to call. I don't really know any of the other girls." Her voice had a deep tenor to it and I had to lean in a bit to hear her over the clacking stoneware, clinking glasses, and roar of chatter in the dining room. I moved the silver-capped salt and pepper shakers out of my way, pushing them next to the artificial flower poking out of a thick bottled vase.

"You haven't made any friends?"

"A couple, but no one to just go hang out with, you know? They're mostly veterans with the team, so they're all tight. I don't really fit in."

I forgot about my notebook and just concentrated on her. "What about the other newer girls?"

She shrugged her naked shoulders and abruptly changed the subject. "Your boss is intense."

I wanted to say, "So are you." Instead I said, "Yeah. But a very good detective. The best."

She scanned the room again, then settled her gaze back on me. "Maybe."

"Selma, are you okay?"

Her expression faltered. "Not quite," she said, her voice low.

A silence hung in the air between us. The pointed peaks of her upper lip and the slight flair of her nostrils at the end of her straight nose gave away the nerves zinging inside her.

She brushed a wing of hair from her face.

"Do you wanna talk about it?" *Since you called me here*, I added to myself.

She arched a brow and seemed to study the people in the room. "My real name is Selma Winchester, not Selma Mann," she said, but stopped as the waitress came to our table. Selma quickly picked up her menu, her painted blue fingernails popping out against the red of her halter.

"Ready to order?" The waitress leaned her weight on one leg and tapped her foot.

I'd hadn't regained my appetite, so I was good on the food front. "Just coffee for me," I said.

The waitress frowned, then sent a hopeful look to Selma.

"The veggie omelet." Selma folded the menu and handed it to the waitress. Her hands trembled as she took a sip of her water. She could say she was fine all she wanted, but it was clear she was freaked out.

"Sourdough, wheat, or white?"

"White, please," she said into her glass.

The waitress stomped away, her white orthopedic shoes gleaming against the dark carpet. I made a mental note to leave her a killer tip for bogarting the table without ordering. We waitresses—even the part-time ones—had to stick together.

"I've been coming to this place since I moved to Sacramento," Selma said. "Maybe too much."

So we were going to go slowly and Selma would set the pace of the conversation. Good to know.

As our coffee was delivered, I remembered what Victoria had said to me that day in the Camacho conference room. Every girl wanted to be a cheerleader—in Victoria's world, anyway. "Has it always been your dream to be a dancer?"

"It was until I realized what it's really all about." She gestured at me, waving her hand up and down. "Look at me. Look at you. Who can see beyond the package? Taping up our boobs and doing a million butt crunches. We're more than bodies, you know, but you sure couldn't tell from the way we're treated."

She was preaching to the choir. I was a Latina woman from a traditional Mexican family trying hard to compete with some tough *hombres* in a man's job. "Of course we are."

"People can't see beyond"—she flung her arms out— "beyond this. I thought being a dancer would be awesome. Freeing. But it's not. It's oppressive."

Hello? Had she seen the outfits we had to wear before she'd signed up? It was total objectification. Not to mention her current ensemble. "If you don't like it, why do you do it?"

"You're perfect, you know," she said, instead of answering my question. "You have perfect breasts." She floated her hands through the air in the shape of an hourglass. "The ratio of your hips to your waist. It couldn't be more ideal." She ran her palms down her sides. "I don't have *that* ratio, but that's what people want. We have to strip it all away."

I had no idea what she was getting at so I sipped my coffee, wishing it had a splash of chocolate and some frothy milk stirred into it. "What do you mean, 'strip it all away'?"

She took a bolstering breath before lowering her voice to a secretive level. "Have you ever heard of *Cuerpo y Alma*?"

I translated. Body and Soul. It rang a bell, but…"No."

"People there see *inside* of you." She put her hands on the table and leaned toward me, lowering her voice even more. "It takes away the importance of the outside package. Do you understand?"

I shook my head, trying to make sense out of what she was saying. "What's *Cuerpo y Alma*?"

She searched the parking lot behind me. "It's where I *belong*," she finally said, drawing out the last word.

"O-*kay*." I was not connecting the dots, and it wasn't from lack of brain cells or effort. "So why not go there?"

Wherever there was.

She hesitated, a long, weighty pause, then finally said, "Because people need real jobs. Jennifer did. We all do. But..."

I leaned closer, hoping we were finally getting to the point of this rendezvous.

"I think the notes we're all getting at the games are because of me."

Phew. She'd had my full attention all along, but now I was giving 120 percent. I opened my notebook and grabbed a pen from my purse. I wrote down *Cuerpo y Alma* and Selma's full real name. Then I prompted her to go on. "What exactly do you mean when you say it's where you belong, and why do you think the notes are because of you?"

She flicked her eyes around, as if she were making sure we weren't overheard. "The package doesn't matter there because people don't care about it."

Either she wasn't making sense or I was slow on the uptake. "I don't understand, Selma."

"It's a naturist resort." There was the low voice again. "You know, clothing optional?"

"Oh." *¡Dios mío!* "Nudists."

"Naturist is more PC, but yeah, it's basically the

same." She shook her head and whatever sadness was in her seemed to deepen. "The outside and inside can't be separated, no matter how much I might want them to be. I can't change who I am."

I tapped the tip of my pen against my notepad, a slew of questions going through my mind. Topping the pile was: *Is it a coincidence that Selma and Jennifer both had ties to nudist resorts?*

"So you go to *Cuerpo y Alma*?"

"As much as possible."

"Selma—?" I said, hesitating because I knew that I had to tread carefully.

She raised her gaze to mine, waiting.

"Did you ever see…" I trailed off. Even though Jennifer was gone, it felt wrong to be the one outing her as a nudist.

A tear slipped down Selma's cheek and she quickly brushed it away. "Yes."

"Yes, what?"

Her voice got small and quiet. "You were going to ask if I'd ever seen Jennifer there. Weren't you?"

I reached into my purse again, this time pulling out the brochures I'd taken from Jennifer's apartment. "I found these in a drawer at her house last night. She was a member?" I asked the question, but I already knew the answer. Although how in the world she hid that from the world when she'd been part of *Living the Royal Life* was a big mystery. Even I would have gotten wind of that, I think, had it been public.

"She was a member there. We both are…were…I still am," she finished.

A wave of knifelike pricks traveled up my back. Now

we were really getting somewhere. "Member?"

Selma lifted her shoulders to her ears, her cheeks turning scarlet. "She pretty much lived there. That's where I met her. She's the one who told me about the tryouts for the Royals."

"So you were good friends?" Selma was young, innocent, and earthy, while Jennifer had had a sleek sophistication about her. They were an unlikely duo, but I suppose a common interest in nudity could be a bonding agent.

"Not good friends, but friends. We spent some time together at NudeStock over the summer."

Every cell in my body went on freak alert. "Um, NudeStock?"

"It's a week of concerts. You know, like Woodstock? They have it every summer. A couple of L.A. bands come up. Some local groups. Vendors have booths around the grass." Her face lit up. "It was fantastic. Amazing to see all those bodies, all those people so sure of who they are." Her eyes sank to half mast, like she was picturing the scene. "They were dancing and singing and just so…so *comfortable* in their skin."

I tried to get a visual on hundreds of naked bodies grooving to rock music, but my Catholic mind wanted to block it. My upbringing ramped up full force and I shuddered.

The waitress came by with Selma's veggie omelet, then quickly disappeared to deliver more food to other hungry customers.

Selma pushed her fork around the plate. "Do you ever get a feeling that you can't quite put into words, but that you just can't shake and you know is right?"

All the time, I wanted to say, but mostly that was related to my family and the unconditional love I had for them, despite their old-fashioned beliefs and their…craziness. My intuition with crimes was more sketchy. "Sometimes."

"I have that feeling. What if her death had to do with her being a member at *Cuerpo y Alma*?" Selma's voice cracked. "I'm scared."

The hairs on the back of my neck stood up. Did she have a reason for believing she was in danger, or had fear seeped in and filled her with irrational thoughts? "Why do you think that, Selma?"

She shifted in her seat. "We have to sign a contract—"

"Right. No dating the players." Which Jennifer clearly hadn't followed.

"No going out unless we're fully presentable—"

"And a morality clause."

Ha. Ditto.

"It doesn't say you can't be a nudist, but you have to be a role model in the community, you know? They wouldn't like it if they found out about her lifestyle."

"Who? Lance and Victoria Wolfe?"

"Mmm-hmm. Jennifer and me…we had to stay away from *Cuerpo y Alma* during filming. No one knew." She choked on her words, her voice straining. "It was like denying who I really was. Am. It still is. Nobody knows."

"Nobody."

"Jennifer made me swear that I wouldn't tell anyone our secret, but what if the Wolfes found out?" Her voice rose at the end as if she were on the verge of tears.

"What are you saying, Selma? You think Lance or Victoria would have killed Jennifer because she broke her contract?"

Selma gave a desperate shrug. "Maybe?"

My hope that this meeting would reveal some great clue faded. I suppose it was possible that someone would kill over a morality clause, but it didn't seem probable. "I think they'd just fire her."

She shook her head. "But there's something going on. First, all those letters. I mean, what are they about? We're not doing anything except trying to live our lives. And now Jennifer." She rubbed her eyes as if she were trying to control her tears. "Sometimes I get the feeling I'm being watched."

Ay, Dios. The girl was on edge. "Have you gone to the police?"

Her cheeks flushed pink. "And say what? That I'm a naturist and I'm scared?" She scoffed. "They'll laugh me out of the station."

She had a point. Other than her intuition, she hadn't provided a single solid reason, and certainly no proof, that Jennifer's murder had anything to do with the broken contract, morality clause, or *Cuerpo y Alma*. Officer Bennett would show her the door and let it smack her on the behind as she left.

Which just made me want to prove him wrong. And as Jack had once told me—and I completely agreed—people kill for the most ridiculous reasons.

I stretched my arms across the table and took her hands in mine, squeezing. "It's going to be okay."

She straightened her spine and pulled her hands away. Her eyes grew wide and she lifted her chin almost in defiance. "But what if it's not? What if she really *was* killed because she belonged to *Cuerpo y Alma*? The letters all say that the writer knows what we're doing. Maybe he or she's giving them to everyone to throw us off the trail. Maybe Jennifer"—she swallowed hard—"and I are the real targets?"

She emptied a tiny container of cream into her coffee, then cut her omelet into bite-size pieces, pushing them off to one side of the plate once they were severed from the semicircle. "You're supposed to be able to be free there and not hide behind the constraints society puts on you. Since your body is exposed, people are supposed to be able to see beyond it." She spoke to her plate, an aching bitterness in her voice. "But what if a killer is hiding there, judging us?"

"But then whoever it is would be a member, too, so why would he or she judge?"

"You don't have to be a member to go," she said after she swallowed a miniscule bite of her omelet.

"How does it work, then?"

"You can become a member or you can pay for day use. Like a campground."

"And what does 'clothing optional' mean, exactly? People can wear clothes if they want to?"

"If it's your first time, they let you work up to taking it all off…if you need to, you know, adjust. But otherwise it means no clothes at all." She gave me an encouraging smile. "It's really freeing, you know."

No, I *didn't* know, and I was A-OK with that. I liked my wardrobe and my Victoria's Secret collection, *muchas gracias*. A little imagination was a good thing in my book. "I'm partial to clothes."

Selma finally worked her way through her eggs in earnest and even dipped into the side of country potatoes.

"It's a way of life, you know? Even when I'm not there, I'm a nudist in clothing. What I wear or don't wear doesn't define me. My clothes can't convey the real me. It's just my body. Being there gives people an opportunity to want to delve deeper and not get stuck at what they think is underneath."

Writing down what she said didn't help me understand it. I glanced at her halter top. It seemed to define her pretty well. Young. Nubile. Sexy. "So you feel free at the resort—not wearing clothes."

"Totally. My parents live at a nudist place up past Napa. I grew up in the life."

Pobrecita. She had a pretty warped sense of what fashion could do for a girl.

She chatted about her naked childhood for a minute before getting back to the point. "Jennifer was spending a lot of time with this one guy she met at NudeStock," Selma said. "She told me about him. Said it was just like in the movies. He saw her from across the grass. He couldn't take his eyes away from her face." Selma's fingers spread across her cheeks. "Her face," she said again, as if those two words held some extra-special meaning.

I was skeptical. I'd seen Jennifer's body. She had a rockin' physique, no duct tape needed. I bet he caught sight of it even if he didn't let on.

"Were they dating?" She wouldn't have had a jersey to add to her collection if she'd been seeing a nudist.

"Dating's so Fifties. People *hook up* at the resort. I know they had a standing meeting. In the hot tub every Monday at six o'clock, or sometimes they'd meet at the bar."

A naked bar. That wasn't something I was dying to see. "Then what happened?"

"They broke it off for a while. She said he wasn't a nudist at heart, but then last Monday, we went over there together after a dance practice. She stopped at the message board—"

"What board?"

"There's a message board just outside the office. People leave notes for each other on it. You know, since we can't carry our smartphones," she said.

"So this guy left Jennifer a message?"

Her head bobbed up and down. "Said he was trying to understand and live in her world." Selma bit her lip, lost in the sadness of her memory. Finally, she came back to the present. "She was mad at first, but then I think she realized that he was a keeper."

After seeing Jennifer's trophies, I could believe it. It seemed to me like she was the one who loved 'em and left 'em. After getting a dose of that herself, maybe she'd reformed.

Selma continued. "I tried to ask her about him, but she kept him private."

"So you never met him?"

"No. I always went with Parker—that's my boyfriend—to our tent."

She left the sentence hanging there for me to fill in the blanks. "Um, tent?"

"People pitch tents or come in motorhomes."

Right. She'd said it was like a campground.

"It's fantastic," she said.

I bet. Not. Jack's bed, now *that* was fantastic. Or at least I *thought* it would be if I ever found myself in it. I refocused. "So you went to your tent…"

"And when we came back out, Jennifer was gone."

"Did she meet up with him again, then?"

Selma absently opened another creamer and poured it into her cup. "Yes."

"And she never told you his name?"

Selma shook her head.

Great. How could I track down Jennifer's nudist lover?

Before I had any ideas, Selma dropped her voice and said, "There's one more thing."

I waited as she poured more sweetener into her coffee, tapping my fingers in a random rhythm against the slightly sticky table.

"Someone graffitied her car," she said.

"What did it say?"

A shudder passed through her and she shook her head, her eyes welling up. She breathed deeply then spat out the words, clipped, to get it over with. "Slut, whore, white trash, traitor. It was all in red."

My skin pricked. To see that kind of hatred and judgment against you would be awful. *Pobre* Jennifer. I might not ever want to go to a nudist resort, but I thought people should have the right to choose and not be judged for it.

"Any idea who could have done it?" Surely not the boyfriend?

"No idea."

"What about other people at the resort? Did she ever have run-ins with anyone else?"

"Not that I saw. Everyone loved her—it was like the whole place was her family. She was everyone's best friend."

I could see that. We hadn't made it to best friends, but Jennifer had been the only dancer to really welcome me into the fold.

Selma paused for a beat, then asked in a trembling voice, "Do you think he killed her? The boyfriend, I mean?"

That was the million-dollar question. "I don't know, Selma." My heart plunged to my stomach. As much as I pushed down the idea percolating in my head, I knew what I should do. What I ought to do. What I had to do.

"The other dancers, do they know about the resort?"

Her eyes widened, her skin turning pale. "No! They wouldn't understand."

I wasn't sure about that. Young, beautiful cheerleaders weren't shy about showing off their bodies. They'd probably dig a field trip to *Cuerpo y Alma*.

"I'm already an outsider," Selma continued. She met my eyes. "You know what it's like. You've seen the girls. They're like a junior high school clique. You have to try to fit in however you can."

Except at the resort. There, everybody was the same. Bare naked. *Ay caramba*.

"We'll figure this out."

"Will you come to the resort? I'll show you around. Maybe you can find something."

The idea had already crossed my mind, but the direct proposition made a knife twist in my gut. First nearly nude as a Courtside Dancer, then totally in the buff at *Cuerpo y Alma*.

My thoughts skipped straight to Jack. The question he'd thrown out at the restaurant the night before shot into my mind. How far *was* I willing to go for my job?

I put off answering Selma, instead asking her, "Have you seen his car? Make and model?"

She shook her head.

Scratch that avenue off my list of possible means to track down a mystery nudist.

A lightbulb suddenly seemed to go off for Selma. "If he killed Jennifer, he would still follow his regular routine, right? So he wouldn't, you know, raise suspicion? They always met at the hot tub." Selma leaned forward as I took a sip of coffee. "I'm meeting Parker tonight. Come with me. You can go, you know, spy at the hot tub."

The coffee caught in my throat. I snatched a napkin and held it to my mouth, trying not to spew it across the table at her. "Tonight?"

Selma brushed away the piece of hair that fell into her eyes. "If he's there, you can talk to him. You'll know if he's the murderer, right?"

Ay, loca. My intuitive powers weren't good enough to judge a naked man in a hot tub and determine if he'd recently killed a woman, as handy as that particular skill might be. I tried to picture myself in the steam bath at *Cuerpo y Alma* making that determination, but the faces bobbing in the water around me were those of my parents and grandparents, my grandmother clasping her beaded rosary between her pruned fingers, praying for my soul in an endless Spanish loop.

I blinked, chasing the vision away. I couldn't tell them about this assignment; that's all there was to it.

I started to wonder how Jack would take it. He understood my passion for this job. He'd been by my side, said we were a team, and didn't mind me shimmying in cheerleading costumes. But a nudist resort was a big step over what I imagined his morality line to be.

I immediately scolded myself. I could tell him—after the fact. Better to ask for forgiveness than permission. That was my motto today. *Mi novio*, Jack Callaghan, could not factor into my career decisions.

Selma tapped her fingernails on her front teeth. *Click. Click. Click.* The sound grated into my brain. "So you'll come?" she finally asked.

I ran through my list of obligations. Dance practice was from three to six this afternoon. No shifts at the restaurant. And so far this was the only lead I had. "I'll be there," I agreed. The thought of pulsing, hot water on my aching muscles actually sounded pretty good.

As long as I had on my swimsuit.

Chapter Thirteen

I stood in the doorway of my cousin-in-law Lucy's house. I'd just dropped the bomb about my destination and Lucy's face exploded with emotion. "You're what?"

My eardrums rattled. "For a case," I explained.

"No way. You can not go there."

I could usually count on Zac's wife to back me up in an adventure whenever Reilly was unavailable. Which was a lot, thanks to her secret affair with Neil. I guess nudist resorts crossed the line, though.

"I thought you, of all people, would understand and be supportive."

"Lola, this is so *not* you. First of all, you believe in accentuating your assets, not showing the full monty."

She led me into the front room of her house, but I stopped and put my hands on my hips. "First of all, I think the full monty only refers to men. And second of all, what do you mean I like to *accentuate* my assets? I think I'm offended by that."

Lucy cocked one eyebrow as she peered down at my outfit, then spread her arms wide and gestured to her own. "Uh, enough said?"

Pft.

"No, not enough said." So what if my new bra, recommended to me by the late Jennifer, enhanced the roundness of my cleavage under my V-neck T-shirt, and my knee-length skirt skimmed my hips in an oh-so-sexy fashion? "You like wraparound pants and fringe"—I gestured to her hippie outfit—"but you bleach your hair and wax your own eyebrows so I know you have some of this in you."

She patted her platinum ponytail. "I happen to like my hair color and I don't want to have furry eyebrows. But I'm a mom."

"And?"

"And I'm a *mom*," she said again, as if I'd understand the second time around.

"And that's synonymous with unsexy in your book?"

She flipped her palm up toward the ceiling. "I'm just saying, *you* wear clothes that show off your body in the best light. My body's past having a best light." She winked. "And what you have going on works for Jack, right?"

I wagged my finger at her. "You're a mom with a killer body. And we are *not* talking about Jack. I don't even think I want him to find out about this. You have to promise. Not my parents, either. So you cannot, I repeat, can*not* tell Zac. Or Chely." My fifteen-year-old cousin had the secret-keeping ability of a Gossip Girl on speed. "Or Antonio."

Lucy frowned. "Why so top secret?"

"Because…" Because I had a job to do, and I knew my family wouldn't approve. And Jack? He'd given me no reason to think he wouldn't be on board with me doing my job, but a nudist resort might push the limits of his understanding. Which would be *no bueno* for our developing relationship. "It's a case. A murder. And if I'd done a better job and found something out"—my voice hitched—"if I'd found *anything* out, maybe Jennifer Wallace wouldn't have died."

"You're going tonight, then?" she asked.

"Yeah," I said, my stomach seizing with trepidation.

She led me into her workroom, a tranquilly decorated space full of browns and beiges, trickling water, and new age music. "A murder to solve. You're going for a good cause. So, I'd say a wax job is in order."

"That's why I'm here. My eyebrows?"

She laughed, *un poquito* diabolically. "No, no, I mean *waxed*."

My heart skipped a beat. "Is that code for something?"

"I could do a Brazilian," she suggested, winking at me. My heart started in again like a sledgehammer in my chest.

"A Brazilian?" Talk about full monty. "I don't think so." Just the thought of it made me nauseous. "I'm good with a landing strip."

"You should try it, Lola. Live a little. I got my friend to do mine a couple weeks ago, after Zac and I hit that rough spot." She winked again. "He *loves* it."

I covered my ears. "La-la-la-la. I don't want to know this." But it got me thinking again. What would Jack like?

She dragged in a deep breath and then said, "You're going to see it tonight, so you might as well hear about it now."

I sputtered. "I'm what?"

She handed me a gown and a paper thong and backed out of the spa room, pressing a button on the stereo as she passed by. Soothing music wafted out of the mounted speakers. "Come on, Lola, a murder? There's no way I'm letting you go there alone. You couldn't pay me to stay away."

She wasn't Mexican and didn't speak Spanish, but the *punto* was implied. If I knew Lucy, she wasn't taking no for an answer. I held the paper triangle attached to a Y-string. "Uh, really?"

"Just put it on." I started to protest again but she held up her hand. "It doesn't have to be Brazilian, *chica*. Don't worry. I'll just clean you up. Make it nice and tidy."

And she closed the door, leaving me alone in her tranquil studio. I sighed. She'd called me *chica*. Lucy was going off the deep end. I undressed, slipped on the gown and thong, and lay down in the lounge chair. I was overdue for a cleanup. Detective work was keeping me too busy.

As I waited for Lucy to return, my mind wandered. How *would* Jack react to my going to a nudist resort? Heck, how did *I* feel about it?

Scared, that's how. On both counts. I rubbed my temples. But it was the most viable lead I had, which meant I needed to follow it.

Lucy rapped lightly on the door and poked her head in. "*¿Lista?*"

I laughed at her horrible accent. "*Sí.*"

She came back into the room, sat next to me, and got to work.

"If you're coming, you'll be lying to Zac and I can't be a party to deception in your marriage," I said as she spread warm wax along my panty line. The warmth was kind of nice. The calm before the storm. "He didn't like the whole rehab thing you helped me with, remember? If he thinks you're at it again, he's going to forbid you from seeing me."

"He thinks it's pretty cool that you're a dancer for the Royals," she said, although I thought I heard a touch of hesitation in her voice. "Here we go." She grabbed hold of the edge of the wax, said, "Take a breath," and *whoomp*, she yanked it off.

I slammed my hands onto the sides of the padded table, bracing my body against the pain. Holy Mary Magdalene, mother of God. "*Hijo de la chingada*," I said through my clenched teeth.

"No turning back now," she said brightly.

I sat up on shaky elbows. "Why do women do this?"

Lucy pushed me down. She spread another layer of wax, checked her work from the last strip. "Because it's sexy," she said as she yanked.

I held tight to the edge of the table, a tear slipping out of my eye. "I always forget how much it hurts."

"It's like childbirth." She grinned. "I'll give you a facial when we're done to make up for the pain."

"C-can't. No time. I go from this torture chamber to dance torture."

"Right. Okay then. I'll just see you tonight. No worries, Lola." She zipped her lips and turned an imaginary key. "I got your back."

It wasn't my back I was worried about at the moment. It was my nude self.

Chapter Fourteen

An hour later I was in Victoria's torture chamber learning new routines and outrageously seductive moves. The other dancers still hadn't completely warmed up to me but Jennifer's death had brought us closer to breaking the ice. They were all subdued, but had started to correct me on moves I was doing wrong. I took their comments with a thank you.

Arriving early to the next game would hopefully let me check out the facilities and snoop, but right now I had other plans. Selma and I gave each other a pointed, silent look. We'd be seeing each other shortly. *A lot* of each other.

I pulled into Camacho's parking lot at six forty-five. Lucy was leaning against her car, her wraparound pants traded in for an aqua tank sundress with a white Egyptian wall-painting design, a fish prominently positioned front and center. I tried to tap into my supernatural powers to see if she had anything on underneath, but X-ray vision wasn't one of my talents, either.

I spotted Selma slouched in her car, her finger tracing her lips. I waved to Lucy and walked over to Selma, knocking on the driver's side window. She jumped, zipping the window down with a jittery hand.

"You got here quickly. Ready to go?" I asked.

"Ready." Her low voice shook.

"Relax, Selma. I'm going to talk to people, ask questions, see if we can find anything out. It'll be fine."

She tapped her fingernails against her teeth.

"I'm bringing a colleague. We'll follow you in my car," I said.

Selma rolled up the window and waited while Lucy got into my car. Then, in a caravan of two, we headed out of Sacramento. Twenty minutes later, we were in an unincorporated country area, heading toward *Cuerpo y Alma*, the clothing-optional resort.

Lucy stared out the window at the passing ponds and fields, horses and cows dotting the landscape. "Jeez, this place is really in the middle of Nowheresville."

"Yep." I eyed her, still trying to figure out if she had on a swimsuit. "So are you really going to go naked?"

She grinned, pulling her platinum hair up into a claw clip. "Totally."

"What did you tell Zac?"

Her grin faded. "I told him I was going out with you for some girl time."

Oh boy. Zac was no fool. He'd see right through that and know we were up to something. "Lucy…"

"Relax. It'll be fine."

I turned right, following close behind Selma. "Are you going to tell him later? *After* my case is solved?"

She turned in her seat. "Lola, I'm my own person. Zac doesn't tell me what to do or what to feel. He knows I love him. He has to trust me and love me for myself. Whether or not I'm willing to go naked at a resort. But don't worry. I won't blow your case."

"If he knew, would he be jealous? You know, because other men would be gawking at you?" It's what I worried about with Jack.

She hesitated, but then said, "A little healthy jealousy never hurt anyone."

"Not true," I said, frowning. "Jealousy is what got him thinking you were having an affair with one of your clients."

"Right. But we're much happier now."

Selma's car turned onto a private lane and I pulled in after her. It was a warm evening. Sacramento just couldn't seem to let go of summer. Anywhere else, October meant cooler weather, which would mean fewer naturists stomping around, exposing themselves to the elements. Which would have been a good thing, in theory. But it was still a smoldering ninety degrees, and I thought that probably meant plenty of people would be milling around in their birthday suits. Which meant maybe I'd find out something about Jennifer.

Selma parked in the visitors' lot and I slipped my car in next to hers. I'd put on a sundress after dance practice and smoothed it down over my legs, adjusting the hem around my knees.

Lucy tucked her purse under the front seat of the car and I did the same, locking up and clutching my keys and three twenty dollar bills in one hand.

Selma stepped out of her car. She had on an oversize

white T-shirt, her bare legs sticking out from underneath. My gut clenched as she leaned in to grab some towels from the backseat of her car and the T-shirt slid up to reveal bare skin.

A la chingada. This was real.

She handed Lucy and me towels. "I keep a bunch in the back so I always have a clean one. You have to have a towel to sit on."

Lucy outstretched her hand. "Lucy. Nice to meet you, Selma. I hope it's okay with you that I tag along."

Selma shrugged. "It's your body. I think it's great that you embrace it."

"Right," Lucy said. "It's great." There was that smidgeon of hesitation again, but she added, "In all its stretchmarked glory."

We followed Selma up the short flight of deck stairs and entered the office. One woman and one man stood behind a counter. Neither of them seemed very glad to be there. Or maybe it was the fact that they were both clothed that had them looking morose. I heaved a sigh, not realizing I'd been holding my breath. I, for one, was relieved at their clothing, even if they weren't.

The woman greeted us, then Selma gestured to Lucy and me. "Tiffany, these are some friends of mine. They're coming in with me tonight."

"Welcome." The woman, Tiffany, greeted us. She pulled out two four-by-six index cards. "Your first time?" We nodded, and she continued. "Wonderful. This way, ladies. I just need to go over the rules."

We followed her through the office, past racks of brochures, dietary supplements, sunscreen, sunglasses, and flip-flops, and out onto an indoor balcony that overlooked a large dance floor. A disco ball hung down from the center of the room, strands of lights draped to the edges of the ceiling.

My gaze extended beyond the disco ball and out through the panoramic windows. The view was breathtaking. A lake was off to the right. Evergreens skimmed the blue sky. And to the left…Oh my. My eyes bugged. A wave of naked bodies moved over the grass. A group of people played volleyball in a sand pit, body parts flinging this way and that.

¡Dios mío! I could feel the nightmares coming on.

I whipped my head around to face the wall in the clubhouse room and my eyelids opened even wider. The wall was covered with framed pictures of naked people. I turned away but flesh and naked bodies danced behind my eyelids, the images burned into my brain.

Tiffany's voice brought my attention back to her and her safely clothed body. I had the feeling I'd seen her before, but if I had, I couldn't place her. Working at Abuelita's, and now seeing all the Royals fans, meant I was in contact with a lot of people. "I just need your names, addresses, and the twenty-six dollar day-use fee."

After I paid for Lucy and me, Tiffany clasped her hands. "The expectation is that when you're on the grounds, you *are* nude."

"I thought we could take our time." Or had Selma been leading me on? *Mentirosa.* She was a good liar.

Lucy wasn't fazed, though. "Great," she said, suddenly enthusiastic beyond reason. She rubbed her hands together like she couldn't wait to strip down to her birthday suit. What happened to the little sliver of doubt she'd had earlier? Was this a midlife crisis for her? Again? But she was a young mom, nowhere near middle age, so that wasn't it. *Híjole.* She was an earth mother type with her blond hair woven into two braids, a leather strap necklace, and her Birkenstocks—always her shoe of choice. Maybe she'd fit in here.

"Okay," I murmured.

"Is this your first time at a naturist resort?"

I smirked. "Does it show?"

She laughed. "Uh, yeah."

I perched on the edge of the bar stool at the café table. "Can I ask you a question?"

"Of course."

Selma craned her head to look out the windows at the people, searching for Parker, no doubt, but Lucy was just enjoying the scenery.

"What's the difference between a naturist and a nudist?"

"No difference," she said. "We prefer to use the term 'naturist' because women tend to be more receptive to the concept if the word 'nude' is removed from the equation. Our philosophy is that we are more accepting of our natural state of existence, uninhibited by the clothing that society restricts us with. We are body and soul, together, intertwined, inseparable."

Sounded like psychobabble to me. "How do men and women deal with each other when they're naked? I mean, what about"—I leaned in—"sex?"

Tiffany smiled indulgently. "Being nude here isn't about sex. In fact, believe it or not, there is probably less sexuality between people here than at a bar off the grounds."

No orgies? No hedonism? I couldn't fathom how that was possible. How could it *not* be sexual?

"I can see you're not sure, Ms…?"

"Cruz."

"Look at it this way. When kids run around the house after a bath, it's not sexual. It's fun. Think of this place as Disneyland for adults. It's like being a kid again. When you grow up this way, it's completely normal." She gestured to her shorts and T-shirt. "Wearing clothes is not."

I'd rather just go visit Mickey Mouse.

Lucy and I filled out the cards. Selma excused herself to the restroom and I seized the moment.

"Tiffany," I said. "A woman Selma knows, Jennifer. She came here a lot and she just died…"

Tiffany's demeanor changed instantly. The faint smile she'd held dropped into a sad frown and her eyes glazed. "I-I've known Jennifer forever," she choked out. "None of us can believe she's dead. Hit us all really hard."

"I can imagine." I paused, hating to intrude on her grief. Finally, I went on. "Selma said she had a boyfriend here?"

Tiffany gathered the cards, her hands shaking slightly. "If she did, she never told me."

Damn. So much for this being easy. "How many people come to *Cuerpo y Alma*?"

She moved back toward the office. "We have more than twelve hundred distinct people through here annually."

¡Ay, caramba! That was a lot of nudists. "And they all check in like we did?"

Tiffany bristled underneath her oversize T-shirt and baggie shorts. "Why are you so curious, Ms. Cruz?"

I laughed, fluttering my hand. "Just nervous, I guess. I knew Jennifer. She loved it here. That's why I wanted to try it, you know? And I'm not sure if her boyfriend here knows about her death."

She considered me and finally said, "People come here confidentially."

Hmmm. Wish *I'd* thought to use an alias. Just in case.

I thanked her as Selma came back.

"I'll show them around," Selma said. I followed her gaze to the wall clock. It was 7:20.

"So, about the clothes?" I asked Tiffany, praying she'd take pity on me and bend the rules a bit.

"You can take a few minutes before you disrobe, but absolutely *no clothing* is allowed in the pool areas."

So Selma hadn't misled me. Phew. I turned to wave and Tiffany leveled her gaze at me. "Absolutely none."

I whipped my head around and frowned at Selma. I'd put my bikini on under my sundress, hoping against hope that they wouldn't be overly strict. "No clothes in the hot tub? Not even a bathing suit? No flexibility?"

"It's a nudist resort," Selma said, leading us down the staircase outside. "Since you agreed to come, I assumed you wouldn't have a problem with it."

She'd assumed wrong. Once again Jack's voice echoed in my head. *How far are you willing to go for your job, Cruz?*

Chapter Fifteen

Selma strode toward the hot tub, peeling off her T-shirt along the way. I gaped at the sight of so much bare skin, sucking in my breath. I turned my back on her, my mouth hanging open, stunned speechless—and saw Lucy slipping one arm through the hole of her sundress. Out popped one breast, free and surprisingly perky considering the three babies who'd suckled it.

I'd known she was going to do it, but seeing it sent a wave of guilt through me. "Lucy!"

"When in Rome," she said, grinning, not a trace of hesitation in her voice. Then she threaded her other arm through the hole and slowly lowered her dress to her hips.

I grabbed her and pulled her to a stop before she could bare the rest of her body. "Lucy, you should rethink this. Zac wouldn't want the mother of his children going naked at a place like this." All the flesh on display. "You don't know these people."

She held on to her dress at her hips. "He doesn't know,

remember? And I'll never see them again." She started inching the dress lower.

"George Clooney is not here," I said, going straight to the man who topped her stripper list. "This is not a fantasy."

"If he *was* here, there's no way I'd drop the dress." She gestured to her breasts. "These have seen a bit too much action to entice a man like George."

"But your husband loves them." They really were quite nice.

"You two coming?" Selma demanded. I turned to find her staring at us in all her hairless glory. My gaze slipped down. She embraced the Brazilian.

My body was still covered by my sundress and Lucy was still topless. We'd be kicked out of here before long, but I was pretty sure I'd discovered my professional boundaries. Partial nudity, okay, but full-on bare-naked Lola? Nope. That wasn't in my P.I. job description.

"Be right there," I said with a nervous wave, racking my brain to come up with a solution. Lucy and I fell into step and I took in the array of bodies around us. No one paid special attention to Selma, but disdainful stares were being lobbed at Lucy and me by the bucketful.

"Guess we're a tiny bit conspicuous with our clothes on," I said.

Lucy stood slack-jawed. "Who knew they came in so many shapes and sizes?"

"Breasts?" I asked.

"Noooo," she said, "but there *is* a lot of variety there, too."

"Oh!" My conscience was having a conflict with my eyes, fighting them about what to focus on. My gaze was on autopilot, though, and drifted down. I had to fight to drag it back up.

I didn't want to look.

I didn't know *where* to look.

A man in his mid-thirties walked by. He was lean and muscular. My gaze drifted down again and Jack flashed into my mind. I'd seen him in his altogether—but it had been through a foggy windshield when we'd been teenagers and I'd been stalking him to hone my investigative skills. I could imagine being with him in the hot tub—

No! I pushed him out of my mind. I caught Selma's eye and notched my head toward the guy. "Is that him?" I mouthed.

She shrugged, but then shook her head. "Don't think so," she mouthed back.

In the pool, a few swimmers floated in the water, reveling in the Indian summer, and three more lounged in the adjoining hot tub. I clung to Lucy, as much to bolster myself as to keep her from dropping her dress. We walked through the gate onto the cobbled brick deck and headed straight for the hot tub. Selma dropped her T-shirt and towel on a lounge chair and stepped into the water.

Lucy turned to me. "Well?"

I shrugged helplessly. What to do? What would my mother tell me? Stupid question. I could hear her shrill voice damning me to hell unless I said a million rosaries and promised my life to God and the convent. I couldn't lead Lucy down this path if I wasn't willing to take it myself. "We should go."

"You have a job to do," she reminded me.

Okay, maybe *she* was the one leading me down the path.

"Yes, but I'm sure I can find other ways to investigate

the mysterious boyfriend."

Selma was already engaged in a subdued conversation with a balding man who was probably in his sixties. Jennifer's civilian boyfriend?

"Maybe," Lucy said, "but are you willing to pass up this opportunity? Life is short, Lola. This is on my bucket list."

Before I could answer, she winked at me and said, "Here goes nothing." Then, quick as a flash, she dropped her dress and passed in front of me, her golden skin nothing but a blur as she plunged into the bubbling water.

¡Híjole!

"Lucy!" I hissed. But her eyelids had fluttered closed and she was moaning. Moaning! "This feels fabulous," she said, a hint of heaven in her voice.

My breath started to come quickly and panic rose inside me. My hand pressed against my chest, comforted by the edges of my swimsuit underneath. It was now or never. Lucy wasn't getting out, so I had to get in. Peer pressure. No matter how old you were, it never quite went away.

I sucked in the deepest breath I could manage and slipped out of my dress, slowly folding it and laying it on a nearby chair. I felt the heat of a hundred eyes on me. It could have been my imagination, but I doubted it, since I was overdressed, even in my bright floral bikini.

I twisted one arm behind me to undo the strap but couldn't bring myself to do it. Mami would be so proud.

Something warm touched my shoulder. I jumped, whirling around, nearly knocking down the woman who stood before me. She was buck naked, except for the sympathetic expression she wore on her face. "They should have told you in the office, hon. Bathing suits are not allowed at the resort."

"Not allowed," I repeated vacantly. "It's my first visit. They said I could take my time."

"Not in the pool area," she continued. "Everyone's nude. No one will care once you're undressed. Right now they care because you're *not*."

In a completely warped way, that made absolute sense. I silently pleaded with her. "I've never done this and I'm nervous. Can I get in first and then take it off?"

She shook her head. "Sorry, no. The first time is the hardest. It's kind of like ripping off a bandage. Do it quickly, and it'll be over."

Selma and Lucy both stared up at me. "Come on, Lola," Lucy said. "Be a risk-taker. You only live once..." I didn't budge, so she added, "It really is freeing. And the water feels great. Totally different without a swimsuit on."

The woman tapped me on the shoulder again. The sympathy was gone and she put her hands on her hips. The pointier parts of her body stood at attention like they could shoot bullets at me if I didn't obey. "Miss," she said, "you need to remove the suit or leave the pool area."

"Okay, okay." *Think, think!* I spied the towels on the chaise longue and grabbed the biggest one. Then, after wrapping it around my body, I carefully unhooked my bikini top and slipped it out from underneath.

I leveled my gaze at her and, holding it out with my fingertips, I dropped it on the pool chair. She watched me like she was ready to call the SWAT team if I didn't fully comply, *muy pronto.*

"Just do it," she said again.

I took another bolstering breath, reached under the towel,

and pulled down my bikini bottoms, laying them next to my lonely swimsuit top. Breathing in and out a few times, towel still a protective armor around my body, I dipped a toe into the water. Warm. Tingling. I could do this. I stepped in, the warm water gurgling around my calves.

"You can do it, babe." The man who'd been chatting up Selma was now directing his full attention to me. I wanted to kick myself for being so stupid. The woman, who was *still* staring me down, had been right. No one would have cared if I'd just done like Lucy. I'd already be safely simmering underwater. As it was, everyone's eyes were on me.

My mother's voice echoed in my head again. "*¿Qué pasa, Dolores Falcón Cruz? ¿Estás loca?! ¿Y con Lucy?*"

In my mind I saw my grandmother crossing herself and fingering her rosary with her gnarled fingers. "*¿Ay, Dios mío, por qué tengo una nieta mala?*"

My whole family flashed before me, judging my actions with disapproving eyes.

Last in line was Jack, and he just shook his head.

I turned to the man who was still staring at me. The muscular guy I'd seen walking by earlier had somehow managed to sneak into the hot tub without my noticing. He watched me, too. Could he be Jennifer's boyfriend?

Selma had said people didn't care about nudity here, but from the lust on the men's faces, I had to disagree. They cared plenty.

"I don't suppose any of you knew Jennifer Wallace?" I demanded. My tone was *un poquito* accusatory, but it was either that or get naked. And I'd discovered something about myself this evening. More is more.

They glanced at each other, then back at me. "Of course.

But she just died," the young guy said. "Come on in. I'll help you take your mind off it."

I cringed. Getting in the hot tub with him wasn't going to redirect my thoughts.

"Do you know her boyfriend?" I asked, swirling my leg around in the water.

They both shook their heads. "Didn't know she had one."

Selma sunk down, her breasts floating at the water line, but her face was tense as she listened. Interestingly, neither of the men paid her any attention. Their eyes were riveted on me and my towel. I could practically see them salivating just to get a glimpse of what I was so carefully protecting.

I wriggled my toes under the steaming water. It did feel good, but my moral compass was pointing away from the pool. "Selma. I think I'll check out the restaurant and bar. There's really no point sitting here in the hot tub."

She gawked at me. "What if he shows up?"

I'd thought the murderer would stick to his routine, but now I was reconsidering. My instincts were telling me the guy wasn't going to show, because he'd said the nudist lifestyle wasn't his natural inclination. "He won't."

The stalwart nude police woman from a few minutes ago brought her hand down on my shoulder again. "I'm going to have to ask you to leave the pool area." Any nicety in her voice was gone.

"Fine, yep, no problem." I stepped back onto the cement, tightened my towel around me, snatched my swimsuit and sundress from the deck, and walked out the pool gate. I waited at the fence. "Selma?"

"Yes."

"Let's go."

She sighed, a mixture of resignation and frustration. She stood up, the water cascading off her in angry torrents.

Her feet slapped against the cement, her towel and T-shirt dragging behind her as she joined me behind the fence. I stared at Lucy, who was still relaxed in the water, eyes closed. "Lucy?"

She peeped open one eye. "I'll stay here. You know, in case you're wrong and he does show up."

Not that she'd know it was him. Selma probably wouldn't, either, for that matter. I eyed the two men in the hot tub. Either one of them could have been Jennifer's boyfriend and we'd never know.

I was torn between wanting Lucy to get out of the water—and be gawked at by the two men in the hot tub—or leaving her here with all three of them naked. Neither was a good option. Then the tattletale woman got into the hot tub and sank down next to Lucy. Having another woman in the mix didn't make me feel better.

I decided then and there that I wasn't letting her out of my sight, not after the jeopardy I'd put her in last time she helped me on a case. "Lucy. Go soak in your own bathtub. *¿Entiendes?*" Lucy had been married to my cousin long enough to understand rudimentary Spanish. "*Ven aquí. Ahorita.*"

With a deep sigh, she managed to get out of the hot tub and wrap her towel around her full hips fairly discreetly. She slung her sundress over her shoulders. I definitely didn't belong in this place, but she wasn't having any trouble with the moral aspect of baring her breasts. She'd had a taste of exhibitionism and seemed to be digging it. She would have been a great hippie.

"Are you sure neither one of those guys is him?" I asked Selma the second we had our flip-flops back on our feet and had started the trek across the grass to the restaurant.

"Not really."

Great.

We passed a wooded area near the parking lot, a cluster of numbered buildings, and a sand volleyball court on the way to the restaurant. Our destination was a square structure across from a grassy area. I rewound my towel around me and clutched my useless bikini and sundress in my hand. Selma started to push the door open but I caught her arm. "Don't we put clothes on in the restaurant?"

She gaped at me. "It's. A. Naturist. Resort."

"*Dios mío*, even in the restaurant? Aren't there sanitary issues? Are the cooks dressed?"

Selma put her hands on her hips, her being naked-as-a-jay-bird preventing her from achieving the indignant effect she was going for. "You can have your clothes on in the restaurant," she finally admitted.

That's all I needed to hear. I slipped my sundress back over my head and released my towel. "Thank God."

I threaded my legs into my bikini bottoms and felt an immediate sense of comfort, then maneuvered my bikini top back on, a Houdini trick I somehow managed to pull off without revealing anything I didn't want to.

"I was hoping you'd see the beauty of being free," Selma said.

"I might. Eventually." Not. More is more. Which in my mind meant the degree of clothes I wore, not whether or not I wore them. I repeated my mantra, trying to cleanse my guilt at even having set foot on the grounds of *Cuerpo y Alma*.

Lucy was at a totally different place than I was. She smiled thoughtfully. "I'm feeling the beauty."

I gaped at her. Who *was* this woman and what had she done with Lucy? "Do you think you might want to put your dress back on in the restaurant?"

Lucy's grin widened. "Are you uncomfortable, Lola? 'Cause I'm kind of digging this."

"Great," I muttered. "I've created a monster."

She laughed, more *at* me than with me. "You have a fabulous wax job and an even more fabulous body. You shouldn't be modest about showing it off."

"She's right, you know," Selma said. "Nothing compares to being free like this. Once you try it you may never go back."

I wouldn't bet on that.

Selma held the door open for us and we traipsed into the restaurant like Charlie's Angels on a dare. Selma skirted in front of us and headed to the bar while I followed slowly behind her, absorbing the environment.

It was a full-service restaurant, complete with a waitress scurrying around in the buff, the view overlooking the lake. A few of the patrons wore clothes, but most of them were stark naked. Thankfully, the tablecloths gave cover to the lower halves of the diners' bodies.

"Unless you're in bed, you know, *after*, there's something very wrong about eating naked," I whispered in Lucy's ear.

Her head bobbed up and down. "I have to agree with you there." Her eyes were darting from one table to the next, one side of her lip rising with each new pound of flesh she registered. "I'd totally lose my appetite if I had to sit next to that." She flicked her chin toward a table in the back.

The furry man there didn't really need clothes to cover up, but a body brush seemed in order.

I nudged Lucy and we sidled up next to Selma at the bar. "This is so, uh, bizarre."

Selma rolled her eyes. "Not really. We were *all* born this way. We *all* have the same parts. Different sizes and shapes, but it's there on every one of us. What's unusual is that we insist on covering ourselves up as if there's something wrong with our bodies."

"I'm down with that." Lucy grinned, but she didn't remove the towel from around her hips.

I folded my arms across my chest like a barrier. "I'm *not* down with it. I don't think there's anything wrong with our bodies, but I do believe there's a time and a place for getting naked."

And for me, the time and place would always include Jack Callaghan.

Selma eyed me. "Let me guess, in the bedroom, right? On the bed with the lights out? I bet your boyfriend would be turned on seeing you here, nude."

Would Jack be turned on?

Three nude people stared up at the television set, watching an NBA game. Apparently being at a naturist resort was like living in Seattle. You did the normal things, simply without clothes—just like you carried on normally in the constant rain of the Pacific Northwest.

I knew I'd never move to Washington.

Laying my towel on the red naugahyde stool, I sat down.

"What can I get for you?" The bartender was a young college-age kid with blond hair and stubble on his face. He wasn't wearing clothes. I concentrated hard not to give in to my morbid curiosity, keeping my eyes on his face.

"I'll have a margarita," I said. Selma and Lucy sat and ordered their drinks. When the bartender returned with them, I wrapped a napkin around the stem of my glass before taking it. No telling where his hands had been.

I smiled at him, fetchingly I hoped. "Can I ask you something?"

He leaned his elbows against the bar, moving his face closer to mine. "Sure thing, peach."

Peach?

"Only I have to ask you something first," he said.

"Okay." No way was I going on a date with a twenty-year-old naked guy. I'd just have to break his heart. I took a long drink and braced myself.

"You know you're in a nudist resort?" he asked.

I sighed. "So people keep telling me."

"Excuse me for stating the obvious, but you don't appear to be nude. You have to be"—he paused—"*nude* at the bar."

I gestured at the diners over the railing. "Some of them have their clothes on."

The bartender's eyes twinkled. "They're in the dining room. This is the *bar*."

Huh. A good Spanish curse word hovered on my tongue, but I resisted spewing it out at him and narrowed my eyes.

He shrugged. "Those are the rules, peach."

I sighed again, more heavily this time. I had a job to do. I stood and slipped the straps of my sundress down over my shoulders, holding the bodice of my dress with my other hand. "Will you answer my question now?"

He was all googly-eyed like I had a sign across my body that said, "Sale item, discounted 70 percent" and I was the last one on the shelf. I got the feeling this guy was not here because of freedom of expression. There was no way in hell I was undressing in front of him.

"Drop the dress first," he said with a wink.

I did, holding it at my waist. Then I reached around my neck to grab hold of my bikini tie. "I'm a friend of Jennifer Wallace. She died yesterday, and—"

"Yeah, that was sad," he said, his face tightening. "You couldn't be part of *Cuerpo y Alma* without knowing her. What a blow—"

Selma interrupted. "Do you know her boyfriend?"

The guy frowned. He ran his hand though his hair, doing something that made his pecs flex. "Didn't know she had one."

Damn it, why'd Jennifer keep her boyfriend so secret?

"She usually met him in the hot tub," I prompted.

He flicked his gaze down, waiting for my disrobing to continue. I pulled the tie a fraction of an inch, a hint of cleavage bouncing at the neckline, but my heart started racing. "Medium build. Dark hair," I said, spouting off what Selma had told me.

The bartender laughed, notching his chin toward the dining room, before settling on me again. "Have you looked around? Male and dark are two things I see a lot of in here."

I batted my lashes, staying focused on his face, trying not to be distracted by the hunger in his eyes. "You sure?"

He winked at me, and an uncomfortable chill ran up my spine. "Actually—"

"Actually, what?" I asked, praying he had a clue.

"She was in here the other night and said something weird."

Lucy and Selma leaned in. "What?" Selma asked, her big

brown eyes open wide.

"She said she was done being told how she was going to live her life," he said, closing his eyes for a second like he was picturing her. "Guess someone did stop her from living it, though."

"Why would she say that?" I asked, still clutching my bikini strings.

He let his gaze travel down my body before saying, "Drop it and we can talk about it all night long."

Guess his grieving was over.

I debated, calculating my next move in this nudist chess game. Did he really have anything more to say about Jennifer? Somehow I didn't think so.

Making my decision, I downed what was left of my margarita. Brain freeze. I pressed my fingers to my temples. "Thanks, but I changed my mind," I said once I could speak again. And then I retied my bikini top, pulled my dress back up, and got the hell out of the nudist bar.

Chapter Sixteen

Selma and Lucy raced after me, catching up once I was outside.

"What Jennifer said to the bartender...she may have been talking about the letters," I said.

Selma's face had taken on the paranoid tinge I was becoming familiar with as she surveyed the surrounding areas. "I was thinking the same thing."

"Excuse me?" A high-pitched voice came from behind us. One of the people who'd been at the bar walked toward us, towel thrown over her shoulder.

Angling my head to the side, I raised my hand. "If you're going to tell me this is a nudist resort, I already know."

She stopped a few feet away from me, feeding her towel through her small hands. "I wasn't going to say that."

I eyed her warily. "You're not the nude police?"

"No such thing." She chuckled softly. "But that's a good one. We should have them here just to keep out the riffraff." Moving a step closer, she dropped her voice. "You're looking for Jennifer Wallace's boyfriend?"

My first potential nude informant! "That's right. Do you know him?"

"Not really, but she and I were good friends. I know she was into him. He saw her for who she really was and didn't want anything from her."

And she didn't want anything from him—like a trophy of a basketball jersey or a photo.

"I ran into her once on the outside," the woman continued. "She was with a man. No one I'd ever seen before, but they seemed comfortable. The thing is, this place was Jennifer's home and I've known her forever. She and I always helped out with deliveries and in the front office, but this one time, when I saw her on the outside, she looked right at me, almost seemed scared, and then she turned her back like she didn't know me."

"So she didn't want whoever she was with to know she came here," I said. "Interesting."

Selma stiffened and widened her stance. "It's the contract we sign. She didn't want to lose her job."

"No, I knew about her morality clause," the woman said. "I think it was more than that. If you're married, you can't come here alone, and they bent that rule for her, but I don't think she wanted to rub anyone's face in her new relationship."

Lucy and I shot a glance at each other and Lucy covered the ring on her left hand. She was married, but they'd let her in. So much for rules.

"Wait," I said. "So was Jennifer married?"

That didn't seem to fit what I knew of her. Unless it was her groupie relationships with the ballplayers that broke up her marriage.

The woman nodded. "To Craig. But they were separated for a long time. Finally got divorced last year."

"Who's Craig?" Lucy asked.

Selma piped up. "He owns the place." She stared at the woman. "They were married? She never told me that."

"Still friends, too. That's the thing about this place. You get deeper and really understand people. She took one of the cottages just down from him when they split up."

Selma was stiff as a corpse. I thought she might snap at the waist if a gust of wind came along. She'd been friends with Jennifer but hadn't known this fact about her, and obviously it upset her.

My head felt ready to explode with this new information but I kept focused. "Can I get your name?"

The woman hesitated, but then said, "Deirdre. I don't give my last name to people here."

I wouldn't, either, but I questioned her about it anyway. "Why not? I mean, if you go for this sort of thing, the people here think just like you."

Deirdre shook her head vehemently. "Perverts are everywhere. I've heard people say that they feel safer here than anywhere else. Some folks even bring their kids and think they're better off here than at the mall, but"—she worked the hand towel, twisting it around and around—"this side of my life is private. Completely separate from life on the outside."

She was more like Jennifer, apparently, than she realized. Now I was curious. Deirdre seemed fairly normal if you overlooked the fact that she was standing here talking to us not wearing any clothes. "So you don't socialize on the outside with anyone you know from here?"

It sounded like we were in prison.

"A few people, but generally, no."

"Do most people here feel that way?"

Deirdre checked behind her. "I can't speak for most people. I have children. Coming here"—she spread her arms—"is my time out. I don't *want* to mix my two worlds. It's private, and most people on the outside don't understand."

Selma wrapped her towel around her hips, shifting her weight from one bare foot to the other, her sandals swinging from her hand. "Just like I told you."

So none of them wanted to let their two worlds collide. Was that why Jennifer had kept her apartment on the outside, even though she had a cottage here?

"Where's her cottage?" I asked Deirdre.

"Down there," she said, pointing toward a long building that looked more like a motel than a series of cottages. "Number Five."

I thanked her as she started to walk back to the restaurant, tossing her towel over her shoulder.

"Let's go," I said when she was gone. I'd managed to keep myself covered, but my grace period would be up before too long. I wanted to sneak a peek at Jennifer's cottage and then talk to the widower, Craig. If he was upset about his failing marriage, about Jennifer's boyfriend, and about her life outside *Cuerpo y Alma*, then he had a damn good motive for murder.

• • •

The three of us—Selma stark naked; Lucy topless, her bottom half wrapped in a towel; and me in my bikini and sundress, just praying the nude police didn't show up and haul me away—stood in front of Number 5.

"I don't know about this, Lola. What if someone catches you?" Lucy whispered at my back as I put my hand on the knob.

"Breaking and entering. All the more reason to keep quiet about our visit here," I said. "Or just entering," I amended when the knob turned and the door opened.

Once inside, I found the light switch, flipped it on, and stared. This place was the complete opposite of Jennifer's other apartment. Her Natomas place had a barely lived-in feel, and the furniture and ambiance had been minimal and unwelcoming. But this place was warm and inviting. From the bright floral cotton couch, the striped armchair, and pine square coffee table to the leaf-green Roman shades and seafoam walls, this place felt like a home.

"Huh." A hypothesis had instantly formed in my head. "She only kept the other place for appearances."

Selma's eyes glassed up. "It's like she's still here."

I didn't believe in ghosts like my grandmother did, but I said a quick prayer anyway. Never hurts to be cautious.

I did a quick search, but nothing struck me as unusual. There were a few pictures scattered around, but not of anyone I recognized. An entire set of dishes was stacked in the kitchen cupboards, along with cooking supplies, food, pots and pans, and everything an ordinary kitchen would have.

The bedroom matched the front room. Same pale green walls; a solid, coordinating dark-green comforter; and even an assortment of clothes in the bureau drawers and closet. Everything a person needed to live comfortably, and mostly unclothed.

"No trophies." I searched under the bed, in the closet, in the bathroom, but there wasn't a single plastic bin with basketball jerseys, pictures, or any other memories from her sports conquests. "She kept everything separate."

"Look at these," Lucy said, holding up a set of silver and royal-blue pompoms. "I was a cheerleader in high school, you know. For about twenty minutes."

"What happened?" Selma asked.

"I didn't really want to sleep with Dirk the Jerk. Star football player," she explained. "Apparently *that* was one of the hazing requirements. Can you believe it?"

She shivered, as if the mere memory of it still disgusted her, but grabbed hold of the pompoms, threw her arms up, and shook them around. Just as quickly, she dropped them back into the bottom dresser drawer next to a box of atomizers and old Courtside Dancer costumes.

We searched for another ten minutes, but not a single thing struck me as unusual.

"I need a computer," I said as we traipsed toward the clubhouse.

Selma grabbed my arm. "You're not leaving, are you? We have to find her boyfriend!"

"We don't know anything about him. She didn't have any pictures of him in her cottage. No notes. No journal. Are you sure he was real? She didn't just make him up?"

Selma waggled her head as she whipped the towel off her hips, trembling even as she tried to come off as defiant— while naked. "No. I did not make him up. He's real."

I got the feeling that Jennifer Wallace had been damn good at keeping secrets—and at keeping her two worlds separate.

"I need to do research," I said. "Try to see who she knows from here that she also knows on the outside. Besides you, of course," I said to Selma, but that one sentence sent my mind reeling. What if Selma Mann was a superstar actress? What if she...?

No. I shook the thought away. I liked Selma. I didn't want to believe she could have killed Jennifer.

But Manny had taught me to form hypotheses and I couldn't ignore this one.

"I'm staying," she said.

"I don't think you should. Are you sure?"

She was a little skittish, but she nodded. "Parker'll be here soon."

She disappeared into the darkness as she passed by a series of outbuildings on her way back to the pool area. As Lucy fell into step beside me, I held my pinkie out to her. "Swear to me that you will not tell Zac we came here tonight."

She held her pinkie up. "I already promised."

I amended the pact. "Until this case is wrapped." She and I both would have to come clean at that point. Just not before.

We laced fingers and shook.

"Can't go back on a pinkie promise," she said.

"Deal."

. . .

In the clubhouse, the former Mr. Jennifer Wallace was nowhere to be seen.

I turned to Tiffany. "Let me level with you." I held out the business card I'd retrieved from my car. "I'm a private investigator. I've been hired to find Jennifer Wallace's killer."

Sort of. To ferret out a rogue letter-writer was more the truth, but I was becoming more and more convinced that the two were related and I couldn't not try to answer the *why* behind Jennifer's death.

"She was married to another nudist?" I asked.

"And she had a boyfriend here?" Lucy threw in, still naked from the waist up. She definitely got into her roles whenever she helped me with a case.

I shot her a warning. We didn't need to play good cop/bad cop, and I wanted Tiffany to be helpful, not feel alienated.

The color drained from Tiffany's cheeks and her hand trembled as she read the card then cupped it in her hand. Her voice dropped and from her quivering chin, I wasn't sure she'd be able to hold back the tears that suddenly threatened. "I'd help you if I could, but I already told you, I didn't know she was seeing anyone. Sh-she and Craig are divorced, but she must have w-wanted to keep her new friend a secret. I don't know, really."

An older man burst into the room, bringing a truckload of energy with him. He ripped off his shirt as he entered, the pile of graying hair on his head matching the thick, curlier hair on his sun-damaged body. But the guy was fit. He gave Lucy and me a cursory look, immediately putting his temper in check. "Who do we have here?"

"Two prospective members," Tiffany said, sticking out her pudgy chin. Her eyes had rounded suddenly and I followed her gaze. She'd left my business card on the counter. Holy mackerel, was *this* Craig?

I'd thought the younger guy we'd seen in the office

earlier had been the ex, but Tiffany's spooked expression made it clear that *this* craggy man was actually Jennifer's estranged husband. He didn't seem particularly mournful at just having lost his wife. And he was too busy making flirty faces at Lucy to notice Tiffany moving across the office and slyly retrieving the card.

I didn't know why *she* didn't want Craig to know I was a P.I. investigating Jennifer's death, but that was definitely my preference. The fewer people who knew—particularly those with motives—the better.

"Prospective nudists," he said. "Nothing I like better than that."

I sidestepped in front of Lucy, holding my arm out. "Great place you have here."

He shook my hand, chuckling. "So formal, miss…"

"Cruz."

"Ms. Cruz. We're very casual here. Call me Craig, and I'll call you…"

Ms. Cruz, I thought, but I said, "Lola." Better to give my nickname than my real name, and better than having Lucy give her name.

I stopped at the rack of sunglasses, hats, and T-shirts. Lucy picked up a tank top, snapped it open, and examined the logo: male and female silhouettes danced in the center of a scroll design. The *Cuerpo y Alma* slogan, *Dare to Go Bare: All Natural, No Additives*, was printed underneath.

Ironic, I thought, *sitting next to protein powders and sunscreen*. Even nudists wanted to look good and avoid skin cancer.

"Is this your place?" I asked.

"It certainly is." He handed me a brochure just like the

one Jennifer had had in her Natomas apartment. If Craig owned the place, did that mean Jennifer co-owned it? Had she kept her percentage after the divorce?

"It's a lot to handle by yourself," I said, trying to sound like a curious nudist and nothing more. "It's a great place."

His giant grin faltered for the briefest moment, but he kept it wide and said, "Used to have a partner, but now it's just me. Tiff here is my right hand," he added, wrapping his hairy arm around Tiffany.

I had a hard time picturing Craig and Jennifer together, but I tried to remember Selma's edict: people here weren't concerned with the outside appearance. Jennifer must have seen something wonderful in Craig—before they split.

"You're leaving?" he asked, loping to the door and holding it open for us.

"Oh yeah," Lucy said, waving her hand like we were old hat at being nudists. "We've been to the hot tub and the bar. Strolled by the cottages and the volleyball courts. Great place."

"We'd love to have you come again," Craig said. He snapped suddenly. "Saturday night."

I sputtered. "W-what?"

"Yep. You think this place is great now? Wait until you come to the Halloween Costume Ball. There's nothing like it. It's the sexiest thing around. Puts those radio Halloween parties to shame," he added with a shake of his shaggy-haired head.

"We'll think about it," I said with a happy wave, wishing upon every star I could see from the window that I wouldn't have to come back.

Lucy tossed the tank top back onto the shelf, right on

top of a row of protein powders. While she fixed it, I asked the only question I could think of that might garner me some information. "We saw the cottages down past the restaurant. Do you rent them out?"

"You in the market?" he asked with a notch of his eyebrow.

I summoned my coy gene. "Could be."

Liar, liar, pants on fire. I added another series of rosaries to my long tally sheet.

He glanced at Tiffany, but she kept her head down, her hand on her computer mouse and her eyes on her monitor.

"We just had one become available. That doesn't happen too often. It'll take me a few weeks to get it ready, but if you're interested," he said, "I'll put your name down."

"Yeah, um, great. I don't think I'd get rid of my apartment, but it would be cool having a place here."

"Lots of folks keep their places on the outside," he said. "As the owner, of course, I don't. Twenty-four-seven right here." He winked. "You always know where to find me." He bent to lower his shorts and my breath caught in my throat. I did *not* want to stick around *Cuerpo y Alma* for another second.

"Yes we do," Lucy choked, grabbing hold of my elbow.

I took her arm at the same time, yanking her out the door. "Talk to you later!" I said over my shoulder.

He stood in the doorway and called after us. "All-righty, then. I'll see you when you come back."

Which, with any luck, would be never.

We hightailed it through the parking lot and toward my CRV. By the time we got to the car, nervous, giddy laughter bubbled up in me. Lucy blew out a raspberry, and we both doubled over, laughing until tears welled in our eyes.

"It takes a special kind of person to call a place like this home," I said after we were calm again.

And I guess Jennifer had been one of them.

"I was getting into it for a while." Lucy blew more air out between her lips. "But I'm over it now. When Craig in there started dropping his drawers—"

She broke off as another onslaught of laughter surfaced. "His willie g-gave m-me the w-willies," she choked out.

That, I thought, was the understatement of the year.

Chapter Seventeen

My cell phone rang first thing in the morning, rousing me from a delightful dream in which I was fully clothed—and so was everyone else. I reached across my bed, grabbing the phone from my dresser. "Hmm?" I said, trying not to sound too sleepy.

"There was a note on my door this morning," Selma's spooked voice said when I answered.

Adrenaline surged through me. I'd thought that maybe the notes had been a decoy to detract from the motive behind Jennifer's murder, but maybe I'd been wrong. Were the other dancers still in danger? "What'd it say?"

Her voice hitched as she read: "'Stop nosing around, or you and your friends will pay the price.'"

My breath caught in my throat. This wasn't some veiled red herring of a threat delivered at a basketball game. This was the real McCoy. Whoever was behind this knew where Selma lived, and that was definitely not a good thing.

"He was there last night. He saw us. He had to."

Just what I'd thought.

She gasped for air. "I don't want to die."

Her mind had gone to the mysterious boyfriend, but mine went to Craig. One of us had to be right.

"Selma." I worked to calm her down, finally saying, "I really think you should stay away from *Cuerpo y Alma*, just for a while. If that place has anything to do with Jennifer's death, you shouldn't be there."

She hemmed and hawed but didn't agree to lay low. I sighed into the phone. There was nothing I could do about that. A nudist had to be free.

I pictured her tiger eyes flashing as she buried the anxiety bubbling up inside her. "I'll be careful, but you find him, Lola."

Exactly what I planned on doing.

• • •

I spent the morning at home. Better to Google *Cuerpo y Alma* on my personal computer than on the office computer, what with all the naked bodies on the screen. I started on the ABOUT US page, reading up on the history of the resort. I learned that *Cuerpo y Alma* had been founded more than thirty years ago and was still run by the same family— Craig's family.

I peered at the pictures, blinking and making a concerted effort to keep my eyes on the people's faces. I couldn't say any of them were familiar, but I clicked page after page after page, thinking I might catch a glimpse of Jennifer and her mystery boyfriend.

Finally, I spotted her mass of blond hair and her huge toothy grin amidst a group. Jennifer was buck naked, just like everyone else. She was next to Craig and another woman I didn't recognize. Deirdre stood a few people away from them. I scanned, searching for Selma, and finally spotted her crouched in front. The backdrop of the picture was a stage.

By the time I registered the concert banner strung from end to end with one colorful word emblazoned on it—Nudestock—my phone beeped with an incoming text.

RED ALERT! Pinkie Promise #EpicFail!!! Zac forced a confession. :(
So sorry, Lola.

No. No, no, no. My heart lurched. If Zac knew, that meant Antonio probably knew. And if Antonio knew, than that meant—

"I heard you got a new hobby," a voice said behind me.

—Jack knew.

I sucked in a mouthful of air, breaking down into a frenzy of coughing. My hand flew to my chest. Not Jack. Antonio.

"*¡Hijo de la chingada!*" My brother. "Tonio, you scared me half to death!"

"Porn, eh?"

"No, not porn." I glared at him. "This is for work."

"Right. Work," he said skeptically.

Before I could swat his arm, a movement in my peripheral vision caught my attention. A shadow, lean and stealthy. The breath caught in my throat again and then Jack appeared.

Damn.

His jaw pulsed as his gaze slid to the computer screen full of naked people, then back to me. "Have fun last night, Lola?"

"Not so much." I clicked the page closed. "I was working."

"Huh. But the Royals didn't play last night." The statement sounded innocent enough, but the blaze behind his eyes made me think it wasn't actually anything of the sort. Damn Lucy for breaking our pinkie-promise pact. I was going to have to come clean with Jack. Which I didn't want to do—not because I thought he wouldn't understand—he was a journalist, after all. He'd gone undercover. He had sources to protect. He crossed lines for his job. But a nudist resort? Did that go too far? I was afraid to face my own boundaries. Was I really not cut out to be a detective? Could I ever be good enough if I had lines I wouldn't cross?

"I had dance practice," I offered. It wasn't a lie. I *had* had dance practice...before I'd gone to the nudist resort.

Antonio didn't blink. "Uh-huh. And after?"

Oh yeah, they knew.

My mind raced as I tried to strategize, but in the end, I gave up. Damn Lucy. I knew I shouldn't have let her come. And damn Zac for then spilling to Antonio and Jack.

"Like I said, I was working."

"Lola." Jack's lips were tight and his eyes narrowed. "Tell me you didn't go to a nudist resort."

I met his scrutiny head-on. "Okay, I won't tell you."

My attempt to lighten the tension in the room fell flat. He didn't smile. Not even the tiniest glimpse of his dimple marked his cheek.

"Jesus," he said as he spun on his heel and paced the living room. Coming back next to me, he raked his hand through his hair, then pointed from me to him. "We're a team, remember? I would have—"

"You would have what, Jack?" I stood, the adrenaline coursing through my body. "Come with me?" Maybe that's what I'd been afraid of. We hadn't made love yet—not from lack of trying. Seeing each other bare-naked at *Cuerpo y Alma* was not what I wanted.

"Hell yes, I would have come."

"I couldn't even do it—"

"That's not the point," he said, although I thought he seemed a bit relieved that I'd confirmed what he'd probably heard from Zac.

"What *is* the point? I have to be able to do my job, but in the recesses of my mind, I'm wondering about what you'll think…or if Sarah has come back and if I should even worry about it because as long as she's around—"

Antonio made a stealthy retreat toward the kitchen. "I'm just going to go. To work. See you kids later." He gave a quick wave, and suddenly he was gone.

"She's *not* around." The floor of the old house creaked as Jack paced.

"For now. Until she runs away from her family again."

"She's not coming back. I won't take her in—"

"What about your sister?"

"Brooke won't take her in, either." He came around to face me. "You can trust me, damn it. You can tell me what you're up to. I want to know."

Wanting to know and being okay with the truth were two different things. Seeing me dance around in a cheerleading costume and stripping at *Cuerpo y Alma* were two different things. "It's a nudist resort. My family will disown me—"

His jaw pulsed. "I'm not your parents, Lola. And I'm not going to stop you from doing your job. If you can't trust me, this isn't going to work."

Salsa lay on the floor by the door, her droopy face curious, following us.

"But I can't pick and choose where a case takes me any more than you can pick and choose where a lead takes you," I said.

Jack sighed. "I know."

I knew he'd been in some dicey situations tracking a source or following a lead for a story. It was his job, and I'd never try to stop him. I didn't think he felt the same about my job—not deep down.

"What about Sarah?" I finally asked. He'd said she wasn't an issue anymore, but as long as she was in his life, she was an issue to me.

He sank down on the couch, his eyes clouding to a stormy gray. "She's not you and *you're* the one I want. Damn it, Lola, I choose you."

My head swam, but I took a deep breath to steady my nerves, wanting to believe him.

We sat in silence for a minute. Finally, I said, "So you don't care that I was at a nudist resort." Not a question, just a statement. And I didn't like the sound of it, either.

He pressed his hands against his face, digging his fingers into his eyes. "Of course I care. You were following a lead. I get that. I want you to be straight with me, Cruz. Do I like that you went there? Hell, no. Why would I want other men to see you naked? Jesus, *I* haven't even seen you naked."

"Not for lack of effort," I said, adding some flirt into my

voice. On both our parts.

Finally, he cracked. "Yeah."

I breathed easier as the tension in the room deflated a bit. I'd discovered last night that I wasn't willing to get naked for my job, but facing that left too many doubts in my mind about whether my parents were right. Maybe I was fooling myself, trying to be something I wasn't cut out for.

"Are you going again?" he asked when I didn't respond.

"If I need to."

He didn't say anything, but his eyes smoldered.

"I have to get ready for dance rehearsal," I finally said, standing. "I'll be back in a minute." I felt his frustrated eyes on my back as I headed to my bedroom to change, Salsa trailing behind me.

Normally, I'd be comforted by the terra cotta silk bedspread, the black wrought iron bed frame, the neatly organized desk and bookshelves (I am my mother's daughter, after all, and cleanliness is next to Godliness), but at the moment I was blind to it. Salsa immediately settled on her pillow, stretching and turning as she found the right position, but I left the door open a crack in case she changed her mind and wanted to go back to the living room with Jack.

I stripped off my blouse and tossed it onto the edge of the bed, wishing Jack and I could get past this, wishing Sarah was a non-issue, wishing my case was solved, wishing I knew for sure that I really was P.I. material.

I unzipped my jeans and was just about to unhook my bra when the bedroom door swung open.

"Lola."

I froze. Part of me had hoped Jack wouldn't be able to stay away. Slowly, I turned, clasping my hands to my chest, holding my black Victoria's Secret bra in place. "*¡Ay, Dios!* Jack. What are you doing?"

He dug his hands into his pockets, dragging his eyes from my body back to my face. Salsa perked up, peering at him curiously, then, as if she knew this was a private conversation, she got up and trotted out the door.

"I don't want to wait anymore," he said.

I felt the rush of air against my stomach, a triangle of black lace showing where my pants were undone. His gaze never left my face, but the heat of it spread like fire over my skin and he seemed to absorb every single detail of my body.

There was a low pull in my abdomen as I shifted my slipping bra back into place. "For what?" I asked, kicking myself after the question left my lips.

He took a step toward me, his voice dropping. "For you. For us."

I took a step back, ending up against the wall, readjusting my suddenly heavy arm against my chest.

He followed, stopping a breath away from me, bracing one hand on the wall above my head. His musky scent embedded itself in my memory banks, something I'd be able to conjure up at will. I gripped the dresser next to me with my free hand, my breath catching in my throat as he pressed his body against me, trailing one finger down my cheek, his chin against my forehead. "Jack—" I muttered as he slowly lowered one knee to the ground. His bent leg brushed against mine, his hands circling my waist, my hips, making their way into my undone jeans. I forced my breath out, my whole body aching with my need for him.

His lips grazed my skin, nipping around my belly button piercing—collateral damage from my first investigation as lead detective. Which I'd grown to kind of like. His hands gripped me, pulling my body closer, if that was possible. "Jesus, Lola, you're killing me, you know that?"

The feeling was mutual. "I just need to know you're only with me, Jack."

He slipped my jeans down my hips. "I am."

My knuckles turned white with the strength of my hold on the edge of the dresser. Was I ready for this? Could I take a leap of faith with him?

"*Belísima.*" He pulled away and stood, stripping off his T-shirt, his lids heavy as he took in every inch of me.

Any words caught in my throat when I saw the curve of his arms, his chest, his taut stomach, wanting to feel them all against me.

My knees buckled and I started to slide down the wall, but his lips found me again. He held me upright as he tugged at my jeans, working them down my legs. I stepped out of them, only black lace and an unclasped bra separating all of me from him.

He kissed my stomach, his hands running up the outside of my legs, making their way down again, then one of them slid up the inside, his fingers skimming the lace. *Dios mío.*

He stood and in one fluid movement, stripped off his jeans, his black boxer briefs riding low on his hips. He caught me again just as my legs were ready to give out completely, and pressed his body against mine.

I leaned my forehead against his shoulder. "Are you sure?" I asked, as much for myself to answer as for him. "I can't change who I am," I added, barely above a whisper.

His hand curved around my back and he dropped his head and brushed his lips against my neck, the heat from his mouth bringing goose bumps to the surface of my skin. He swept my hair away from my ears, circling my silver hoop earrings with his fingers. "I don't want you to."

"I have to be able to do my job—" I moaned when his teeth tugged at my earlobe.

"Just trust me."

He searched my face when I didn't answer.

I tried to steady the rise and fall of my chest, unclenching my hand from the dresser and skimming his hair, his cheek.

His breathing was heavy. There wasn't a trace of a smile on his face. This was what torture was like.

I held my breath as my thoughts grew fuzzy. I started to move my arms, the straps of my bra dangling from them. Then, slowly, I let the lace slip away from my body.

I heard the sharp intake of his breath before I saw the intensity of his face. The next second, his lips were on me, his tongue exploring every inch. His touch sent an electric charge through my body.

Just when I was sure I couldn't take another second, he stopped, nuzzled his way to my mouth, and kissed me, hard and insistent, more urgently than I thought possible.

Dios mío, I needed him.

He held me close as he edged me away from the wall and over to the bed, laying me down as he propped himself above me, taking me in with aching, hungry eyes. "Finally."

I backed away from any thoughts of Jack's past, the notches on his bedpost, his one long-term girlfriend. I didn't want to think about any of that now. I reached for him, my body moving under his, arching up.

He pulled away, skimming his lips down my body before

he found the lace barrier and slipped it off me. He paused, his lips curving up. "Mmmm. That's *very* nice."

I felt the blush rise on my cheeks. The wax job. "It was provisional. In case I had the guts to be a nudist for a day."

He lifted his smoldering gaze to mine. "Really? Not for me?"

I smiled just a little. "Well," I confessed, "you crossed my mind…"

He gave a devilish grin, taking another look. "Uh-huh. That's what I thought." Then he slipped his boxers off and crawled back up to me like it had always been meant to be, like there was no other place he belonged. Home.

Chapter Eighteen

"You sure you have to go?" Jack asked as I came back in the room after a speed shower. He lay in my rumpled bed, still naked.

Being with him for the first time was both beyond anything I'd imagined and not nearly enough. "I do if I want to keep my cover and solve my case."

Which I did. More than anything.

He looked wolfish and ready for more.

Almost anything.

I crossed the room, bent down, and kissed him. Part possessive, part hungry, part —

"You will," he said as he pulled me down on top of him.

My eyes closed and I breathed him in. I'd been waiting for this moment since I'd been in high school. Now I thanked God that I'd had time to grow up and appreciate making love with Jack as an adult rather than as a teenager. Poor Greta Pritchard had lost out.

It took work, but I finally pried myself away from him

and with another kiss, wiggle of my hips, and a wink, I was out the door. And feeling like a bubble ready to burst. As if I were still in high school, I felt an urgent need to tell someone about the amazing experience I'd just had. But who? Reilly was out of the question. My sex life might become pillow talk for her and Neil, and I definitely didn't want that. My sister, Gracie, was teaching school. No dice there. Lucy was a possibility, but she was probably working, and besides, I now knew that my schoolgirl giddiness would get back to Jack if I told her.

Which would be *no bueno.*

I'd whispered it to Salsa as I left, but now I jammed in my Bluetooth and dialed my oldest childhood friend. I couldn't tell anyone I was undercover as a Courtside Dancer. I couldn't tell anyone I'd been to *Cuerpo y Alma.* But I *could* tell Coco Sandoval that my long-awaited passion for Jack had been realized…in a big…and multiple…way.

"It's done," I blurted the second she answered.

"Lola? *¿De qué estás hablando?*"

"Jack Callaghan…and me. We—"

Her screech drowned out the rest of my sentence. "You did not!" she said after she recovered.

"*Sí, dormimos juntos,*" I said, sure the glow was still on my face.

"So you two are…*¿qué? ¿Amantes? ¿Novios?*"

Hmmm. Were we lovers? Boyfriend/girlfriend? "*Somos socios,*" I said as I merged onto the freeway. Partners. A team. I liked the sound of that.

She asked a million more questions, most of which I declined to answer. Not so schoolgirl after all. I didn't want to kiss and tell *everything.* Before long I was at the arena.

"Gotta go, Coco. See you at *Ambrosía*."

I didn't know when I'd be able to salsa dance at our favorite club again, but whenever it was, I'd make sure Jack was right there with me.

Ten minutes later, all thoughts of him were relegated to the back of my mind. I was out on the court going through the dance routines and listening to the *chisme* about Jennifer's death. I tried to pick up any bit of information that might help me with my investigation. Any inkling that anyone—besides Selma—knew about Jennifer's other life.

By the time practice was over, I'd found out from some of the girls that Jennifer had grown up in a tiny rural town just outside of Sacramento, that she'd been married and still used her ex-husband's last name—both things I already knew—and that while she loved lemon meringue pie, she was a health nut, she had a standing appointment with the team nutritionist, belonged to a local gym and went religiously, and had less than 17 percent body fat, something the other dancers had been envious of.

The one thing none of them mentioned was her being a nudist.

After we'd all showered and changed, I tried to catch Selma's attention, but she'd already scurried out of the arena. Heading for *Cuerpo y Alma*, no doubt. For once, the arena was nearly deserted. Time to sleuth around the Royals' locker room.

I waited until the coast was clear, then I strode down the wide, cavernous hallway, on the hunt for some clue that would show me how Jennifer Wallace's two worlds had collided.

• • •

As I rounded a corner, the sound of men's voices bounced off the walls and came at me. I slung my workout bag over my shoulder and plowed on with sure footsteps. As long as I acted like I knew where I was going and that I belonged, no one would question me.

The hallway curved. The locker room was just around the next bend, but the voices were growing closer. My goal was to search the locker room—specifically, to scour the lockers of the ballplayers Jennifer had broken the rules with. It was possible one of them was the mysterious boyfriend from *Cuerpo y Alma.*

I didn't hold out much hope for the theory—six-foot-five-plus inches of naked man would surely attract attention. Selma had caught a faraway glimpse of the guy and she hadn't mentioned *those* stats, so it felt like a long shot. But I had to try.

My other theory was that one of the trophy wives had had a hand in Jennifer's death. Jealousy was a powerful motivator.

I followed the hallway around the last turn before the locker room and froze. The two men I'd heard were suddenly in front of me. I immediately recognized one as the Royals' trainer, Steve, and the other as his brother, Larry.

"Hi," I said. They appeared exactly the same as they had when I'd first met them. Not exactly pudgy, but not super-fit, either. Slightly receding hairlines. Ruddy cheeks. And talking sports.

"The new dancer, right?" Steve asked, pointing at me and then snapping his fingers. "Can I help you? This area's off-limits to you girls."

I bristled at the dismissive way he said "you girls," but

I kept my expression innocent. "Oh, I didn't know. It's so cool to be down here. I was just taking it all in." I pointed to the locker room behind them. I upped my innocent act, gave a little flip of my hair. "Is that where you work on the players?"

"That's right." Steve glanced at his brother, then at me, giving a shrug. His cheeks lifted as his lips curved up. "It's Lola, right?"

"Good memory."

"I make it my business to know everyone. This is my brother, Larry."

Larry plunged his hands into his pockets and shuffled his feet, dipping his chin in acknowledgment.

"Let's give you a quick tour, shall we? It'll be our secret," Steve said. He maneuvered himself between Larry and me, draping his arm around my shoulder as we walked toward the locker room. "Larry's a big fan of the Royals. Pays to know the trainer," Steve said in an almost conspiratorial tone. "Never miss a game, do you, Larry?"

Larry uttered a quiet *mmm-mmm* as his brother dropped his arms from our shoulders and opened the door to the locker room. He ushered me inside, talking in a low voice to Larry before falling into step beside me again.

I was a black belt in kung fu and could take care of myself. Part of that meant paying attention to the niggling feelings I got in my gut. And right now my gut was telling me that something didn't feel right. A wave of unease coiled through me and I suddenly knew I was being manipulated. A tour of the locker room from Steve in return for what?

I moved ahead of the brothers, casually opening random lockers, oohing and aahing at the contents of each one. I'd already done this with the ball boy, and nothing new had materialized since then. Big surprise. This place was devoid of clues. But there had to be something. Anything. Jennifer didn't die for no reason.

Steve and Larry were both quietly watching me, Steve with overt curiosity and Larry with a sad intensity.

Maybe behind the closed door…

"My office," Steve said, spreading his arm toward the room I'd seen him in during my brief tour with the ball boy.

He opened the door and I poked my head inside. The huge room held a massage table; a gooseneck light; two vinyl-covered beds; privacy screens; cabinets; and the biggest, tallest stainless steel bathtub contraption I'd ever seen.

"This is a lot of equipment," I said, coming back to the giant bathtub. "That's huge."

"Has to be able to cover the extremities, hips, and backs of pro athletes, and you know how big they are."

"I didn't before I got this job." I laughed. "But now I do." The height of the pro players made Steve, Larry, and any other Joe off the street seem positively tiny.

As I tried to figure out how to bring up Jennifer without it coming out of the blue, Steve prattled on. "Lots of turmoil right now."

Boo-ya. The perfect opening. "Right. Really sad. Did you know Jennifer?"

Steve cleared his throat as Larry dug his hands deeper into his pockets and stared at the ground. "*Every*one knew Jennifer," Steve said after a loaded pause.

I blinked, playing the part of innocent dancer rather than private investigator. "I thought she was married?"

"Where'd you hear that?" Steve asked, waving away the

very idea. He moved to the counter, absently tossing tubes of ointment into a drawer, moving a canister of protein powder into one of the cupboards, and throwing a soiled white towel into the laundry bag sitting in the corner. "She had boyfriends. Lots of 'em. Heard the police found some interesting things at her apartment."

I wondered if he had been one of her boyfriends, so I watched him with eagle-eye attention as I fished. "I actually heard she dated one of the players?"

Steve scoffed. "One?"

"What do you—"

"Stop." The word snapped from Larry's pursed lips like a bullet from a gun.

Steve's eyes pinched together. "Larry," he said, a heavy warning in his voice that piqued my curiosity.

"I know you didn't like her, but she's dead." Larry's chin still pointed toward the ground, but he raised his eyes to Steve. "Even she deserves respect."

Ay, caramba, the brotherly love was strung tight right now. I got the feeling that Larry was the voice of reason to Steve's strong personality. Maybe he'd reveal more about the late Jennifer Wallace.

I tried to melt into the shadows, except there were no shadows in the all-white trainer's room. So I took a step backward, listening, hoping they'd forget I was there.

"I know she's dead, Larry—"

Larry's voice dropped to a low, menacing level. "Murdered. And she was—"

"What?" Steve flung his arms up, frustrated. "She used you, man." He patted the air in front of him, placating his brother. "She used me. She used everyone. Surely you can understand that."

But apparently Larry didn't see things the way Steve did. He shook his head, his ruddy cheeks turning blotchy. "Uh-uh. She didn't—"

"She didn't what?" I slapped my hand over my mouth. Had I said that aloud?

Yep, I must have, because the team's trainer suddenly stood ramrod straight and whipped his head around to stare at me.

The niggling feeling in my gut intensified. My mind scrambled. There wasn't any love lost between Steve and Jennifer, that seemed clear. And if the trainer thought Jennifer had wronged his brother, could he be the one behind her death?

Or what if he'd been one of Jennifer's conquests?

Oh boy.

Steve took a step toward me and I suddenly felt like a trapped animal. I raced through my options. I could take him down with a quick upward thrust of the heel of my hand against his chin, followed by a knee to the groin. But while that was something Dolores Cruz, P.I., would do, it was not something Lola Cruz, Royals Courtside Dancer, could pull off without raising some serious eyebrows.

I wanted to keep my cover intact so I plastered a bewitching—or what I hoped was bewitching—smile on my face, threw my hand up in a wave, and backed toward the door. "I'm so sorry about Jennifer," I said. "She seemed like such a great girl."

Larry's expression softened. "She was. She didn't deserve what she got."

"Nobody deserves murder," I said.

Steve stopped. "Have you always been a dancer?"

"N-no," I said, shrugging. "I got lucky getting this gig. It's tough to make it through auditions, but the team lost someone—"

"Another girl who didn't get what she deserved," Larry said, shaking his head.

She'd gotten what she wanted, if not what she deserved. "She's engaged, isn't she? To a player?"

"But had to leave the team," Larry snapped. "Damn hypocrites if you ask me."

"Yeah, maybe they should change the rules, since everyone seems to be doing it," I said, noticing how nobody quite knew if Rochelle Nolan had been fired or had quit. It was all very vague. "Thanks for the tour. I have to go," I said, pulling the door open.

"Lola." Steve moved toward me, but I was already in the hallway, the door closing behind me.

Voices drifted our way and just as Steve caught the door and stepped into the hallway, Victoria and Lance Wolfe rounded the corner.

Victoria looked at me, then at Steve, then back at me. She raised her pencil-thin eyebrows, asking a silent question. Lance wasn't as subtle. "Well, well, well. Overtime with the trainer, Lola?"

I forced a laugh. "Steve and Larry were just giving me a tour. Great equipment," I added. "Top-notch facility."

Victoria and Lance started walking again. I went with them, wondering who else was having an affair with a player and won-dering how Larry knew so much about the dancers.

I felt the weight of Steve's gaze on my back until we disappeared from his sight.

"What was that about?" Victoria asked once we were in the clear.

Good question. "I'm not really sure. Larry's upset about Jennifer's murder. He got mad at Steve for not showing more respect." I glanced at the dance coach. "Did you know Jennifer, um…"

She glanced at Lance before answering. "Broke the rules? Yes. I was aware."

Lance just frowned, disappointed. In his players? The dancers? Probably both.

Not the answer I'd expected, either, Lance, I wanted to say, although it didn't surprise me that Victoria saw and knew everything related to her girls. "If you knew, why—"

"Why did I keep her?"

She had an irritating habit of finishing my sentences, but I let it go. "Yes. Since Rochelle had to leave for the same thing."

"Because she was one of the best. A pro. Vanessa will take her place, but she doesn't have the same rapport with the girls. Jennifer's shoes will be tough to fill."

Like any good P.I., I followed the immediate line of questioning that arose. "Did Vanessa know she was next in line for captain?"

Victoria shook her head, her perfectly coiffed hair remaining perfectly in place. "We don't have a set hierarchy on the team. She wouldn't have known, no."

I pondered this—and the inner workings of the dance team—as I left the arena. My direct line of questioning wasn't leading me to any answers. I headed straight to Camacho & Associates. The whole *Cuerpo y Alma* thing was still front and center in my mind. I couldn't help but feel like it was related to Jennifer's death somehow, someway. Vanessa killing Jennifer so she could become team captain seemed far-fetched. And at this point, I had no connections between the resort and the team—other than Selma.

Chapter Nineteen

The second I set foot in Camacho's, Reilly, in all her orange-haired glory, dragged me into the bathroom and said, "*¡Ven, ven, ven!*"

"*¿Qué haces?*" I asked her, following up with the English translation, "What are you doing?"

She let the door close behind her but quickly opened it again, poking her head into the hall.

"Reilly? What's going on?"

"*Chisme*," she said under her breath. "The best *chisme* ever. E-V-E-R. *E-ver.*"

"*¿Qué?*" I leaned against the sink and waited, trying not to get too excited. Reilly used to be the gossip queen, but since her clandestine affair with Neil had started, she'd gone hit or miss with dishing the office dirt.

"Remember the job I was doing for *el jefe* a while back?" she asked, closing the door again and coming to stand next to me.

"How could I forget?" She'd been babysitting Manny's

daughter. The daughter no one had known he'd even had. The daughter I'd seen in the back of Manny's truck. Same olive skin, same chiseled features, and a sweet rosebud mouth that had to have come from her mother, whoever *she* was.

"I got some goods."

Oooh, this had the potential of being *really* good *chisme*. "On his ex-wife? *Dígame*," I said, on the edge of my seat. Gossip about Manny was something she had to tell me right this minute. He was my mentor, and a super-ex-cop-detective, but he had Javier Bardem charisma and the mystique of Amaury Nolasco—with hair.

She darted her heavily lined eyes around as if someone might materialize out of thin air. "It started last night. Neil and me, we were, um, you know…"

She trailed off, giving me time to fill in the blank.

"Got it. Moving on." I circled my hand to keep her talking.

"He gets kinda chatty afterward, and he let it slip that *el jefe* and Tomb Raider Girl broke up because of the ex-wife and the daughter. Turns out she doesn't want to be a step-mommy."

I stared. "No, really?"

Her eyes scanned the tiny bathroom again—still no ghosts. She leaned in closer to me and dropped her voice.

"Yup." That was it. Just yup.

"Huh."

Reilly primped in the mirror, fluffing her Crayola-colored hair and pinching her cheeks. "That's all I have."

"Good *chisme*." But with nothing more to gossip about, we headed back to the conference room, which was as quiet as church during Easter Mass. Who knew where the rest of the associates were? All I cared about was that Sadie was not in my business, which meant I could continue my research on any connections between Jennifer Wallace, *Cuerpo y Alma*, and the Royal Courtside Dancers.

. . .

I'd come to believe that the least likely suspect is often the one who's guilty. I didn't like Trainer Steve, but that didn't mean he was guilty of murder. Rochelle didn't have a motive. For Victoria and Lance, maybe, since they were the ones with the double standard, but not for Jennifer. I kept circling around to Selma, much as I didn't want to ride that train.

She was the sole connection between the dancers and *Cuerpo y Alma*. She was the one who supposedly caught a glimpse of the mysterious boyfriend. She thought she had something to lose if her naturist habit came out.

Pero I felt like I was missing something about the big picture. Where was Manny when I needed him?

Oh right, in the midst of *As Camacho Turns*, a P.I. *telenovela*.

I hadn't had any real contact with the players, and nothing led me to suspect any of them. The wives were a possibility, but no one had surfaced as a likely suspect. And what about the other Courtside Dancers? They were the most unlikely suspects in my mind, but it was possible one of them had a grudge against Jennifer. Knowing women and their petty jealousies, it wasn't outside the realm of possibility.

Of course I had no hard evidence against any of them. Manny's rule of thumb was to form a hypothesis, but I didn't think an imaginary grudge between women would really fly with him as a viable hypothesis.

Which led me right back around to Selma Mann. I couldn't believe the youngest dancer on the team and a naturist at heart could be a murderer, but I'd been surprised before.

I sat down at the conference room computer and Googled her.

And found *nada*. White Pages listings and Facebook didn't give me anything. Selma Mann might be the only person in the world, besides me, who didn't regularly update her Facebook status. I didn't keep an active page because it didn't really go hand in hand with being a private investigator. I wasn't sure it went with being a nudist, either.

Selma's last status update was from a few weeks ago. It was a quote:

"The only thing wrong with nudity is a society that says nudity is wrong." –Bill Pacer

Whoever Bill Pacer was.

I read response after response, backtracking when I saw Jennifer Wallace's name and her comment.

"The nakedness of woman is the work of God." –William Blake

Ten people had liked her quote. I went down the list. Selma had liked it. So had Larry Madrino…

I clicked on his picture and leaned closer. Larry Madrino was Trainer Steve's brother. And he liked Jennifer's William Blake quote.

I kept reading, stopping again when there was another response from Jennifer.

If only some people would see that nudity means lack of clothing. Sexuality is different. It's a state of mind. Why can't people separate the two?

Selma, Larry, and seventeen other people had liked her comment. Selma responded with:

Get naked. Clothes belong in the closet.

Not to Jennifer. Her apartment's closet had been practically empty, which still struck me as strange. Even a nudist had to dress up. Unless it was simply a love nest. Whatever clothes she wore in were the clothes she wore out.

I clicked on Jennifer's name, but someone had changed her wall to a Rest in Peace message. I couldn't see any status posts, but I could see her friends.

Which meant I could see who else might have crossed between Jennifer's two worlds.

I scoured the list of her friends, jotting down the names of anyone from the dance team, the basketball team, or *Cuerpo y Alma*. The list grew and grew as I clicked on name after name and saw interests and organizations.

"What's wrong?"

Reilly's voice brought me out of my Facebook daze. I peered up at her. "What? Nothing."

She made a face at me, squinting her eyes as if she could read my mind if she tried hard enough. "You're sighing. More like heaving, actually."

"I am?" I was? "I guess I was just thinking about how much information this is to sift through."

She hovered at my shoulder, staring at my list of names. "Yikes."

My thoughts exactly.

"Nudists, huh? I'm not sure I'm down with that, but I'll go the distance for you, Lola. No one will ever be able to say Reilly Fuller isn't loyal and willing to do whatever it takes for a friend. So what are you going to do? Can I help? I'm really not sure about the whole nudie thing, but Neil might like it—"

"Whoa, tiger." I patted the air to get her to simmer down. "No one said anything about going back to the nudist resort." And seeing Reilly and Neil in their altogether, together, wasn't high on my list of things to do.

Although…

"If I get the member list from *Cuerpo y Alma*, I might be able to cross-reference." I grabbed my cell phone from my purse, pulling out one of the brochures I'd taken from Jennifer Wallace's dresser. I dug out the rest, rifling through them until I had the resort front and center. Nice. The number was right there on the front of the pamphlet. I dialed. "Please let Tiffany pick up."

No such luck. It was a man, and I was pretty sure the deep, laid-back voice belonged to Craig Wallace, ex-husband to Jennifer. "All natural, no additives when you dare to go bare at *Cuerpo y Alma*," he said.

I made my voice bright, batting away the flapping *mariposa* wings in my stomach, but before I could say anything, he continued. "Ms. Cruz, I knew you wouldn't be able to stay away."

"Caller ID?" I asked, thinking, not for the first time, that I needed to get an incognito phone with a fake ID. Technology was great, but it definitely posed problems for surreptitious investigative moves.

"I like to know everyone here, and everything that goes on here, so, yeah, caller ID."

I'd been avoiding it, but if Craig was that tuned in, and he had an emotional connection to Jennifer, maybe he needed to be my go-to guy at the nudist resort.

"Craig, right?" I asked, making sure I was talking to the sun-scorched, wrinkly skinned nudist. I clutched the brochures, trying not to stare at them. But I couldn't pull my gaze away. I listened, zeroing in on the numbers Jennifer had scribbled in the corner of each. What did they mean?

"The one and only. I remember you," he added with *un poquito* of an accusation. "You and your friend are coming to the Halloween Ball. You can be my guests and I'll give you a personal moonlit tour of the grounds."

I tried to detect the leer in his voice that I was sure was there, but really, he just sounded more hang-ten than creepy. "Oh, well, thanks so much, but I already took a tour—"

My mind hiccupped. Wait a second. I'd been on the grounds. I stared at the brochures, trying to remember. Lucy, Selma, and I had walked from the hot tub, past the parking lot, past some storage buildings…*numbered* storage buildings.

I tried to remember how many buildings there were. Three? Or maybe four?

Jennifer had written *#1* and *#2* on the different brochures. Could it be related?

Craig's voice brought me back to the phone call. "Oh no,

no buts," he said. "It's tomorrow night and everyone will be here. It's the biggest party we have at *Cuerpo y Alma*. And the only one that allows a wee bit of clothing," he added, as if he could read my mind and knew that there was no way in hell I'd be going to a Halloween party—or anywhere, for that matter—stark naked. "You just have to be creative."

I'd been asking myself if I'd really be able to do it—and flaunt it—if it meant I could bring Jennifer's killer to justice. At this moment, talking to Craig, the answer was a definite no.

"I work tomorrow night," I said, stalling for time. The Royals had a game, but I could go to the party afterward. To get a closer look at those buildings.

"After you get off work. We won't start the party without you."

I must have sputtered into the phone, because he quickly followed up with, "Kidding. The party gets going around ten or eleven."

Maybe I'd be done. Unless the buildings turned out to be a big clue and I found a killer to follow. Or something. "I'll think about it."

"Okey-dokey, then," he said.

I came back around to why I'd called in the first place. The member list. "Mister…er, Craig…" There was no way I could ask him about the people who came to *Cuerpo y Alma* without telling him who I was. I grimaced, imagining the phone call I was going to have to make to Jack in a minute. "Uh, thanks again for the invitation. I guess I'll give it a go. Sounds like fun."

If he was surprised he'd convinced me to come, he didn't show it over the phone. He rattled off a few details, then hung up, leaving me wondering just what kind of skimpy, yet chaste, costume I'd be able to pull together by tomorrow night.

Chapter Twenty

I spent the rest of the afternoon scouring Jennifer's Facebook friends for any stray connection or clue as to why she might have been killed. I found Craig, Deirdre, Victoria, and Selma, but not Lance, Tiffany, Carrie, Vanessa, or any other Courtside Dancers. They'd all left Rest In Peace comments, noting how much she'd be missed and how devastating losing her was, but no one had left a comment saying, "I killed her!"

Big surprise.

Unfortunately, the word "Guilty!" wasn't stamped on anyone's forehead, either.

After I added some notes to the whiteboard bullet points I'd started on the case, I stood back to consider. Steve had acted so oddly but I couldn't fathom a motive. Given more time, maybe. Larry had known Jennifer and he'd stood up to his brother as her defender. His presence was all over her final Facebook page. I'd heard from the dancers, and from Steve, that Larry attended every game. Which meant he could be the letter-writer.

A niggling sensation started inside me, working its way from my gut to my head. What if *he* was the boyfriend she met at the hot tub? Was that even possible? Selma had said something about the guy not being comfortable with the nudist life—Larry seemed conservative to me, what with his beige Dockers and plaid button-down shirts. He didn't strike me as the nudist type, but my brief experience at *Cuerpo y Alma* told me that naturists came in all shapes and sizes, and trying to pigeonhole them into being a certain way wouldn't get me anywhere. I needed an open mind.

Would he strip it all off for a woman?

For Jennifer?

But then why kill her? Had she broken it off with him? Had the green-eyed monster reared its ugly head when he found out about her other conquests?

All speculation, which wouldn't convince Manny I was on the right track, and certainly wouldn't close the case for Detective Bennett.

But it did make me hungry.

Hmph. I capped my markers, tidied up my file on Jennifer, and headed outside. Sure, it was October, but my jeans and blouse stuck to my body, the definition of stretchy redefined as they hugged every single curve I had. I hightailed it to Abuelita's, changed into my work uniform—black pants and a white peasant blouse—and scarfed a bowl of *sopa de calabaza*, which Papi'd made with fresh pumpkin. As I started work, I wondered if there would ever be a day when I could stop helping out at the family restaurant.

"*Mira*, Lola!" My cousin, Chely, skipped into the restaurant, skidded to a stop in front of me, and tossed her textbook and binder onto the counter. "My cheerleading coach showed me this cool move!"

I'd been holding my own and hadn't needed private cheer lessons from her, but watching her slide into the splits, then pop back up as if she were a rubber band made me cringe. I was only twenty-nine and I could do a high kick Bruce Lee would have been proud of, but the splits? No way.

"So you like cheerleading?"

She shrugged. "It's okay. I mostly like it because my mom doesn't." She grinned. "She can't say anything about the makeup or the outfits, because they're required."

"*Ay, Chely.* Your mom's just—"

"Pink and blue and butterflies for the *quinceañera*, remember?"

How could I forget? Her fifteenth birthday celebration had coincided with my first big case.

"But we made it work," I reminded her.

"Yes we did." She slugged my arm, snatched up her chemistry book and binder, and scurried off to the break room to get ready for work. I finished filling the chip baskets, worried that if I didn't solve this case, I'd be out of a job and, *ay caramba*, I'd be grateful to be a waitress at Abuelita's.

• • •

Three hours later, my shift was almost done and I was no closer to figuring out an idea for a costume to wear to the *Cuerpo y Alma* Halloween Ball. Glancing at the clock above the cash register, I spewed out a sigh of relief. Eight forty-five.

"I'm outta here at nine," I said to Antonio as he passed by, carrying a bussing bin of dirty plates.

"Take care of table twelve."

I stared him down. He and our father ran the restaurant, but Antonio was handling more and more of it. The pressure was getting to him. No small talk. No friendly brother of the year.

He stopped at the In door to the kitchen and turned back to me. I hadn't budged.

"*Ahorita, por favor*," he said, faking a grin.

I saluted him. "Ay, ay, *capitán*."

"Funny, Lo," he said. "I have a lot on my mind, it's late, but it's still swamped. I need you to stay late."

"Fine," I said. At this rate, I'd be wrapping myself in Saran Wrap for a costume. Which probably wasn't a bad idea.

A wave of dizziness fluttered through my body. I needed to sneak in something to eat. Something more than pumpkin soup.

I delivered an order to a rowdy group of teenagers in the back and headed to the kitchen. I had to eat...*now*. I couldn't come up with a costume idea—plus solve Jennifer's murder—on an empty belly. I grabbed a handful of chips from the warmer and scanned the lobby. The customers kept coming. Good for business, but that didn't help me with my schedule.

I turned to head back into the kitchen, stopping when I spotted a vibrant head of red hair. I'd only seen that color hair on one person—Jack's sister, Brooke. She was a Sacramento cop, but instead of her blues, just then she wore a sweater, jeans, and boots. She was as ready for fall as I was.

I started toward her for a quick hello but froze in my tracks. She was arguing with a woman—a tall, blonde, pretty woman—pulling her toward the door by the sleeve of the woman's ratty sweatshirt.

My breath caught in my throat, my head suddenly full of cotton.

Sarah.

She was back.

And she looked right at me, her mouth curved up in a smirk.

My sister, Gracie, who was also filling in tonight, breezed up to the hostess station, counted out a stack of menus, and called, "Sanchez, party of six. Sanchez?"

Just like in the movies, as the group of people stepped forward and Gracie led them to the dining room, the door to the restaurant opened and a breeze fluttered in. A flash of panic zipped across Brooke's face. Sarah's lips twisted.

And there, darkening the door, was the perfect specimen of a man—something I now knew from my own personal experience—Jack Callaghan.

• • •

I leaned against the wall and watched as if it were one of Mama's *telenovelas* come to life right in front of me. My own personal soap opera, complete with a movie star hero. Sandy brown hair, golden-honey skin, a body that had already turned my insides to goo, smoky blue eyes.

And a crazy ex-girlfriend who just wouldn't stay away.

¡Dios mío! Forget that damn dimple. How dare he? How could he have come here to Abuelita's with…with… *Sarah*? And after our night together…

He saw Brooke, who mouthed something to him and still looked like a deer caught in the headlights of an oncoming semi-truck. Jack scowled at her, then turned to Sarah. He stood with his hands in the front pockets of his jeans, listening to whatever Sarah was saying, but, as if he could sense me, his gaze turned in my direction.

The color drained from his face. Guess he hadn't expected me to be here tonight.

Busted.

I suddenly felt weak in the knees and inexplicably hot. I lunged into the kitchen. The Sarah problem wasn't resolved, that was clear, but I didn't have to see them together

My dad pushed four steaming plates forward on the stainless steel warming shelf.

"Food's up, Dolores. Table five. *¡Ándale!*"

"*Hijo de la chingada*," I swore under my breath, cursing my father's timing.

I tightened my uninspired ponytail. I was worse for wear after a long day, and my coppery salon highlights were probably as dull as a tarnished pot. I ran my fingers through the few strands that framed my face. If I was going to witness the demise of my brand new relationship with Jack, I would do it with style.

I headed toward the oval mirror by the kitchen's In door. I was a five-foot-seven-inch woman with boobs, hips, and killer biceps. I'd never be a supermodel, but I was okay with that because I could take any empty-headed stick woman in a dark alley—or anywhere else. Including *la pendeja*, Sarah.

But as I started to pinch my cheeks and swipe my lips with the MAC O I had in my pocket, my dad slammed his hand down on his cutting board. "The food is ready, Dolores! *¡Pronto!*"

"*Lo siento, Papi.*" There was no more stalling.

I balanced three plates with my left hand and took the fourth in my right. Sure, it *looked* precarious, but I'd been working at Abuelita's since I was thirteen. I could waitress with my eyes closed. I backed out of the kitchen, pushing the door open with my foot.

The door swung closed behind me. I swiveled my body and glanced around; every noise in the restaurant seemed magnified. The clock's ticking sounded like a woodpecker nipping at my skull. The clatter of the late-night dinner customers was a low buzz in the back of my brain.

Instantly, my eyes locked with Jack's. The sides of his lips tugged downward. Was that helplessness I detected? Or was it resignation?

Sarah stood straight and tall, like she was rooted to the ground and refused to budge. Brooke whispered something in Jack's ear. His eyes never left me, but he lips moved as he responded to her.

Something didn't feel right. The plates I carried wobbled and I shifted to rebalance, still watching him. Watching them.

The kitchen door swung out behind me, creaking a warning. Somewhere in the recesses of my mind a voice screamed, "Move out of the way!" *Pero*, too late. *Smack!* The door swung open, hitting me squarely on the ass, plunging me forward into the dining room.

I struggled to keep upright as refried beans and clumps of Spanish rice careened through the air. The plates crashed to the floor. There was a silent moment before applause broke out in the restaurant with the loudest whoops, whistles, and hollers coming from the table of teenage boys in the back.

A flurry of Spanish flew at me from my grandparents'

regular booth in front.

Muttering a guttural animal sound, I pulled myself upright. I stepped back and turned around, facing the swinging kitchen door. I still held one plate in my right hand; only half the food had flown off it. It was a small save, hardly worth celebrating, but it felt like a victory.

It was short-lived.

The kitchen door flung open and banged against me again. The plate in my right hand smashed against my chest.

"*Híjole.*" I dropped the plate, jumping up and down, fanning my hands in front of me. "Hot! Hot!" It didn't do a bit of good. *Mole* sauce oozed down my blouse, scorching my skin. With clawlike fingers, I pulled the cloth away and blew on my burning chest.

"Lola!" Antonio stood holding onto the pass-through door to the kitchen, his face grim. "What the hell are you doing?"

I stared him down. "What am *I* doing?" I hunched forward, trying to keep my blouse away from my skin. "What are *you* doing, Tonio? That's the *Out* door!" My eyes bulged and I threw out my arms. "*Mira.* Look at me!"

A disbelieving huff escaped his lips. "Yeah. You're a mess."

Using every ounce of inner strength not to slap him silly, I turned to take in the Mexican feast on the floor. Then I scanned the dining room. My table of teenagers was still sniggering, but the clapping had stopped.

"Oh, and you're right," Antonio said from behind me. "That's the Out door and I was going *out* of the kitchen. You're not supposed to just stand there." He moved next to me and bent to pick up the ceramic shards.

I stood, slack-jawed. He was right. It had been my fault.

As I picked up the pieces of broken plates, I scanned the waiting area—then blinked. Jack, Brooke, and Sarah were gone. So much for a committed, caring relationship where one person checks on the well-being of the other after a hot plate of chicken in a rich sauce scalds her.

Antonio snatched a precarious piece of chicken from my sleeve. "Who're you looking for?" He plopped it in his mouth while I crouched on the floor, flabbergasted, still holding my shirt away from my chest.

"No one. Absolutely no one." Because it looked like Jack had made his choice.

Antonio raised an eyebrow at me then leaned through the swinging door to the kitchen. "Accident, Pops. We need a repeat of table—"

He flicked his chin up. "What table?"

I held up five fingers.

"Table five's food. Lola, um, dropped the plates."

I heard my father curse in Spanish as Chely burst through the kitchen door, grinding to a halt when she saw me. She threw up her hands, her mouth in a circle. "Oh, man. What happened?"

"It wasn't me, *tío*," she called to my dad. "I'm glad it wasn't me. You father would have fired me on the spot."

I resisted the urge to flip someone off—Antonio, my table in the back, the empty space where Jack had been— and finally dropped my hand, defeated. "I'm going upstairs."

I stomped through the kitchen and went straight up the back stairs to the break room. I'd avoided the mirror in the kitchen, but now that I was alone, I beelined to the bathroom and closed the door. My eyes involuntarily squeezed shut. I pried one open, peered in the mirror—and stifled a scream.

It was so much worse than I'd thought. Bits of chicken clung to my hair like globs of fat. My flirty white peasant blouse was completely covered with brown sauce. *Mole* was *not* a good accessory.

Cursing, I unbuttoned the blouse and slipped it off, knocking chunks of chicken to the floor. My olive skin was smeared darker with the sauce, blotchy red from the heat. I wiped away a layer of goo. No blisters, *gracias a Dios*.

I untied my apron and peeled off my pants, tossing the whole outfit into the laundry bin. I couldn't throw it away without trying to salvage it, but I couldn't wear it home. I also couldn't put my street clothes back on.

"*Cabrón*, Antonio. This was an expensive bra, too." Fifty dollars down the drain.

I stared at myself in the mirror. The splatters of sauce on my face were like chocolate freckles. The *mole* had slipped under my bra and adhered the fabric to me like a second skin. My 34-C breasts might as well have been covered with *ganache*. I turned around and peeked over my shoulder to see if any of the mess had found its way to my backside. What a blessing. My butt was *mole*-free.

I groaned. Who was I kidding? I was a disaster.

"Lola?"

"Thank God, Gracie," I said when I heard my sister's voice. "Did you hear what happened? God damn Antonio! I'm so mad at him. He owes me a bra—"

"Do you need anything?" she interrupted through the door.

"Yeah. *Mami's* housedress."

"*¡Cómo no!*" I heard the horror in her voice. "Really?"

"I have no choice! The sauce got on everything." I pushed open the bathroom door. "Look at me." I tugged the front of my bra down to show Gracie the evidence. "I'm a mess!"

I waited for sympathy and instead saw her frozen face gaping at me. "What?"

She turned toward the door of the break room. "Lola— don't—" she choked.

My head felt spongy and everything came to a screeching halt. I pivoted and saw Jack leaning against the doorjamb.

Chapter Twenty-One

Jack's eyes slowly skimmed my body and the heat of humiliation—increased by the fact that Sarah, the girlfriend who wouldn't go away, was somewhere nearby—rushed through me all over again.

Somehow I managed to step my lead feet back into the bathroom and slam the door. Leaning against it, squeezing my eyes shut, I made the sign of the cross and prayed this would end quickly. A light tap sounded through the door, followed by Jack's husky voice. "Come on, Lola. We need to talk. It's not what you think."

I knew it wasn't, but I didn't like how seeing Sarah made me feel. I wanted Jack, and I wanted him to myself.

"About what?" I asked, a frog firmly stuck in my throat. I was Magdalena Falcón Cruz's daughter, which meant I was nothing if not stubborn.

"I didn't think she'd come back," he said, "but she did."

"No kidding."

"Damn it. I told her I was done. I told her parents I was

done. I told Brooke to stay the hell out of it. Sarah showed up again anyway."

I laid my hand flat against the door, imagining it matched up with his. "I can't do this, Jack. Not after we…" I swallowed the lump climbing up my throat.

He was silent for a beat, then said, "Come on. Open the door, Lola."

I counted in my head. *Uno. Dos. Tres. Cuatro. Cinco. Seis.* And then I cracked open the door.

He paced, raking his hand through his hair as he turned back to me. "I really thought it was taken care of."

So maybe he wasn't the *mujeriego* I'd ranted about a few minutes ago, but would we ever be free of Sarah? "Guess you were wrong."

He closed his eyes for a minute, breathing in. "I'm trying. She just showed up and called me from in front of the restaurant."

Frustration seeped out of him and into me. I swallowed the rant I felt creeping up again.

"Here. Why here?"

He cocked his head slightly, raising his brows in a *why do you think?* way.

"Because of me," I said. Great. "Is she Glenn Close? Is she going to go psycho on me?"

"No," he said, but there was the tiniest hesitation before he spoke again. "No."

"I don't have a rabbit."

"That's good," he said with a smirk.

Salsa's droopy face floated behind my eyes. "If that's a joke—"

He pushed the door open, another wave of humiliation

washing over me. Jack had come back to see to me—in all my *chonis*, bra, and *mole* glory—but knowing that Sarah had returned to Sacramento put a damper on everything.

"She's not violent," he said.

"*Gracias a Dios*, because she had a *Jagged Edge* thing going on in her eyes."

"Brooke has her corralled. I should go deal with this, but you have to trust me, Cruz."

"I'll try," I said.

He brushed the backs of his fingers over my cheek. "I meant everything I said earlier."

I bit my lip. That felt like eons ago, but it had only been this morning. In my head I'd erased everything I'd said when I'd seen Sarah, Brooke, and Jack in the lobby. But I believed him.

"Are we okay?" he asked. Before I could answer, his cell phone rang.

I folded my arms over my sauce-covered chest, scowling at the phone. That Sarah had some nerve.

He checked the screen, his jaw tensing. "It's Brooke." He answered, his face grim as he listened, and a few seconds later, he hung up. Everything in his eyes said that he wanted to stay, but he moved toward the door. "I have to go."

"Yeah. I'll just talk to you later," I said. I knew this wasn't easy for him, *pobrecito*. It wasn't easy for either of us. Sarah was a big old thorn in our collective side.

He leveled his gaze at me like he was trying to read between the lines. "Yes, you will," he said, and he lowered his head and kissed me. "Good sauce," he said, touching his tongue to my lip.

I wanted to drag him down to the ground and let him

lick the *mole* sauce right off of me. "Good luck," I said as he left the bathroom. And then he was gone.

My heart still beat in my ears when Gracie knocked on the open door a minute later. "You okay?"

"*Fantástico.*" Not.

She handed me Mami's worn embroidered Mexican dress. I slipped it over my head, looked in the mirror, and spread my arms wide. All I could do was laugh. A sad, angsty laugh, but I certainly wasn't going to cry. Jack and I had something. We really were a team. He just needed to keep Sarah on the bench for good.

Gracie batted my arm. "You don't look so bad…really," she said without much conviction.

I pulled another bit of chicken from my hair. Yes, I did. "I gotta go," I said, trying to button up my thoughts about Jack. About us. "I have to figure out a costume for a party tomorrow."

Her big brown eyes grew instantly wide. "*¿De versa?* Where? I wanna go to a Halloween party!"

"Uh, *no*, you don't want to go to this one. It's for work."

She folded her arms over her chest, looking way too much like our mother. "Lola, what are you up to?"

I'd already said too much. If Gracie knew the truth, our mother could guilt it out of her. I squeezed her arm. "Not a thing. I gotta go," I said. I grabbed my purse and scurried down the stairs, determined to figure out a costume so I could infiltrate *Cuerpo y Alma*, get their member list, cross-reference with Jennifer's friends, and figure out who killed her. And why.

Maybe by then, Jack would have taken care of, again, what to do about Sarah.

Chapter Twenty-Two

By game time the next day, I hadn't heard from Jack and I still had no brilliant costume idea, but I'd fallen into a routine with dance team warm-ups, makeup, and costuming. I almost felt like a pro. The buzz in the dressing room was subdued, but the women were charged up.

"This one's for Jennifer," Victoria Wolfe said to us as we headed through the tunnel to the arena. "Make her proud."

Selma's lower lip quivered. Carrie dabbed her fingertips below her eyes. Vanessa bowed her head. Invoking Jennifer's name sent a ripple through me. I'd hardly known her, but I was definitely going to give it my all tonight. I could only imagine what Victoria's words meant to the other girls.

I followed Selma in the line, running behind her as we shimmied onto the court, cheering and riling up the crowd. We stopped to work our own sections of the arena, clapping and pumping an arm every now and then.

As soon as I could, I yelled over the crowd. "Selma!"

She glanced at me, never breaking her rhythm.

"Are you going tonight?" I asked.

She whipped her head toward me, the tiniest hiccup in her step-tap movement. "Going where?"

"To the Halloween party, you know?" I prompted.

"Totally," she said, her grin growing bigger at the mere idea. "Are you?"

"I'll be there," I said, but I wasn't nearly as enthusiastic as she was. "What's your costume?"

"It's a surprise," she yelled with a wink, "but it's super sexy."

Hijole. My mother better start praying for me now. This was going to be a big hedonistic, erotic ball, I just knew it.

"Hey," I called, wanting to get an answer to one question that had been bugging me. "What's in those buildings on the grounds?"

She drew her eyebrows together. "Where?"

"Off by the parking lot? There are a couple of buildings—"

"Oh! Yeah, I know what you're talking about." She shrugged. "No idea."

The song ended and I scooted over next to her. "Did you ever see Jennifer go into them?"

Her mouth gaped and she stared at me. "Is this a clue? Do you think they have something to do with this?"

"Just following a hunch."

Finally, she shook her head, turning back to the section of the crowd she was working. "I never saw her head over that way."

Before I could prod her to think harder, I heard my name bellowed from the crowd. "Lola!"

I peered into the stands. The royal blue and white

blended together. It was impossible to pick one person out of the slew of fans.

"Lola! Up here!"

I lifted my gaze higher and saw a big blue foam hand, one finger pointing up. Then I saw electric orange hair. Reilly. My gaze slid left. Next to her was Neil. And next to Neil was a stony-faced Manny.

My heart dropped to the bottom of my gut, but I chased it back up again. Better that they were here than at *Cuerpo y Alma* tonight.

I felt the heat of someone else's stare. Or maybe it was the burning of thousands of eyes on me—I couldn't really tell. I turned and saw someone standing in the tunnel entrance. I finally recognized who it was.

Larry Madrino. But what I didn't know was if he was staring at me or—

I squinched my eyes, trying to follow the angle of his gaze. A chill wafted over me. The invisible line from his eyes led straight to Selma. She must have felt the intensity of it, too, because her attention shifted to the tunnel and she fluttered her hand at Larry.

I whipped my head around to scrutinize Larry again. It could have been my imagination, but he seemed to hesitate before waving back at Selma.

"Lola!" Reilly had climbed down to the bottom row of seats, and she flagged me down from the railing. "*Ven aquí, chica!*"

I held up my hand to tell her to hold on a minute. Something wasn't right about the way Larry was staring at Selma, but when I turned back to the tunnel, he was gone and Victoria, headset firmly in place and mouth moving, had taken his place. All the dancers knew to clue into Vanessa, who had taken Jennifer's place as our team captain. Even from clear across the basketball court, I could see she'd taken her cue from Victoria. She rolled her hand in the air, her signal for us to gather in the center of the court for our first routine.

Reilly would have to wait.

So would Larry. I put them out of my mind for the time being, got through the moves without any major flub-ups, and headed back through the tunnel for the first costume change.

• • •

Nearly two hours later, the game was finally over. I'd searched for Larry again, but if he'd stayed at the game, he hadn't sat in his premium seats. The wives and girlfriends sections were filled to capacity, but no one seemed angry, distraught, or murderous. Reilly, Neil, and Manny were nowhere to be found, absorbed by the departing crowd.

It was now or never. Following my gut, I hurried down the corridor leading to the trainer's room. I didn't know what I'd say if I ran into Larry, but he'd left the game and no letters had been delivered. Coincidence?

One quick peek through the small window in the door showed Trainer Steve attending to one player in the giant stainless steel soaking tub. Another leaned back on the exam table, drinking from a red plastic cup as he waited for his turn with the trainer.

No Larry.

I ducked out of view before Steve could see me. Barely. I started back down the hallway toward the exit, tossing a new question around in my head. Larry and Jennifer had been friends. Had he known about her proclivity for nudity?

I turned the corner and sped up. For a while, I'd wondered if Selma, the one common denominator between Jennifer's two lives, could be the killer. But now I was back to thinking it might be Larry. If he hadn't liked the fact that she'd been a nudist… I had a sudden twining knot in the pit of my stomach. There was something about the way he'd been staring at Selma…

Oh no. Could she be next?

What if he knew about the Halloween bash? My pulse ratcheted up. What if he was on his way there right now?

I snatched my cell phone from my bag and dialed Selma, rushing to the parking lot. She answered before the first ring stopped and blurted, "You're not backing out, are you?"

"No!" I said, then calmed my voice. Spooking her wouldn't help. "I'm on my way home to change. Where are you? Wanna drive together?"

"No. I'm halfway there. I'm meeting Parker before we head into the party," she said, the message in her voice crystal clear. *¡Ay, Dios!* Some before-bash nookie was on their party plan. That was more than I needed to know. On the flipside, if she was with Parker she'd be safe.

"Selma," I said, "could Larry Madrino have known Jennifer was a nudist? That you're one?"

"Steve's brother? I don't think so. He's so straitlaced. He wouldn't have understood."

I couldn't quite bring myself to warn Selma about Larry—I was part of the *Innocent Until Proven Guilty* camp—but I did tell her to be careful. "Call if you need me," I said.

"No cell phones inside, remember?"

Right. "So I'll just see you at the party then."

At home, I threw together the best costume I could. With no more time to waste, I wrapped myself in a trench coat and tiptoed down the front staircase of the flat above my parents' house, praying to *la Virgen de Guadalupe* that I wouldn't run into anyone. Especially Magdalena or Gregorio Cruz.

"*¡Dolores!*" My mother's voice shot out the front window as I descended the stairs in front of it. "*¿Adónde vas?*"

One prayer that wasn't answered. "Just going to a Halloween party, *Mami*." I held the trench coat tighter and hurried down the last few steps.

"*Espera*," she barked, and I instantly halted. No matter how old I was, I was pretty sure she'd have that effect on me.

"I'm late, *Mami*," I said, turning to her.

Her face blurred through the screen, but her frown and her scrutiny of my coat were unmistakable. "What is under that?"

"*Nada*. Don't worry. It's just a costume."

"*Dolores Magdalena Falcón Cruz*," she said, squinting her eyes as if that would help her see through my coat.

My grip on the heavy fabric tightened. I could ignore her and start walking again. Or I could tell her no. But both of these would get me nothing but a whole lot of grief, pretty much for forever. The home-cooked meals would be spooned out with a scowl and a heavy dose of guilt, and the prayers for my soul would triple.

Not worth it.

I cracked open my coat, just wide enough for her to see the plaid skirt I had on.

She squinted her eyes, frowning. "*No entiendo.*"

I wasn't about to show her the rest. She'd never understand the sexy schoolgirl outfit I'd scrounged together. I'd cut an old pink-and-black-plaid skirt into an ultra mini— *un poquito* too mini, actually, since I'd gone with a lacy black thong underneath to give the illusion of nakedness. Unless I could keep my coat on, I wouldn't be bending over at *Cuerpo y Alma.*

I wore black high-heeled pumps on top of a pair of pink and black argyle knee socks I'd found in the bottom of my drawer right on top of my first surveillance pictures of Jack and Greta Pritchard.

I went braless under a stretchy white knit top, leaving the buttons undone. The distance between the top's knot under my breasts and the band of my skirt was interrupted by my belly button ring.

Hopefully it wouldn't be my only souvenir from a has-been career.

The ensemble was topped off with a pair of fake glasses and my hair pulled into two low ponytails. I was every high school boy's fantasy.

My mother would not understand any of it.

"*Está bien*, Mami. It's just a costume."

As she shook her head, I seized the moment and hurried down the sidewalk to my car. "*Hasta más tarde*. I'll be home late. Don't wait up."

Chapter Twenty-Three

Away from the prying eyes of my mother, I tucked in my Bluetooth earpiece and called Manny.

He answered with a clipped, "*Dígame.*"

Verbose, Manny was not. Just a *tell me* was all he needed to say.

"I've got a hunch about the Jennifer Wallace case," I said. Cut to the chase was always the best M.O. with Manny. No small talk. No frivolities. No *nada*. Nothing but business, and the occasional intense expression that made me think he knew everything about me—which made the hair on the back of my neck stand up.

"Hypothesis?"

"Larry Madrino. Steve Madrino is the trainer for the Royals. Larry is his brother, a fixture at all the games and, I think, may have been in love with Jennifer." We'd both seen Jennifer's love trophies, so I didn't need to explain to *el jefe* that she didn't love Larry back. "He had motive and opportunity."

"How are you going to prove it?"

The very question I'd been asking myself all evening. "I'm going to finish up a different lead first. I have a list of Jennifer's Facebook friends. I'm going to cross-reference them with the membership at *Cuerpo y Alma* and see if any match. If they do, I'll follow those up. If they don't, then that's another finger pointing at Larry."

He grunted, but I sensed it was a grunt of approval. "Get back to me when you find something out."

He was the boss. It was a given that I'd report back to him. "*Por supuesto*," I said.

My finger itched to dial Jack, but I resisted. He said he'd talk to me later. Whenever he'd dealt with Sarah—again. Which must not be done yet.

And I had a job to do. I'd think about him later. Instead, I called Lucy, immediately launching into her for telling Zac about our field trip to the nudist resort.

"I'm sorry, Lola. Really. I tried, but you were right. He knew we were up to something. I had no choice."

I sighed. "I know."

"Marriage."

"Yeah, marriage."

"What are you doing tonight? It's almost Halloween!"

"*Nada*," I said, hoping she wouldn't remember the Halloween Ball Craig had told us about.

But she did. "Oh my God, you're going, aren't you? I promise I won't tell this time. Lola, you cannot go back there without me!"

"I don't know what you're talking about."

"*Pft*. Yes, you do. You're going to that costume ball."

I couldn't lie to her. "If you say one word, I'll never speak to you again." A totally empty threat, because life without Lucy would be way too dull, but still…

"It's a naughty ball," she said, barely holding in her giggles.

"And I made myself a naughty outfit, so *no es problema*."

She squealed, demanding to know the details. I filled her in on the plaid skirt, the sheer top, and the knee socks.

"And nothing underneath? Lola, I'm shocked. No, I'm flabbergasted. No, no, I'm stunned speechless."

Speechless would be a good thing. "One word," I said. "Thong."

But I might as well have been stark naked by how guilty I felt.

"Ohhhh." I could hear the disappointment in her voice, but she covered it up the next second with her own one word. "Bra?"

"Nope."

"What color is the top?"

"White."

"Hmmm."

Hmmm, indeed. Another reason I hadn't been able to open my trench coat for my mother. Perky dark nipples on a brisk night and thin, knit white fabric did not go together. Of course, chances were that I'd be overdressed compared to the nudists. "And you're just going to be in and out of there?"

"Assuming Tiffany or Craig will let me have a peek at the membership list."

"You sure you don't want to wait and go tomorrow? In the daylight?"

That idea was a lot more appealing than the event I was

about to experience, but I couldn't put it off. I told her about my worry for Selma, my theory about Larry, and then said, "It can't wait."

And it couldn't.

Chapter Twenty-Four

Cuerpo y Alma's parking lot was overflowing. Everybody loved a good nudist Halloween bash, it seemed. After I found a parking space, I sat in the safe cocoon of my CRV, ogling the nudists' bare bodies as they headed inside. Most of them weren't so much wearing costumes as strategically placed accessories.

As I watched the skimpy costumes parade by, I shook my head. *¡Ay, caramba!* Since when did Mardi Gras beads and a sequined mask constitute a costume? A couple passed by the passenger window of my car and I couldn't help but stare. The man was entirely red, from head to foot, and wore devil ears and carried a pitchfork. The woman had flames painted on her body with bursts of fire centered on her breasts.

Body paint. I knocked the heel of my hand against my forehead. Of course!

I had a sudden feeling of relief. Magdalena Cruz may not have approved of my costume, but I was positively relieved at how blissfully covered I was compared to what I was seeing.

Leaving my trench coat behind and bolstering all my Xena strength, I headed in. A knot of guilt formed in the pit of my stomach anyway, and my heartbeat felt like a jackhammer had taken over. Having Lucy with me the first time I'd been here had been a huge confidence booster. Handling this leg of the investigation solo? *Un poquito* scary.

I hesitated at the door to the office, my hand on the knob.

"Going in?" a woman said behind me.

I tried to answer but ended up staring at her elaborate costume. She was painted like Poison Ivy from Batman, complete with shading on the leaves twining around her limbs.

"Y-yes," I said.

My first order of business? Talk to Tiffany about getting a copy of the member list. I turned the knob and went in, Poison Ivy and a group of other partygoers right behind me. I backed up against the shelf, knocking over supplements and nudist knick-knacks in my hurry to move out of the way. I started to straighten them up, darting to the counter when the front office was finally empty. Only one woman remained. She wore a long dark wig, heavy eye makeup, black lipstick, and a chain belt slung low on her hips. And nothing else. She had to be Elvira. Or Morticia Addams. AKA Tiffany.

"Hey, remember me?" I asked her over the low, driving beat reverberating through the walls. It took her a few seconds, but when recognition finally dawned, she darted a glance behind her. In case Craig had slipped in unnoticed and heard who—or what—I really was? "The detective," she said to me when she turned back around. "Your costume's not exactly nude."

"I thought sexy and suggestive was okay for this?" According to what Craig had said on the phone, or had that just been a ploy to get me here? I cringed inside, but outside I just remained *muy* calm. "I don't think I could pull off the schoolgirl thing if I took off anything else."

She seemed to consider. "Maybe," she said with a shrug. "I guess it'll be okay."

"I don't plan to stay long. I was hoping I could go through your member list." She shook her head and opened her mouth, but to shush her I held up the tub of protein powder I still held. "Wait. Hear me out," I said, quickly putting the tub back on the shelf. "I have Jennifer Wallace's Facebook friend list. I just want to cross-reference to see if anyone is on both."

"There will be—"

She broke off as a few more costumed nudists came through the office, signed in, and proceeded into the banquet hall where the party was. The music grew louder as she opened the door, fading again as it closed after her.

I waited until we were alone again, then said, "I know. Selma Mann. You. Craig. Dierdre. But I need to know if there are others."

Her dark, goth eyebrows furrowed. "Why? What good will it do? It's not like she was killed because she was a naturist."

"Actually, we don't know *why* she was killed; that's the point. She was divorced. She had quite a few boyfriends. She kept parts of her life pretty hidden. And it seems as though maybe somebody didn't like that. I'm trying to figure out who that might have been."

"Naturists are gentle. They're real, you know? They wouldn't get mixed up in anything sordid like murder, and she didn't mess around with a bunch of boyfriends."

"She had an apartment—"

"It's a cottage—"

"No, no. I mean in Sacramento."

Tiffany cocked her jet black brows at me like I was crazy. "I've heard what people are saying about her, but they're wrong. She didn't have another apartment. She still owned this place with Craig. She had her cottage here. She didn't need anyplace else."

I let this information trickle through the crevices of my mind. Either Tiffany didn't know Jennifer very well, or the apartment with all the jerseys and pictures of men didn't actually belong to Jennifer. What if it was a front for someone else? Selma?

I kept my thoughts to myself and went back to my goal. The membership list. "I just want to see if I can figure out who killed her."

Tiffany frowned, considering, then shook her head. "I just can't do that." She leaned toward me, lowering her voice. "If Craig found out, I could lose my job."

I didn't want her livelihood put in jeopardy, but I needed to see that list. "He won't find out. Tiffany, Jennifer was murdered. The police think that apartment was hers. You're saying it wasn't. I need to find out the truth and I need your help."

Another group of nudists barreled through the lobby on their way to the party—a body-painted Scooby led the way, followed by X-rated versions of Shaggy, Fred, Thelma, and Daphne. They glanced at me, each of them scoping me out with a full up and down perusal. Fred's eyebrows pulled into a *V* and Thelma adjusted her fake thick black glasses. "Britney Spears, or are you from the old Van Halen video?"

Shaggy guffawed and slapped his bare leg. "'Hot for Teacher,' right? Smokin', dude!"

"You got it. Doing it different tonight and actually wearing some clothes." I could almost feel my nose growing. "Who knows what'll come off later?" I added with a wink.

"Now you're talking," Shaggy said with his trademark warbly voice. "Catch you inside, schoolgirl."

I threw up my hand in a flip wave, trying to mask the ick factor rolling over me. Cheesy pickup lines were bad enough in a good situation. Coming from a naked Shaggy, they were downright disgusting.

"You got it," I managed, then quickly turned my back and pretended to examine the supplements and knick-knacks on the shelves while they checked in and finally passed through the door to the party.

As soon as they were gone, Tiffany beckoned me over. "I'll let you see the names, but Craig'll be back any minute and he'll fire my ass if he finds out. You better hurry!"

I didn't waste a single second. I threw the tub of powder back onto the shelf and practically catapulted across the small room and over the counter. "So how do you keep track of the guests?"

Tiffany had a wary eye on the door, but she pulled out a card file and set it on the counter. "Everyone has to check in here. We take the information card to verify the ID, collect the usage fee, and that's it."

"What about your computer?" I asked.

"I'm setting it up, but it's not ready yet."

¡Ay, caramba! Not only did they live without clothes, they'd been living without technology. "So anyone can come at any time."

"Right. A membership entitles you to certain perks, but otherwise, we're open to the public."

"And you never saw Jennifer with anyone in particular?"

She shook her head. "She knew everyone."

Which made it difficult to hone in on her special friend.

I reached for the cards, but Tiffany zipped her mouth shut as a woman, wrapped in toilet paper, sauntered into the office. She checked in, then sashayed through the door to the party room.

Tiffany's voluminous chest rose and fell with her breaths. "You have to hurry," she said nervously. What, did she think Craig could materialize out of thin air?

"I will." I put my hand on the index card file she'd set on the counter, but she held tight to it. "I promise," I added when she didn't let go.

Finally she released it to me. "Don't tell a soul," she said, her voice low. "This place is an oasis for people. A sanctuary. It's private."

"Got it." The door opened again and the partygoer turned sideways to fit through the opening. Clear and white balloons attached to her bod, hitting the doorjamb as she passed. "Sorry. Omph! There we go."

As she muttered to herself, a red flag shot up in my head. That voice. I turned to face the door. "Lucy?"

She maneuvered the last balloon through the door and whipped around to face me, her grin wide and toothy. "In the flesh."

I couldn't believe she'd said that with a straight face. She had a shower cap on her head, rosy cheeks, balloons from her torso to her shoulders, and below the waist she had a blue tutu.

"Is that supposed to be water?" I asked, poking my finger at the tulle.

"Clever, right? It's Mia's. Zac helped me with it."

My brain screeched to a halt. She'd used her daughter's tutu and—"Zac *helped* you? As in your husband *knew* you were coming here?"

She gave a sheepish grin. "I couldn't really hide it from him—"

I sputtered, steam gathering in my head, but she hurried on. "It's okay, Lola. He didn't tell a soul, I promise."

Tiffany glared at Lucy. "You didn't tell me you were married last time. You can't come in without your spouse."

"No problem," Lucy said brightly, adjusting one of her balloons.

Another red flag shot up. I grabbed her arm and yanked her aside. "No problem? What do you mean, no problem?" I said more harshly than I'd intended, but I had a sinking suspicion that I wouldn't like what she was going to tell me.

She shook her arm free. "He didn't want me to come alone. H-he'll be here in just a minute."

My head suddenly felt stuffed with cotton. "Here? He's coming here?" Zac…my *primo*…my *cousin*…at *Cuerpo y Alma*? My *tía* Marina already thought I was corrupting my niece, Chely, what with my independent streak and P.I. job. Now *la familia* Cruz would blame me for bringing Zac and Lucy to a nudist resort. *Dios mío.*

But behind the counter, Tiffany gave a satisfied dip of her chin. "Good." Then she glanced at the wall clock.

"Ticktock," she said.

Right. Craig could waltz through the door any minute. I prioritized my thoughts. Membership list first. My cousin showing up here second.

Tiffany led Lucy and me into a room next to the office and handed me several more plastic boxes filled with file cards just like the ones we'd filled out the day we'd come with Selma. "Everyone's in here?"

"Yes. Now hurry," she said, scurrying back out to the front when the front door slammed and we heard the excited voices of more naked partygoers.

"Who's the target?" Lucy asked, peering at the cards over her shimmering balloons.

I swallowed my anger at Lucy for telling Zac about my plan tonight, pushing it into the same compartment in my mind where Jack and Sarah and my future were hiding. "Anybody who's a member here who's also on this list," I said, producing the printout of Jennifer Wallace's bazillion Facebook friends.

Lucy eyed the list skeptically. "Really? I don't have a photographic memory."

Neither did I, which was why I'd spent two hours alphabetizing the names and organizing them so I could scan by the first letter of the last name.

We put the list between us. "I'd have made a copy if I'd known you were coming to help me."

"You're a detective. I figured you'd deduce that there was no way I'd leave you alone at this place."

It *had* occurred to me, but I never thought Zac would be down with it. And would be coming, too.

I slammed the door on my thoughts and focused on the

job at hand, peering through my fake glasses and tossing one ponytail behind my shoulder. Lucy was already sifting through her stack of index cards, glancing at the name then quickly cross-referencing on the printout before discarding it.

I did the same, and one by one, the stack of cards showing who was both a member of *Cuerpo y Alma* and a Facebook friend of Jennifer's grew bigger.

Tiffany poked her head in a few times to check our progress. So far, Craig hadn't shown up. Our luck held until we'd gone through the three containers full of cards. "Thirteen people," I said when we were finished.

"But you can eliminate a few of them, right?" Lucy asked. "Selma. The woman Dierdre. I don't think she could hurt a fly. Tiffany. Craig—"

I wish. "Can't eliminate anyone."

A man's voice, loud and boisterous, shot through the closed door and Lucy and I both froze. I held my breath, ready to bolt. But the low, soothing murmur of a woman's voice cut the tension in the air. Not Craig. I released the breath I'd been holding. My hands trembled at the thought of being discovered searching the files, such as they were.

"We can't eliminate any of them, Lucy," I said as I scribbled down the information from each card. Which wasn't much. Gathering information about its members, growing a mailing list, or anything else that required more than a name and e-mail address wasn't high on *Cuerpo y Alma*'s marketing plan. "Everyone's a suspect."

And really, since once a person was on the grounds, they could conceivably be anyone they wanted, who knew if the cross-referencing was completely accurate? They didn't check IDs. A person could pretend to be anyone they wanted.

Something about the idea of a person pretending to be someone else struck me, but I couldn't pinpoint why. I let go of the idea as we heard more voices pass through the lobby, and the rhythm of the music changed. I recognized Beyoncé's voice telling the guys in the room to put a ring on it, followed by the crowd shouting, "And nothing else!" So they'd adapted this song to a nudist anthem.

"Let's go," I said, pushing away from the table.

I snapped my head up as Tiffany burst through the door. Lucy lurched into the edge of the table, surprised, and *Crack!* one of her balloons popped.

"He's coming," Tiffany hissed, snatching the card files from the table and shoving them back onto the bookshelf where they'd been.

I jerked as my heart catapulted into my throat. What now? I quickly folded the list of Facebook names into a small square, jamming the paper into my knee sock.

She rolled her hand in the air as if that could speed us up. "Hurry!"

We moved, making it to the front room barely a second before Craig, dressed as a construction worker with a tool belt slung around his hips, a yellow hardhat—*y nada más*—marched through the door.

Chapter Twenty-Five

Another group of people was right on Craig's heels. Behind me, Lucy screeched. I tore my gaze away from Craig, the naked Village People construction worker, and turned to the new revelers.

There was a familiar face. I swallowed. Did a double take. Oh boy. Zac. I quickly dipped my head, squinting my eyes a moment later as I peered up. He was my cousin. Curiosity about what costume he and Lucy had rustled up for him got the better of me.

I dared to focus as Lucy raced past me, her balloons bobbing around her. Zac was bare-chested, a kids' pool float around his hips. Bright blue bike shorts. *Phew!* I breathed out, relieved that I hadn't corrupted my *primo*.

Lucy fell into Zac's arms, bending at the hips so she wouldn't crush her balloons or the aired-up duck floatie he wore. I couldn't help but laugh. Water, bubbles, and a rubber ducky. They were so sweet together at the nudist resort Halloween bash.

The other people who'd come in weaved around them. I studied each one, combing through my memory to see if any of them had been in the photos at Jennifer Wallace's house.

None of their faces set off alarms in my head.

"You're here," a man's voice said in my ear. "I knew you'd come."

"Craig," I said, turning to him, pretending to be the best new, reluctant nudist I could muster. Which wasn't a stretch.

"Are you checked in?"

"Lucy and I are. Her husband isn't."

"Tiffany," Craig said, an unspoken command in the one word. He never took his eyes off me. Which meant he must have really been over Jennifer.

Tiffany took out a new index card and slid it to Zac. "Name and e-mail address," she said.

Zac walked toward the counter like he was a prisoner about to walk the plank rather than a man about to party with a bunch of nudists. "Do I have to give my real name?" he muttered in my direction as he passed.

"No," I said.

"This is your doing," he said to me in Spanish, talking from between clenched teeth.

"I didn't ask either of you to come," I answered back under my breath. Speaking Spanish was like a secret code language and it came in handy sometimes. Like now.

"How about a personal tour of the grounds?" Craig asked, dropping his arm across my shoulders and guiding me away from Zac.

A shiver wound through me, but I pushed away the creepy factor of taking a private walk with an X-rated construction worker. "Definitely," I said, walking quickly toward the door, forcing his hand off my shoulder.

"How are you doing, Craig?" a woman's voice said. I turned back to see Deirdra, the woman who'd chased down Lucy, Selma, and me outside the restaurant last time we'd been here. She was dressed as Cleopatra, with an Elizabeth Taylor–style cornrowed black wig and gold tassels, but minus the toga. Gold bracelets climbed up her arms and a wide belt was slung low on her hips.

"Hanging in there, thanks," Craig replied.

"Something wrong?" I asked.

He took off his hardhat, scratching his head. "My ex-wife died a few days ago."

I shot a glance at Dierdre. Had she asked him about Jennifer for my benefit? She winked, confirming it.

"Wow," I said, jumping at the opening and turning back to Craig. "I'm sorry to hear that. Do you have kids? That would be awfully hard."

"No. No kids." He shrugged, putting the yellow hat on and pushing it down on his head with the palm of his hand. "She lived here, so we still saw each other, but we'd both moved on, you know?"

Which explained the private tour of the grounds I was about to get.

I let my eyes open wide. "Is that the cottage you said is available?"

"Sure is. If you want to rent it out, you'd be right down the hall from me," he added with a wink.

"Rent it out? Lola," Zac said with a hiss. "*Ven aquí.*"

I turned and frowned at him, making angry eyes. Then I turned to Lucy. She got the message. She put her hand on Zac's arm and whispered something in his ear. He visibly relaxed, but I still thought he'd rather be anywhere but here, and I got the impression that he definitely didn't trust what I was doing or what Craig was saying...or maybe both.

I shifted my thoughts back to my investigation. Did Jennifer's affairs have anything to do with their divorce? "I'm not sure about giving up my apartment," I said.

"Lots of people transition slowly. Jennifer—that's my ex-wife," he clarified, since, of course, he didn't know that *I* knew who she was, "was the only person I knew who never hesitated in her commitment to the naturist lifestyle."

Based on Selma's inner conflict, I had to believe that was true. The only problem was that I knew Jennifer *did* have another place on the outside. "She must have been really special," I said.

"She would've thought you have too many clothes on," Craig said.

I grimaced at his suggestive tone, but my thoughts spiraled. I'd seriously considered Larry might be Jennifer's murderer and the mysterious letter-writer. Against my will, I'd wondered if Selma could be involved. But what about Craig? Could he be an Academy Award–caliber actor, completely fooling me about his nonchalance over Jennifer's death? Or had he really still been in love with her, found out about the affairs, written the letters, and then killed her?

"I tried to leave something to the imagination," I said.

"You did." He skirted around me, pulling open the door that led to the event room. Beyoncé was done singing about rings on her finger, another song had ended, and now the first strains of Michael Jackson's "Thriller" played. I leaned against the banister. Squeals erupted from down below. Red plastic cups were held high into the air. The people scurried toward the center of the room as the song played. As if expertly choreographed, the people started the "Thriller" zombie dance. If I hadn't been on a case, determined to figure out what this place had to do with Jennifer's death, I'd have laughed at the naked spectacle. Instead, I let Craig lead me to the stairs. A quick search of the room told me that if Larry were here, it might be more difficult to find him than I'd thought. Nudist costumes didn't just mean a mask and nothing else.

At the bottom of the stairs, I spotted what had to be the most creative costume I'd seen so far. A woman in roller skates glided by. She had a thick rope tied around her waist. A man with a cardboard crank attached to his back, his face and body painted at the joints so he resembled a wind-up Ken doll, held onto the length of rope and pulled her across the floor.

Recognition dawned. Selma Mann.

So the wind-up toy had to be Parker, her boyfriend, and their pre-party party must be over.

"Selma!" I called, waving my hand in the air. I couldn't believe it, but I was sort of getting used to seeing naked people. I hardly flinched when Parker turned full frontal on me, and only jumped a tiny bit when Craig's muscular arm brushed against mine.

Like an ice skater, Selma lifted one straight leg in front of her as she glided along the floor, pulled by Parker. She saw me, and her brightly painted cheeks rose as her hot pink lips formed an *O*. She yanked on the rope until Parker stopped, then she skated over to us, towing her boy-toy behind her.

"Not bad, Lola. Kinda conservative, but I'm impressed."

"She could stand to lose some of it," Craig said.

Selma tilted her painted face, considering me. "She should take off the shirt but leave on the tie."

Suddenly, Selma lunged toward me and grabbed the knot of my shirt from between my breasts. My first instinct was to knock her hands away and block her with my fisted forearms, but I kept myself in check. She knew my purpose here, but no one else did, and I couldn't overreact.

"Come with me; I'll help you," she said.

I stepped backward but she'd picked the knot and my shirt started to fall open. Craig's eyes were glued to my chest, so I grabbed the flaps of the shirt and held them closed. "I'm okay, really."

Before I knew what was happening, Craig was behind me, his hands on my shirt, tugging it down to slip it off my shoulders.

This time my instincts kicked in and I didn't fight them. I raised my arms. "*¡Basta!*" I snapped, using every ounce of reserve I could muster to stop myself from stomping on his exposed toe. But I swung around to plunge the heel of my hand against his chin. He tried to hold onto my shirt as I moved away from him, but I gripped tightly in front. This shirt was coming with me.

"Just the tie, huh? Remember, this is only my second time here," I said with a nervous laugh. "I need to work up to it, and this is allowed." I quickly retied the ends of the shirt, but with my cleavage plumped I felt exposed by the sheer fabric and the short skirt.

"Work up to what?"

A shiver swept over me at the gravelly voice. My biggest underlying anxiety about the night, aside from potentially facing a killer, was the fear that Jack might show up, but it turned out I'd miscalculated. This was worse.

Manny Camacho stood behind me.

In black leather pants and bare-chested. No *panza* for him. Not even a single bit of fat, let alone a belly. Manny had *un cuerpo espectacular*.

What in the hell was my boss doing at *Cuerpo y Alma?* Another shiver danced over my skin and I swallowed. *Híjole.* Was he a member?

"*Nada*," I said just as Parker wound up the rope attached to Selma's waist, rolling her toward him. She lifted her hand in a quick, horror-stricken wave. She didn't want to be recognized by Manny. Without even so much as a *ta-ta*, she skated away.

I pushed my fake glasses up the bridge of my nose. "Wait, I want to talk to—" I started to say to her, but I zipped my lips as a woman came up behind Manny, her red-tipped fingernails scraping his skin as her hand snaked over his shoulder. Oh God, was he back with Isabel? Had he brought Tomb Raider Girl?

But then the woman moved to his side and I saw that it wasn't Manny's model ex-girlfriend.

It *was*, however, the sexiest policewoman I'd ever seen. The black, shiny bodice of the dress only half covered her breasts, and the skirt was shorter than mine—and that was saying a lot. A sexy thigh holster held a fake gun and a pair of handcuffs dangled from a clip on the holster. She'd rounded out the costume with slinky black fishnet stockings.

My eyes flew wide open. I recognized her immediately. Her velvety hair cascaded down her back. A black choker encircled her long neck. Oh. My. God. Victoria Wolfe.

Here. With Manny.

The world was off its axis, especially because I knew that I had my Victoria's Secret thong on underneath my schoolgirl skirt, but I wasn't so sure she had on anything. And from the glimmer in her eyes, I got the distinct impression she wouldn't mind arresting Manny, slapping her handcuffs on him, and frisking him.

"Good to see you, Lola," Manny said, his gaze boring into mine with such intensity that a shudder fluttered over my skin.

I swallowed, finding my voice, keeping my cover in front of Craig but wanting to know what the hell was going on. "I never expected to see you here."

"I read something about this place," he said slowly, and I suddenly knew exactly what he'd been reading. The whiteboard for the case at the office. I swallowed. Was he checking up on me and my ability to do my job?

"I heard about it from a friend," Victoria said, and I got the very definite impression that the friend had been Jennifer. But if she knew that Jennifer came here, why hadn't she mentioned it?

"Decided to check it out," Manny said, his gravelly voice sounding like it had an extra layer of rocks in it. His lips were drawn tight and his nostrils flared. He wasn't entirely comfortable. Good to know Manny had limits, too. I'd often wondered.

"Dragged him here in my car is more like it," Victoria said with a demure laugh. "I'm always willing to try new things. Lance? Not so much. Do you know I parked behind those buildings, as close to the front entrance as I could, just so he wouldn't back out."

"Wait," Craig said, suddenly speaking up. "You all know each other?"

"He's a Royals fan," I said, shoving my nerves away.

"Aren't we all? You a player?" he said to me, his thin lips quirking up at his joke.

"A dancer," I said. And with any luck, that gig would be up soon.

There was a pause as he processed this, and I knew just what he was thinking. Had I known Jennifer?

"How did you say you found out about *Cuerpo y Alma*?" he asked me, as if he were trying to figure out if it was a coincidence that I was here, or if I'd come because I knew he murdered his ex-wife. Which, of course, I didn't know and wasn't even sure I believed, since I had no evidence.

I kept playing along, darting quick glances at Manny and Victoria to keep their lips zipped. "A friend," I answered.

"Well," he said, extending his hand to Manny. "Royals fans are always welcome here. So are the Royals themselves," he added, indicating one particularly tall man dressed as a gladiator. I recognized him but didn't remember his name or number.

"So I noticed," Manny said, glancing at a group of people who'd painted half their naked bodies blue, the other half white.

I couldn't help but notice that Craig didn't comment on my boss being overdressed, and he certainly wasn't trying to strip his black leather pants off of him like he'd tried to remove my shirt. I shook my head.

"*Mujeriego*," I muttered. Craig was a big-time player with a wide-open field of women right here in his yard. All the more reason to be a nudist—er, naturist.

Manny's dark eyebrows shot up. He'd understood me. I shrugged. Let him think I was talking about him. He did have a girlfriend. And an ex-wife, so the fact that he was here with Victoria—and without Lance—meant maybe calling him a player wasn't too far off the mark.

As if he could read my mind and decided to act the part, his eyes smoldered and slipped down to take in my costume. His lips parted, just slightly, but enough to know he liked my psuedo-innocent costume *un poquito* better than he liked Victoria's bad-girl get-up.

"How about that tour?" I said to Craig, once again feeling overly exposed even though I was one of the most clothed people around.

Across the room, I saw Lucy and Zac dancing. Or Lucy dancing and Zac staring vacantly, still shell-shocked. His horror-filled eyes roved the room, stopping every now and then on a body before moving on. I didn't blame him. One thing I was learning was that nudists came in every shape, size, and age, and no matter what those factors were, they had an underlying confidence about them. They were proud of their birthday suits.

"Sure thing," Craig said, "but I need a couple minutes. Gotta check the food tables." He turned to Victoria. "Good to see you—"

"Going to be quite a night," Victoria interrupted, throwing her shoulders back, preening like a peacock. All for Manny's benefit, I suspected. Or maybe for the guy she waved at across the room. *Pobrecito* Lance.

As Craig wandered off toward the buffet, I called after him. "I'm going to get some air." He nodded at me, and then his bare behind disappeared in the sea of naked bodies.

I wheeled around and threw my hands on my hips, staring at Manny and Victoria. "Why are you here?"

"We saw your notes on the whiteboard," Manny said.

Victoria chimed in. "I knew Jennifer came here, but I never imagined…Do you really think there's a connection? Does this place have something to do with Jennifer's death?"

"That's what I'm hoping to find out. Nothing makes any sense. She had her place in Natomas, but her ex-husband says she only lived here. She kept this place a secret, but you know about it, so who else does? She had a boyfriend but no one can tell me who he is, and that doesn't quite jive with all the jerseys and pictures we found at the apartment. Nothing makes a whole lot of sense," I said again.

Manny's dark eyes narrowed. "We'll circulate in here," he said.

"I'd say call me if *you* find anything, but no cell phones."

Victoria was already scanning the crowd. In case things with Manny didn't work out? I had another moment of sympathy for her husband. The way she was eyeing the gladiator made me wonder if she ever broke her own rules.

But that was not for me to worry about. I was going to take a self-guided tour of the grounds.

I walked across the courtyard, past the pool area. A few people soaked in the hot tub, but otherwise the grounds were deserted. I headed around the pool, and just as I was about to turn right, in the direction of the restaurant, the squeak of a door opening drifted through the air. I turned toward the row of buildings along the edge of the grounds, bordering the parking lot.

I moved closer, peering into the darkness, my breath catching in my throat when I saw a dark shadow move from one building to the next. I went with my instinct. Whoever it was had to be doing something they shouldn't be.

A flurry of nerves hit the pit of my stomach. I had no plan. I'd come tonight to ferret out information, not to chase down a bad guy. No weapon, other than my black belt in kung fu. With no backup. I moved forward anyway, stealthy as a cat on the hunt, curious. And suspicious. But I stopped abruptly when a hand came down on my shoulder.

A scream shot up my throat, but another hand clamped over my mouth, stifling it before I could unleash it into the quiet night.

Chapter Twenty-Six

"Shhh. Lola, it's me."

Jack? My senses were tingling and I suddenly felt something hard against my hip. *¡Ay, caramba!*

My heart stopped. I slowly turned around and—

Breathed again. His idea of a skimpy costume was right up there with Manny's: shirtless. Only instead of the black leather that Manny had on, Jack was wearing jeans and chaps, and the hard thing I'd felt was a toy gun holstered and slung low on his hips.

He held his finger to his mouth. "Shhh."

"How did you…? Why are you…?"

He answered in one word. "Zac."

I cursed my cousin under my breath, but then I knew Jack Callaghan had my back. *Mi amor.*

"So you came to help?"

He lowered his chin, giving me a look that I translated in my head to mean, *Are you serious? You at a nudist resort, left to your own devices?* His smoldering gaze dropped to my pink and black mini *mini* skirt and knee socks. "Where else would I be? After our last conversation—"

I put my finger to his lips. "I hardly remember that conversation, *pero gracias*."

His slow perusal of me, and the pause at my bare belly—and above—made my skin blister and my knees go weak. "Brings back a few high school memories," he said, his dimple etching into his cheek as his lips curved up.

"Of who? You and Greta Pritchard?" I batted my eyelashes at him.

"Hardly," he said, and I remembered how he'd said he'd had a crush on me back then. If only I hadn't been his best friend's little sister.

The wait had been worth it.

"What are you spying on?" he asked.

Back to business. I notched my head toward the building. "Someone's in there."

He used two fingers, pointing toward a cluster of trees along the edge of the property. I followed him, tiptoeing so the heels of my shoes wouldn't sink into the soft ground.

I turned back to the buildings and crept forward. Jack didn't make a sound, but I knew he was right behind me. The buildings were each lit by a single wall-mounted lamp, giving off just enough light to see the shape of the structures but not any details.

"Who is it?" Jack whispered, his breath in my ear sending a shiver down my spine.

"I don't know."

"Does it have something to do with your case?"

"Jennifer had some numbers written on brochures I found in her apartment. I was thinking they might correspond with those buildings. And now someone's in them, and at this hour? And during the party? Seems odd, *pero no sé.*"

"Oh no. No Spanish right now. English only, *por favor,*" he said.

I turned and saw the heat in his eyes—was it from my costume, speaking to him in my native tongue, or both? "*Lo siento*—oops." I put my fingers to my lips, smiling innocently and tossing my ponytails back. "I mean, sorry."

"*Cruz.*" A definite note of warning tinged his voice.

"*Callaghan.*"

The squeak of a door stopped our flirting cold. I whirled back around, peering through the bush in front of me. A person stopped in the threshold. Whoever it was looked right, then left, then straight ahead. My skin crawled as I felt the gaze settle on me, but Jack and I stood as still as stone Aztec ruins. The building was open and the light was on inside, but even with the outdoor lamp, it was too dark for me to see who stood there, so it was impossible for anyone to see us hidden behind the shrubbery.

I held my breath and waited. Finally, the person moved, leaving the doorway and turning right, past the first building and into the parking lot.

I darted a quick glance around. All the partygoers were inside the main building behind us. The lights blazed from the event room. No one else was outside.

The coast was clear and there wasn't a second to waste. I reached behind me, wrapping my hand around Jack's wrist, then pulled him forward. "*¡Vente!*" I said with a hiss, then I let go and sprinted as fast as I could in my short skirt, braless top, and high heels.

I had seriously underestimated how long it would take

to run across the grounds where I'd been hiding to the building with the open door. I plowed on, glancing back just long enough to know that Jack was right behind me. With my skirt flapping up and down as I ran and nothing but a black lacy thong on underneath. *Ay, Dios.*

And then he was in front of me, easily passing me up as my foot landed in a divot, my ankle twisting under me. I bit back the yelp that shot up my throat.

He reached for me, grabbing my arm but still pulling me forward. "You okay?"

"I think so." I shook off the pain radiating from my ankle and kept going, limping slightly, until we were finally within ten yards of the door.

Jack made it to the threshold first, urging me on. "Hurry up."

Just then, a movement to the left caught my eye. Shit.

Jack must have read my expression. "Hurry, Lola."

I made it to the small cement pad in front of the door, the pain in my ankle like a knife through the bone. Damn high heels. I couldn't put my finger on what I heard, but I knew whoever we'd seen leave the building was almost back. Before the person could round the corner, Jack grabbed my hand and yanked me inside.

His voice dropped to a low hiss. "Over there," he said, dragging me toward a freestanding shelf. We slipped behind it just as the *thump, thump, thump* of footsteps hit the cement floor.

Chapter Twenty-Seven

It was impossible to see a thing and we didn't dare move. As it was, I was pretty sure whoever was in the building with us could hear my pounding heart.

I zeroed in on the sounds, hoping to get some clue. Woman or man? Larry? But if he'd had a thing for Jennifer, what would he be doing here now that she was gone?

The sound of a cardboard box being shoved aside was followed by a low grunt, the patter of footsteps, and the slam of a door.

"Shit, this is crazy," Jack whispered.

He could say that again.

I stood, my ankle buckling under me, but Jack was there with his arm around me. A slice of light shone through the window. My eyes adjusted, and I registered the shadowy details of the ten-by-ten room. Boxes. Shelves. And more boxes. I grabbed the first one I saw, ripping it open and peering inside. It was full of tubs of the containers sold in the resort's front office. "Protein powder."

"It's just a storage facility," he said, but then he shook his head. "Why would someone be loading up boxes of this stuff now, in the middle of a party?"

"It has to be Craig," I said. "He told he had to check the food supply before he could give me a tour, but he could have easily slipped out here." He'd been married to Jennifer. A new idea slid into my mind. "What if…Oh boy, what if he's doing something illegal here and she found out about it?"

I searched my memory for the sound of his footsteps as he'd walked away, but the music had been too loud, and were bare-feet footsteps really identifiable, anyway? Then it dawned on me. I'd heard the *thump*, *thump*, *thump* of shoes on the floor, not the *slap*, *slap*, *slap* of bare feet.

"Maybe he put on shoes to come out here," Jack suggested when I told him why it probably wasn't Craig we'd seen.

"Maybe." But my gut said *no*, and one thing my superstitious *abuela* had taught me was to always follow my gut.

I closed the flaps of the box and shoved it aside. "Let's check another one."

"Over there," Jack said, pointing across the room.

A few boxes were missing from a shelf. Those had to be the ones just taken out of the building.

I took a step, hobbling as fast as I could, the pain spiraling around my ankle. Jack was ahead of me, tearing into a box from the shelf he'd pointed out. "More protein powder," he said.

He quickly closed the flaps, rearranging the boxes so the one he'd opened wasn't on top. The low buzz of a phone sounded from just outside the door, followed by a clipped,

"What?"

I gasped. We hadn't found anything, and now we were on the verge of being caught. Caught doing what, I didn't know, but I still didn't want to explain why we were here.

Jack and I stared at each other, then in perfect unison, we both dropped to our knees. I moved first, scurrying around the corner of the shelf. It was only after I started crawling, the cold air from outside blowing into the building and chilling the flesh of my bare behind, that I remembered what I wasn't wearing. Full coverage *chonis*. Damn. I could almost feel the heat of Jack's gaze on my backside, but there was nothing I could do about it at the moment.

I hurried. Jack hurried. We rounded the corner just as the door opened and a man said, "Done."

Not a good enough sampling to identify a voice—if I even knew who it was.

He must have hung up the phone. The next second, the *thump* of footsteps pounded against the cement, coming to a stop in front of the shelf we'd just been at. Another box slid from it, then more footsteps out the door, but this time, the light went out, the door slammed shut, and Jack and I were alone.

Chapter Twenty-Eight

I counted to ten in my head, in case whoever had been here decided to come back.

"He's gone," Jack said, his voice sounding loud in the hollow darkness of the storage building.

"...*ocho, nueve, diez*," I muttered, finishing my count. Then I cocked my head to the side, flipping my ponytails back as if that would help me hear better. All was silent. "Yep."

Jack stood, then held his hand out so I could grab it and stand without putting too much weight on my foot. "Any better?" he asked.

"Maybe. I think so."

He started toward the door as I processed my thoughts aloud. "So someone was loading up a delivery of protein powder at, what, like, ten thirty? Eleven?" The numbers on Jennifer's brochures must not be related to these buildings at all. It was a dead end.

Jack, ever the investigative reporter, poked his head out

the door into the darkness, then turned back to me. "Let's check the other buildings." He grabbed a nearby tub of protein powder and placed it between the door and the jamb. "In case we want to come back in here," he explained.

Ah, *mi amor*! I knew I liked him for his brains. "Good thinking," I said, crinkling my nose as my fake glasses slipped down. If I'd had a pocket, I would have tucked them away. But I didn't, so I slid them back into place and followed Jack out the door, testing my weight on my ankle. So far, so good.

He glanced down at it a few times. "It's fine," I said under my breath, although I knew a whopping dose of Advil was in my future.

He tested the door handle of the second building. Locked. I limped around to the side of building two while he jogged to the others. I cupped my hands and peered through the window. Not much to see but shadows. Except—

A hand came down on my shoulder. "It's me," Jack said quickly enough that I could stifle the yelp hovering on my tongue. "They're all locked."

"What does that stuff look like to you?" I asked, pointing to the window.

"It's dark in there," he said, but he did exactly what I'd done, cupping his hands and peering through the glass. "Furniture. Chaise longues and stuff."

My shoulders sank. "Yeah, that's what I thought, too."

We went back to the first building. "We have to be missing something," I said. My instincts couldn't be wrong on this!

He followed me inside, closing the door behind us. We didn't dare turn on the lights, but after another minute, my eyes adjusted, the moonlight streaming in enough to show us the shelves.

"What do you think you're going to find?" Jack asked.

"Good question. I don't know." Something tickled the back of my brain, but I couldn't drag it out to the surface. "There's nothing here, and yet…"

He walked alongside the shelves, touching the boxes and moving them to look behind. I went the other direction, doing the same, but stopped when the box I pushed nearly flew off the shelf. I shoved it out of the way, touching the one below it. "Jack," I called.

He was by my side in a flash, standing behind me as I opened the box. "Empty?"

I turned and saw all his bare-chested glory. I swallowed the lump that rose in my throat. "Um, yeah. Empty." I averted my eyes. "Why would there be empty boxes stacked here?" We went through a few more. Empty, each and every one, but shelved as if they were full of tubs of nutritional supplements.

Bending over, I peered between the shelves, leaning in to reach for the wall. Only it wasn't a wall, it was—"A door."

I pulled my head out from between the shelves, straightened up, and turned to find a smoldering, almost pained expression on Jack's face, his gaze directed at my backside. *Ay, caramba.* Not now. If I couldn't let my mind wander there, neither could he. We'd have plenty of time for that later.

I stood and snapped my fingers. "Callaghan. Focus."

He blinked, his eyes still dark and seductive, but his attention back where it should be. "A door." Then, as if a lightbulb turned on, he repeated, "A door?"

"*Ayúdame*," I said, slipping into Spanish. His curiosity bypassed his desire, because he grabbed the end of the shelf and slid it back enough that we could fit behind it.

The whole time, that niggling feeling kept tapping in the recesses of my mind. I could hear Jennifer's voice telling me something…something important. *Pero*, what was it? Manny's voice came next. "*Just wait. It'll come to you. Remember your hypothesis.*"

One of my hypotheses was that Larry Madrino had some jealous, unrequited love going on for Jennifer, but that just didn't feel right. Manny's voice popped into my head again. "'*Doesn't feel right' isn't enough. Hard and cold facts, that's what you need.*"

"It's unlocked," Jack said, and just like that, Manny's voice was gone.

We stepped inside. There were no windows, so I closed the door behind me and ran my hand along the wall. Finally, I found it and flipped it up.

Ceiling-mounted fluorescent lights flickered on and the room was suddenly blazing with brightness.

Jack and I stared at the long, rectangular table, the buckets, the tubing, and the glass jars in the center of the room. "Is it a meth lab?" I asked when I found my voice again. It had to be. Why else would all these chemicals and supplies be here? I could see the headline now:

RURAL SACRAMENTO NUDIST RESORT FRONT FOR CRYSTAL METH LAB

Jack's jaw pulsed as he walked around the science lab setup.

I read the names of the chemicals. Benzyl Alcohol and

Benzyl Benzoate, whatever *that* was. Grapeseed oil. Beakers and needles. And testosterone cypionate.

After a minute, he turned to face me, the color draining from his face. "Shit."

"What?" What could a chemist make with testosterone cypion— "Holy Mary Mother of God," I said. "It's not meth, is it? Someone's making steroids."

Chapter Twenty-Nine

I grabbed Jack by the arm, an idea crashing into my head. "The drug scandal with the Royals a few years ago."

Jack's expression was grim. "What about it?"

My heart raced. We were close to the answer, I could feel it. "Players were suspended."

"Right. Lance Koning and Mike Javorski."

Those names. My breath caught in my throat. "Twenty-three and fifty-one."

He tilted his head, studying me.

Lines criss-crossed in my head, making me dizzy. "I saw those jerseys at Jennifer's house." Numbers 23 and 51. The trophies she'd had tucked away in her box. The gladiator from the party spun into my head. Number 11, Christof.

Jennifer's words floated back to me. "She majored in chemistry," I told Jack.

He leaned against the table, cupping his hand to his chin, crossing one leg over the other. He was one part sexy cowboy, one part brainy journalist. "Who?" he asked.

"Jennifer Wallace."

"How do you know?"

"She told me."

His brows lifted.

"I know," I said. "Not your stereotypical cheerleader."

"And you think—"

My skin tingled with the thrill of discovery. What if Jennifer hadn't been an innocent in all of this? "It's possible. If Jennifer used this place to make some sort of super-steroid, she could have sold it to the players."

"Okay. But how would she distribute it?" Jack asked. "It's not easy to run a drug operation."

In my mind's eyes, I saw Steve's training room. He'd had tubs of protein powder in his cupboard. I gasped. I'd thought Larry had something to do with this, but…

"Through the trainer." I shoved the glasses up the bridge of my nose. "That has to be it. She made it and Steve Madrino distributed it." I gestured in the direction of *Cuerpo y Alma*. "And what a perfect cover. Who would ever suspect a chem lab *here*?"

We both turned toward the main room of the storage building. "So the stuff in the tubs isn't protein powder; it's a steroid powder," he said.

A charge zipped through me. "It has to be."

"One question, Cruz." Jack held the door open and I skirted past him, still limping, back into the main area. "Who killed her?"

I didn't know *who* killed her because I didn't know *why* she was killed. It was *un problema*. "The letters to the dancers," I muttered. "Who would have access to the ball boy to deliver them?"

"The players, the other dancers, the fans—"

"Not really, though." I whirled around to face him, flipping my ponytails behind my shoulders. "They sort of had access, but not really. Not all the time. Only one person has constant access—" Something else Jennifer had said hit me. "*¡Dios mío!*"

"What?"

But before I had a chance to tell him my theory, the door to the storage building banged open and there, in the darkened doorway, a backlit glow around him, stood a very angry matador.

Chapter Thirty

Holy mackerel. The plot thickened. I moved toward the matador. But I stopped as Jack's hand grabbed the low waistband of my skirt and held on tight.

The man ran his fingers over the brim of his sequined hat and stomped his booted foot. The hard muscles of his legs pulsed below his black satin underwear.

A scream rose in my throat, but the laugh that surfaced battled it. I fought the conflicting urges by sucking in a deep breath and twirling one ponytail. "Is that you, Larry?" I asked, making my voice playful and innocent.

He stepped across the threshold, flashlight in hand, whipping the black, red-lined cape around himself. The door slammed behind him. "You shouldn't be here."

"How did you know?"

"The owner's going around asking everyone if they've seen a spicy schoolgirl. The second I heard the name Lola," he hissed, "I knew it was you. What are you doing here?"

I braced myself, rooting my feet to the ground. Only my

left ankle wobbled and I hissed in a pained breath. Under normal circumstances, I could take down a grown man, but right now I was only operating at a brown-belt level.

I snuck a glance at Jack. He met my gaze and a silent laser of understanding shot between us. He had my back. Literally.

"The truth, Larry?"

"Of course."

"I'm trying to find out who killed Jennifer."

He stared at me.

"You were the boyfriend Selma told me about, right?" I asked.

His lower lip quivered under his beaded eye mask. "We were in love, you know," Larry said. The tortured expression on his face eased my nerves. Manny might need proof, but my instincts were telling me that Larry hadn't killed Jennifer. "She tried to get out, but—"

"What do you mean, get out?" Jack asked, his hand still on my lower back. "Get out of what?"

He flung his arms around. "This. This stuff. This…mess. It's worse than a gang. Once you're in, you're in. I accepted her for who she was. I didn't care about her ex-husband. About this place." He gestured to the back room Jack and I had just come from. "About that."

"So she wasn't working alone?" Jack asked.

I sucked in a breath, hating to kick a man when he was down. I did it anyway, in the name of truth. "Your brother?"

But Larry recoiled. "Steve can be an idiot," he said, "but he's no mastermind criminal. No." He glanced behind him at the closed door, as if whoever he was about to rat out was standing on the other side, ready to burst through and take him down.

He ripped off his hat, the skin of his bald head glinting in the indirect beam of the flashlight. A few lines in my head miraculously straightened out, something else Jennifer had said to me pinging to the forefront of my mind.

"*Dios mío*," I muttered for the second time, the gladiator floating to my head again, followed by the drawer of atomizers in Jennifer's un-lived-in apartment.

Jack moved his hand, on high alert. "What?" he asked, and just as I was about to tell him who I thought might have been Jennifer's partner-in-crime, the door behind Larry swung open and I found myself staring into the eyes of a killer.

Chapter Thirty-One

Victoria Wolfe's silhouette darkened the doorway, the details of her police/vamp costume suddenly ironic. Officer of the law. Right. "Well, well, well," she said, all breathy and harsh. "Guess the party's moved down here."

"Seriously?" Jack hissed in my ear.

I nodded as Larry whipped around at the sound of her voice.

"Victoria," he said, low and menacing, as if he were challenging a bull with a taunting, "*¡Andele, toro!*"

"Larry." She *tsk*ed, then drew the gun from her thigh holster. I peered at it in the dark. It wasn't a prop for her costume. *Hijo de su madre.* It was a freaking semiautomatic.

Damn, she'd waltzed right into the party with a loaded weapon. The woman had *huevos*.

"You should have left well enough alone," she said to Larry.

His fists bunched the fabric of his matador cape. "You killed her. I loved her, and you killed her."

Victoria stood tall, staring him down. "She had a choice, Larry. We had a good system; you know we did."

"She would have kept your secrets—"

Victoria shook her head and let out a low, contemptuous laugh. "She didn't, you fool. You're here. That means she told you."

A shiver danced over my spine. Victoria hadn't known for sure that Larry knew until this moment.

"Why'd you hire me?" I asked, stepping forward as if I could protect Larry.

"My husband," she answered, adding with a snicker, "marriage is about compromise. He was insistent. I knew Manny Camacho was good, but I thought *you*," she said, pointing her finger at me, "might be too green to actually figure things out. Now I have to clean up another mess."

I'd been listening to everything she'd said, but my brain suddenly hiccupped. Victoria had wiggled her fingers in a flirty, familiar wave to the gladiator. Number 11 from the Royals. Christof. She knew him. Like really *knew* him.

And just like that, another piece of the puzzle slipped into place. Victoria *did* break her own rules by fraternizing with the players!

The facts were still muddy in my head, but slowly, they were coming into focus. The apartment in Natomas didn't look lived in because it *wasn't* lived in. Not by Jennifer, anyway, who had her cottage here at *Cuerpo y Alma*. But it had been used. By Victoria.

"Those pictures and the jerseys at the Natomas apartment," I said. "They weren't Jennifer's, were they?"

"Of course they weren't," Larry snapped. "She owned that place for the tax write-off, but she never used it."

Of course! "They were yours," I said to Victoria. "Your love nest?"

"We had a deal," Victoria said. "She helped me. I helped her. She had loans to pay off. It was a good arrangement until she went and fell in love. Pft." She held her gun steady. Impressive, especially given her three-inch high heels.

I might not have a gun, but I'd shot plenty. Target practice was one of Manny's steadfast rules. Knowing everything about being a P.I. was one of mine. Getting a better look at Victoria's gun, I saw that it was probably a Ruger 380.

My heart dropped to the pit of my stomach. Not again. Jack and I had been in this situation before, only it had been at a marina and he'd been shot. Now, his smoky blue eyes narrowed as he listened to the story unfold. I wouldn't let him get hurt again.

"Who else is involved?" I asked, stalling for time. Had it been Steve we'd seen hauling boxes out of the building? I'd thought it was Craig, but maybe I was wrong. If it was Steve, and he came back, surely he'd help us. Larry was his brother, after all.

"I'm not a fool, Lola. Why do you think I showed up when I did that day you were snooping around the training room? Not coincidence, I assure you. I've had a close eye on you since day one. I'm certainly not going to tell you anything that could incriminate me—"

"So you're not going to kill us?" Relief flowed out of Larry.

"Of course I'm going to kill you. Like I said, I'm no fool. I'm cautious. That was Jennifer's problem. She couldn't help getting involved with you, Larry. Couldn't help bringing you here even though I told her not to."

I felt the brush of Jack's fingers against mine. I snuck a glance at him but couldn't read his face. He clenched his jaw, his lips drawn tight. He was either ready to go down with me in a blaze of glory, or he was thinking, not for the first time, that getting involved with me was *muy* bad for his health.

If only we had telepathy so I knew what he was thinking and he knew about my plan.

Which at the moment didn't actually exist.

Not that kicking Victoria in the sternum, thereby dislodging the gun from her grip and sending her teeth chattering, was much of a plan. But it was the best I could come up with. I had some experience attacking people with guns, and it was never pretty. I was a kung fu fighter, but a strong high kick was no match for a shooting bullet. Didn't matter. I had to try.

A shadow moving outside the window caught my eye. Victoria was ranting at Larry and didn't seem to notice the slight notch of my chin. But Jack did. His gaze flickered, just barely, and I knew he'd seen it, too. Victoria's accomplice, come back to get more of the goods?

"Manny will figure this out," I said, hoping my plan would prevent the worst from happening until he did.

Victoria just threw back her head and laughed. "Not after I'm done with him, he won't. A little role-play during sex goes a long way." She gave me a good once-over, then scrutinized cowboy Jack. "You two won't have a chance to experience that firsthand, I'm sorry to say."

Oh no. *Somos amantes*, I thought. We were lovers—one time counted, *¿de veras?* Heat rose from my heart to behind my eyes. I *wanted* to role-play with Jack. I wanted to do *everything* with him. I flipped my ponytails back, pushed my fake glasses up my nose, and squared my shoulders.

Victoria Wolfe was going down. *Punto*.

"Trust me," she said. "Manny Camacho will be eating out of the palm of my hand before the night is through."

I shook my head. I didn't believe Manny could fall that easily. He was an honorable man. I couldn't imagine he'd compromise a case or the truth…even for a good lay.

I moved forward. "Not another step," Victoria snapped.

Manny's rules echoed in my mind. *The first rule of private investigation is self-preservation. You can't help anyone if you're injured, arrested, or dead.*

I'd decided that the second rule was to preserve the lives of the ones you loved. Namely, Jack Callaghan. I had a feeling that Sarah, the escape artist, would continue to be a thorn in our sides, but I wasn't going to let her ruin another minute of my potential life with the man I sort of…almost… might very soon…love. I had to trust him—just like I wanted him to trust me.

I thought back to my first meeting with Victoria. Did she know about my black belt? For the life of me, I couldn't remember, but I didn't think it had been mentioned. There'd been a lot of talk about my curves and physique, but not much about my skill set as a detective.

I stood even with Larry. He was frozen, his mouth open, his eyes glistening. I had a feeling that Victoria's words had hit home with him. He'd never get to role-play—or do anything—with Jennifer again. The idea had taken hold. He trembled, ready to go into a tailspin.

I put my hand on his shoulder. "Larry?"

Victoria heaved out a put-upon sigh, as if Larry's anguish

was seriously cramping her style. "Please," she said. "It's not like you would have lived happily ever after. I know you couldn't stand this place, but it was where Jennifer belonged."

"I-I was learning to like it," he said, his lower lip quivering.

She quirked a sardonic smile at his matador getup. "Is that why you came tonight? To fit into her world? Since you can't have her anymore?"

Dios mío, did the woman have no shame? *¡Qué bruja!*

Larry's entire body suddenly trembled. I stared at him as his pasty skin took on a tinged red hue, creeping up his legs, his torso, his neck, and concentrating on his cheeks.

"Okay there, Larry, just relax," Victoria said, patting the air with her empty hand. "I didn't mean anything by it."

But Larry was too far gone. I took a step to the left as his foot scraped against the ground. *Ay caramba.* He wasn't the matador after all. He was the bull.

Before I could high-kick the gun out of Victoria's hand, he charged.

Chapter Thirty-Two

The gun went off, the loud *pop pop* of two shots sounding almost like booms. Deafening in the small storage building. I careened backward, my weak ankle buckling under me, and fell against Jack, who pushed me upright. I zeroed in on Victoria and Larry. He had her up against one of the shelves. Cardboard boxes filled with Victoria and Jennifer's special steroid concoction crashed to the ground.

Victoria craned her head as another carton hit the floor. "Damn it, Larry," she said, hissing through her teeth.

Jack and I glanced at each other. Instantly, we went into action. With super stealth, he circled around behind the shelf. Adrenaline kicked in. My ankle throbbed, but the pain was dulled by my survival skills.

Larry was summoning up gumption I hadn't known was in him. His hands encircled her wrists, but she clutched the gun, grunting and struggling as she tried to angle the barrel downward to point at his head.

Victoria was strong, but Larry was stronger. He pushed

her arm down and away.

I took a page out of Jack's spy book, but moved at lightning speed. It didn't matter. She caught my eye, her neck strained, blood vessels popping under her skin. Slowly, she fought Larry until the gun was trained on…me.

Shit. No more time to waste. I ducked, trying to stay out of the line of fire. Another booming *pop* sounded. "*¡Hija de la chingada!* What are you trying to do?"

"I still have four left," she said with a hiss, struggling against Larry to move her wrist and retrain the gun.

"No," I said. "I do." And I lunged. In one quick move, I snatched the gun from her hand and yanked the handcuffs from the holster clip on her outer thigh.

"Coming over," I yelled, tossing the cuffs to Jack. We were synchronicity. He snatched them from the air and without even a second of hesitation, he snapped them onto her right wrist.

I slipped the gun into the back waistband of my skirt and grabbed her cuffed wrist, edging Larry out of the way and jerking her forearm until she had to turn her back on me.

Larry twisted her left arm down and around, locking it behind her back. As I slapped the other handcuff on her, the doorframe splintered with a loud *crack* and the door flung open. Manny rushed in.

I stared at him, then at the gun he had drawn. Where had he hidden *that*? My gaze slipped down his black leather-clad legs hitching at…aah, an ankle holster. Nicely played, *Señor* Camacho. Nicely played. "How'd you know we were here?"

"Craig couldn't find you." He met my gaze, his eyes dark and intense. "I asked myself, where would Dolores go? Easy.

To the most remote place on the property, probably alone. And here you are."

"Not alone," Jack ground out. I could almost hear his fists clench. Having Manny know me that well wasn't his idea of a good boss/employee relationship. Couldn't say I blamed him.

"So I see," Manny said. "*Buen trabajo, Sargenta.* You, too, Callaghan," he offered stiffly.

I took the compliment, but Jack glared. Manny would become best buddies just as soon as Sarah and I did… which would be never. We each had our baggage. The only difference was that mine was my boss and I'd never slept with him or been engaged to him.

I shoved Victoria toward Manny. "Meet Jennifer Wallace's murderer." She glanced back at me, and I added, "Guess you won't be able to role-play after all."

She blinked slowly. Not a single bit of remorse flitted through her eyes.

I thought about her poor deluded husband, Lance. *Pobrecito.* He'd certainly been duped. Victoria had said he'd been the reason they'd come to Camacho & Associates in the first place. Unless…

I'd assumed Lance wasn't involved, but what if Craig was innocent and Lance wasn't? What if *he'd* been the one we'd seen carrying off boxes of the protein powder steroid?

"Your husband," I said. I bent down and slipped my fingers into my knee sock, fishing for the list of *Cuerpo y Alma* members who matched Jennifer's Facebook friends. I felt the heat of Manny's stare. And Jack staring *him* down. Oh boy.

I turned my back, quickly scanning the list. No names

had shown up on my part of the list, but what about the members Lucy had compared? I glanced at the names on her list. Lance. Lance. Lance. Nothing yet.

And then suddenly two names magnified. There they were in black and white. It was no surprise they'd been her Facebook friends, but seeing them on the *Cuerpo y Alma* list? That was a whole 'nother thing.

They froze on my lips as my gaze drifted over Manny's shoulder. Two men stood there, both of them staring at Victoria, utter horror and disbelief on their faces.

One was in costume, painted blue and white like a die-hard Royals fan. The other was in plain clothes.

Steve Madrino and Lance Wolfe.

Chapter Thirty-Three

I hadn't been able to see the man carrying boxes out of the storage building. It could have been either of them. Behind the two men, I saw a figure moving across the lawn. It was like a bad B-movie moment. Hair whipped in the wind, breasts bounced up and down, and the tail of a rope dragged across the ground.

Selma.

She ran across the grass, skates still on her feet. Closer. Closer.

Manny took hold of Victoria's handcuffs. He didn't know about the accomplice. He headed toward the men to lead Victoria out of the building.

That's when I saw it.

The slightest movement. The touch of his thumb to his ring finger. Lance Wolfe's heart was breaking at the sight of his wife and the knowledge of what she'd done, while Steve stood still as a mountain lion on the hunt, ready to pounce.

"Selma!" I yelled.

Manny stopped.

The most obvious person.

Victoria was right. It had been a pretty slick operation. They made the steroid powder and Steve Madrino, the team's trainer, had administered it to the players. He'd had tub after tub after tub of the stuff in his training room.

The most obvious suspect.

Steve turned. Perfect. I sprinted forward, did a hop-skip, and thrust a high kick to his chest. My ankle nearly exploded from the impact, but he lost his balance and stumbled back.

Lance grabbed for him, and Selma airplaned her arms as she tried to stop, nearly losing her balance on the soft earth.

"Your rope, Selma!"

Bless her naked heart. She didn't ask questions, she just undid the knot of the rope around her waist, throwing it to me just as Steve regained his balance and started running.

Larry took off after him, his matador cape flying behind him. Hopping on one foot, I threw Jack the rope. He ran, and not twenty seconds later, Larry had tackled his brother and Jack had hog-tied Steve, Victoria's partner-in-crime, with Selma's pull-toy rope.

All in a day's work.

Chapter Thirty-Four

"So Steve wrote the notes to try to scare Jennifer back into cooperating," I muttered, fitting the last few puzzle pieces together.

I hobbled across the parking lot, leaning against Jack's arm for support. I glanced up at him. Would we ever have normal dates that didn't include near-death experiences?

"*¿Cómo estás*, Callaghan?" *Mi amor*, I added in my head, finally believing we had a chance.

He squeezed my shoulder. "Doing okay. Gotta love the hazards of your job. But your ankle?" He peered down at the knot under my pink and black knee socks.

"It's not so bad." I was sure my mother or grandmother would have some old-world Mexican homeopathic remedy for it and I'd be good as new in no time.

A smile played on his lips. "You're a tough one, Cruz."

"Just call me Xena. And you wouldn't have it any other way."

"No, I don't think I would." He put his finger on the

bridge of my fake school girl glasses, pushing them back into place. "Now, about that role-playing later…" he said, his suggestive grin widening.

My nerves zinged, but before I could answer by jumping up and down and clapping in true schoolgirl fashion, Manny appeared out of the shadows. "Nice kick, *Sargenta*. Took him down easy."

Jack tensed beside me, releasing his supportive hold on me, and I cursed Manny and his impeccable timing.

But I liked the hard-won compliment. "*Gracias*."

Craig had called the police. The fact that Sadie Metcalf leaned against her sporty car meant that Manny had probably called her. Their love-hate relationship was still a mystery, but one to be thought about at another time.

I spotted Lucy and Zac sauntering across the parking lot. More of her balloons had popped, and judging from the lightness of his step and the curve of his lips, he was ready to go home and pop the rest. So he'd adjusted. A while ago, I wanted to kill him for telling Jack I was here, but Jack had helped me solve this case. He had my back. And he wanted to role-play. Zac was forgiven.

Reilly and Neil stood next to a thirty-something dark-haired man. He was neat and tidy in khakis and a Polo shirt. Next to him stood a rumpled man with a bad comb-over. *Hijo de su madre.* Detective Bennett and my old friend Detective Seavers.

Bennett watched me. He ran his finger under his shirt collar, clearly *un poquito* hot and bothered as I closed the distance between us. Meanwhile, Seavers's bushy unibrow pulled together as he gave me a good once-over. "You again?" He notched his chin toward Jack. "And your *friend.*"

"Solved another case for you," I said, hopping the last few steps to alleviate the shooting pain in my ankle. I felt my cleavage jiggling and under the downturned parking lights, I was pretty sure my tight white shirt didn't leave much to the imagination.

"So I hear," he said.

A breeze kicked up my skirt. I pushed it down, but not before anyone who was curious got a glimpse of my sheer thong and bare behind.

Bennett cupped one hand behind his neck and quickly turned away. Manny's entire face darkened, his eyes smoldering. Sadie scowled.

So plenty of people were curious. But only Jack was entitled to the whole shebang.

I patted Neil's shoulder as I passed him. He had a lovesick-puppy expression on his linebacker face and only had eyes for Reilly.

And Seavers? He was made of steel. He didn't flinch. Didn't blush. Wasn't fazed at all by my skimpy clothing, my belly button ring, or the quick glimpse of my bare skin. He cleared his throat. "You'll go that last mile to close a case, won't you, Ms. Cruz?"

Reilly silently clapped, cheering me on. She threw me a thumbs-up sign, then snuggled close to Neil.

I thought about what Seavers had said. Would I go that last mile? That had been the big question. How far was I willing to go for my job? What *were* my boundaries?

I answered Seavers, but my words were mostly for Jack. He had to know, once and for all, that there were some lines I wouldn't cross. "I used to think so, Detective, *pero* my mother taught me well. There are some things I won't do and some lines I won't cross."

Jack had folded his arms over his bare chest, his expression a mix of a wolf ready to protect his mate and a lion ready to devour her.

Which meant he was ready to devour *me*.

Turns out my costume wasn't too far off the mark. I was a good Catholic girl who pushed the boundaries, yes. But unless Jack Callaghan was in the picture, and the setting was *muy privado*, I kept my clothes on.

Acknowledgments

I like to say that Lola Cruz is my alter ego—if I were a twenty-nine-year-old smokin' hot Latina detective. She lives in my head, and thanks to my husband's family and culture, she comes alive on the pages of the Lola Cruz novels. So thank you to Carlos for his love, support, and for bringing such a rich culture into my life.

As always, a big thanks goes to Holly Root, Lola's first and loudest cheerleader; to Libby Murphy for her tireless— and, at times, laborious—editing; to Stacy Abrams and Suzanne Johnson; to Danielle Barclay for all that is to come; to the Lit Girls; to Lyn Bement for her teaching moments, her Spanish expertise, and attention to accent marks; and to the real Selma Mann, an inspiration and a great sport. Thanks to Heather Howland for her artistic vision and to Liz Pelletier and the Entangled team for...*everything*!

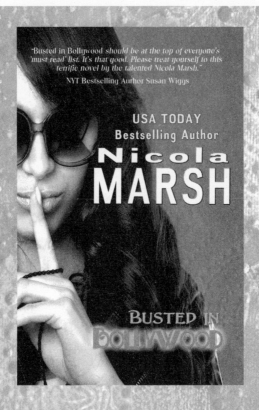

Keep reading for sample chapters of
BUSTED IN BOLLYWOOD
by USA Today Bestselling author Nicola Marsh

Shari Jones needs to get a life. Preferably someone else's.

Single, homeless and jobless, Indo-American Shari agrees to her best friend's whacky scheme: travel to Mumbai, pose as Amrita, and ditch the fiancé her traditional Indian parents have chosen. Simple. Until she's mistaken for a famous Bollywood actress, stalked by a Lone Ranger wannabe, courted by an English lord, and busted by the blackmailing fiancé.

Life is less complicated in New York.

Or so she thinks, until the entourage of crazies follows her to the Big Apple and that's when the fun really begins. Shari deals with a blossoming romance, an addiction to Indian food and her first movie role, while secretly craving another trip to the mystical land responsible for sparking her new lease on life. Returning to her Indian birthplace, she has an epiphany. Maybe the happily-ever-after of her dreams isn't so far away?

Chapter One

Look up *stupid* in the dictionary and you'll find my picture.

Along with revealing stats: Shari Jones, twenty-nine, five-seven, black hair, hazel eyes, New Yorker. Addicted to toxic men like my ex, cheesecake, and mojitos (not necessarily in that order), and willing to do anything for a friend, including travel to India and impersonate aforementioned friend in an outlandish plot to ditch her fiancé.

See? Stupid.

"You're the best." Amrita Muthu, my zany best friend who devised this escapade, cut a wedge of chocolate cheesecake and plopped it on my plate. "Have another piece to celebrate."

I loved how she always had cheesecake stocked in her apartment freezer but as I stared at my favorite dessert I knew I couldn't afford the extra calories. Not with my destination of Mumbai—land of food hospitality—where I'd be bombarded with rich, sugar-laden treats that I'd have to eat to be polite.

Despite my Indo-American heritage, *jalebis, gulab jamuns,* and *rasmalai* are not my idea of heaven. The sickly sweet morsels were a testament to years as a fat kid, courtesy of an Indian mother who wasn't satisfied until my eyes—as well as my waistline—were bulging from too much food.

"Eat up, my girl," Mom used to say, shoveling another mini Mount Everest of rice and *dahl* onto my plate. "Lentils are strengthening. They'll make you big and strong."

She'd been right about the *big* part. Still waiting for my muscles to kick in.

But hey, I survived the food fest, and thanks to hours in the gym, smaller portions of *dahl* (yeah, I'd actually become hooked on the stuff), and moving away from home, I now had a shape that didn't resemble a blimp.

"Shari? You going to eat or meditate?"

"Shut up." I glared at Amrita—Rita to me—then picked up my fork and toyed with the cheesecake. "Too early for celebrations." *Commiserations* were more likely if this wacky plot imploded. "You're not the one spending two weeks in Mumbai with a bunch of strangers, pretending to like them."

"But you don't have to pretend. That's the whole point. I want you to be yourself and convince the Ramas I'm not worthy of their son." Rita stuck two fingers down her throat and made gagging noises. "Bet he's a real prince. Probably expects the prospective good little Hindu wife he's never seen to bow, kiss his ass, and bear him a dozen brats. Like that's going to happen."

She rolled her perfectly kohled eyes and cut herself another generous slab of cheesecake. Curves are revered in India and Rita does her heritage proud with an enviable hourglass figure.

"You think my naturally obnoxious personality will drive this prince away, huh? Nice."

Rita grinned and topped off our glasses from the mojito pitcher sitting half-empty between us. "You know what I mean. You're flamboyant, assertive, eloquent. Except when it came to your ex." She made a thumbs-down sign. "I'm a wimp when it comes to defying my folks. If anyone can get me out of this mess, you can."

Debatable, considering the mess I'd made of my life lately.

"No way would I marry some stooge and leave NYC to live in Mumbai. Not happening."

She took a healthy slurp of mojito and ran a crimson-tipped fingernail around the rim of the glass. "Besides, you score a free trip. Not to mention the added bonus of putting Tate behind you once and for all."

That did it. I pushed my plate away and sculled my mojito. The mention of Tate Embley, my ex-boyfriend, ex-landlord, and ex-boss turned my stomach. Rita was right—I *was* assertive, which made what happened with him all the more unpalatable. I'd been a fool, falling for a slick, suave lawyer who'd courted me with a practiced flair I'd found lacking in the guys I'd dated previously.

I'd succumbed to the romance, the glamour, the thrill. Tate had been attentive and complimentary and generous. And I'd tumbled headfirst into love, making the fact he'd played me from start to finish harder to accept. Maybe I'd been naïve to believe his lavish promises. Maybe I should've known if something's too good to be true it usually is. Maybe I'd been smitten at the time, blinded to the reality of the situation: an unscrupulous jerk had charmed me into believing his lies to the point I'd lowered my streetwise defenses and toppled into an ill-fated relationship from the beginning.

"Oops, I forgot." Rita's hand flew to her mouth, a mischievous glint in her black eyes. "Wasn't supposed to mention the T-word."

I smirked. "Bitch."

"It's therapeutic to talk about it."

Morose, I stared into my empty glass, knowing a stint in India couldn't be as bad as this. If there's one thing I hate, it's rehashing the mess I'd made of my love life. "What's there to talk about? We're over."

"Over, schmover. If he came groveling on his Armani knees you'd reconsider." She jabbed a finger at me. "If he comes sniffing around you again I'll kick his sorry ass to the curb."

"I already tried kicking him to the curb and now I'm homeless and unemployed."

Three months later, I couldn't believe he'd played me, thrown me out of his swank Park Avenue apartment, and fired me all on the same day. So what if I'd called him a lying, sleazy bastard with the morals of a rabid alley cat? If the Gucci loafer fit…

Rita refilled my glass, her stern glare nothing I hadn't seen before. "He'd reduced you to ho status. He paid your salary, your rent, and left you the odd tip when he felt like it."

She stared at the princess-cut ruby edged in beveled diamonds on the third finger of my right hand and I blushed, remembering the exact moment Tate had slipped it on. We'd been holed up in his apartment for a long weekend and in the midst of our sex-a-thon he'd given me the ring. Maybe I'd felt like Julia Roberts getting a bonus from Richard Gere for all of two seconds, but hey, it'd been different. I loved the guy. He loved me.

Yeah, right.

Tate had strung me along for a year, feeding me all the right lines: his wife didn't love him, platonic marriage, they never had sex, they stayed together for appearances, he'd leave her soon, blah, blah, blah.

Stupidly, I believed him until that fateful day three months ago when someone at Embley Associates, one of New York's premier law firms, revealed the latest juicy snippet: Tate, the firm's founding partner, was going to be a daddy. After years of trying with his gorgeous wife, nudge, nudge, wink, wink.

Say no more.

Unfortunately, Tate had tried some schmoozy winking with me to gloss over his *'I was drunk, she took advantage of me, it won't change a thing between us'* spiel. I'd nudged him right where it hurt and things had spiraled downhill from there.

Hence, my homeless, unemployed, and dumped status.

I folded my arms to hide the offending bauble—which was so damn pretty I couldn't part with it despite being tempted to pay rent. "Your point?"

"Forget him. Forget your problems. Go to India, live it up."

"And save your ass in the process?"

Rita grinned and clinked glasses with mine. "Now you're on the right track."

"I must be crazy."

"Or desperate."

"That, too." I shook my head. "Have you really thought this through? Word travels fast in your family."

"We've been planning this for a month. It'll work." Rita lowered her glass, an uncharacteristic frown slashing her brows. "You've been living here. You've seen my mom in action. You know why I have to do this."

She had a point. While every aspect of Rita's Hinduism fascinated an atheist like me, her double life was exhausting. Her folks would be scandalized if they knew she drank alcohol and ate beef, forbidden in her religion. But according to my inventive friend, who liked to stretch boundaries, cows in New York weren't holy and the alcohol helped her assimilate. Likely excuses, but living beneath the burden of her family's expectations—including an arranged marriage to a guy halfway around the world—had taken its toll. She needed to tell her folks the truth, but for now she'd settled on this crazy scheme to buy herself time to build up the courage.

I could've persuaded her to come clean, but I went along with it because I owed Rita. Big-time. She'd let me crash here, she'd listened to my sob story repeatedly, she'd waived rent while I fruitlessly job-searched. Apparently out-of-work legal secretaries were as common in job interviews as rats were in the subway. Didn't help that the low-key, detail-oriented job bored me to tears in my last year at Embley Associates, and I'd been wistfully contemplating a change. Therein lay the problem. I needed to work for living expenses and bills and rent but my personal fulfillment well was dry and in serious need of a refill.

Another reason I was doing this: I hoped traveling to Mumbai would give me a fresh perspective. Besides, I could always add actress/impersonator to my résumé to jazz it up when I returned.

"Telling your family would be easier." On both of us, especially me, the main stooge about to perpetuate this insanity. "What if I mess up? It'll be a disaster."

Oblivious to my increasing nerves, Rita's frown cleared. "It'll be a cinch. My aunt Anjali's in on the plan, and she'll meet you at the airport and guide you through the Rama rigmarole. She's a riot and you'll love staying with her. Consider it a well-earned vacation." She clicked her fingers and grinned. "A vacation that includes giving the Ramas' dweeby son the cold shoulder so he can't stand the thought of marrying me. Capish?"

"Uh-huh."

Could I really pull this off? Posing as an arranged fiancée, using a smattering of my rusty Hindi, immersing in a culture I hadn't been a part of since my family had moved to the States when I was three. Though I was half Indian, spending the bulk of my life in New York had erased my childhood memories of the exotic continent that held little fascination for me. Sure, Mom told stories about her homeland and continued to whip up Indian feasts that would do a maharajah proud, yet it all seemed so remote, so distant.

It hadn't been until I'd become friends with Rita, who worked at Bergdorf's in accounts—and who gave me a healthy discount once we'd established a friendship—that my latent interest in my heritage had been reawakened.

Rita had intrigued me from the start, her sultry beauty,

her pride in her culture, her lilting singsong accent. She encapsulated everything Indian, and though my life had temporarily fallen apart thanks to the Toad—my penchant for nicknames resonated in this instance, considering Tate *was* cold and slimy—the opportunity to travel to India and help Rita in the process had been too tempting to refuse.

"You sure this Rakesh guy doesn't know what you look like?"

"I'm sure." Her smug smile didn't reassure me. "I'm not on Facebook and I Googled myself three times to make sure there were no pics. You'll be pleased to know I'm decidedly un-Google-worthy. As for the photo my parents sent before they left… well, let's just say there was a little problem in transit."

"Tell me you didn't interfere with the U.S. Postal Service."

"'Course not." Her grin widened. "I tampered with the Muthu Postal Service."

"Which means?"

"Mom gave Dad a stack of mail to send. He was giving me a ride, and when he stopped to pick up his favorite tamarind chutney I pilfered the envelope out of the bunch."

"Slick."

"I think so." She blew on her nails and polished them against her top, her 'I'm beyond cool' action making me laugh. "Besides, we look enough alike that even if he caught a sneak peek at some photo, it shouldn't be a problem."

Luckily, I had cosmopolitan features that could pass for any number of backgrounds: Spanish, Italian, Portuguese, or Mexican. Few people pegged me for half Indian, not that I'd played it down or anything. In a country as diverse as the

U.S., an exotic appearance was as common as a Starbucks on every corner.

"I like your confidence," I said, my droll response garnering a shrug.

"You'll be fine."

"Easy for you to say." I twirled the stem of my cocktail glass, increasingly edgy. "Even if this works, won't your folks fix you up with another guy?"

"Leave my parents' future matchmaking propositions to me." She snapped her fingers, her self-assurance admirable. "If they try this again, I'll pull the 'I'm your only child and you'll never see me again' trick. That'll scare them. I would've done it now but they've planned this Grand Canyon trip for a decade and I would've hated seeing them cancel it, and lose a small fortune, over me."

She paused, tapped her bottom lip, thinking, as I inwardly shuddered at what she'd come up with next. "Though I do feel sorry for them, what with Anjali being their only living relative, which is why I pretended to go along with this farce of marrying Rakesh in the first place."

"You're all heart."

She punched me lightly on the upper arm. "You can do this."

"I guess." My lack of enthusiasm elicited a frown.

"Here's the info dossier. Keep it safe."

She handed me a slim manila folder, the beige blandly discreet. Welcome to my life as a 007 sidekick. Halle Berry? Nah, I'm not that vain. Miss Moneypenny? Not that old, though considering the time I'd wasted on Tate, I was starting to feel it.

"My future as a single woman able to make her own life

choices depends on it."

I rolled my eyes but took the folder. "I know everything there is to know about the Rama family. You've drilled me for a month straight."

"Okay, wiseass. Who's the father and what does he do?"

I sipped at my mojito and cleared my throat, trying not to chuckle at Rita's obvious impatience as she drummed her fingernails against the armrest. "Too easy. Senthil Rama, musician, plays tabla for Bollywood movies."

"The mother?"

"Anu. Bossy cow."

A smile tugged at the corners of Rita's crimson-glossed mouth. "Sisters?"

"Three. Pooja, Divya, and Shruti. Watch them. If the mom's a cow, they're the calves."

Rita's smile turned into a full-fledged grin. "And last but not least?"

"Rakesh Rama. Betrothed to Amrita Muthu, New York City girl shirking her familial responsibility, besmirching her Hindu heritage, shaming her mother, disappointing her father, embroiling her best friend in deception—"

"Smartass."

Rita threw a silk-covered cushion at my head, and thanks to the four mojitos I'd consumed my reaction time slowed and it hit me right between the eyes. Reminiscent of the lapis lazuli paperweight I'd thrown at Tate as I slammed out of his office that last time. Pity my aim wasn't as good as Rita's.

Her scheme might be crazy but I knew I was doing the right thing. India would buy me some thinking time about what I wanted to do with my life.

I dribbled the last precious drops from the mojito jug into our glasses and raised mine in Rita's direction. "To Bollywood and back. Bottoms up."

· · ·

"Oh. My. *God*."

Shielding my eyes from the scorching glare of Mumbai's midday sun, I ran across the tarmac like a novice on hot coals, seeking shade in the terminal yet terrified by the sea of faces confronting me. How many people were meeting this flight?

A guy jostled me as I neared the terminal, my filthy glare wasted when he patted my arm, mumbled an apology, and slid into the crowd. I wouldn't have given the incident a second thought if not for the way his hand had lingered on my arm, almost possessively. Creep.

I picked up the pace, ignoring the stares prickling between my shoulder blades. Were the hordes ogling me, or was that my latent paranoia flaring already? *There's the imposter—expose her.*

I battled customs and fought my way through the seething mass of humanity to grab my luggage from the carousel. Caught up in a surge toward the arrival hall, *culture shock* took on new meaning as men, women, and children screeched and waved and hugged. On the outskirts I spotted a woman holding aloft a miniature Statue of Liberty, like Buffy brandishing a cross to ward off the vamps.

I'd laughed when Rita told me what her aunt would use to identify herself at Mumbai airport; now that I'd been smothered by a blanket of heat and aromas I didn't dare identify, jostled by pointy elbows, and sweated until my peasant top clung to my back, it wasn't so funny.

I used my case as a battering ram as I pushed through the crowd toward the Statue of Liberty. I'd never been so relieved to see that lovely Lady and her spiked halo.

"*Namaste*, Auntie," I said, unsure whether to press my palms together in the traditional Hindi greeting with a slight bow, hug her, or reel back from the garlic odor clinging to her voluminous cobalt sari.

She took the dilemma out of my hands by dropping the statue into her bag and wrapping her arms around me in a bear hug. "Shari, my child. Welcome. We talk English, yes?"

Holding my breath against the garlic fumes, I managed a nod as she pulled away and held me at arm's length.

"That naughty girl Amrita didn't tell me how beautiful you are. Why aren't you married?"

Great. I'd escaped my mom's Gestapo-like interrogations only to have Anjali pick up the slack. I mumbled something indecipherable, like 'mind your own business,' and smiled demurely. No use alienating the one woman who was my ally for the next two weeks.

"Never mind. Once this Rama rubbish is taken care of, maybe you'll fall in love with a nice Indian boy, yes?" Anjali cocked her head to one side, her beady black eyes taking on a decidedly matchmaking gleam.

I don't think so! I thought.

"Pleasure to meet you, Auntie," I said.

Rather than quiz me about my lack of marriage prospects she beamed, tucked her arm through mine, and dragged me toward the exit where another throng waited to get in. "Come, I have a car waiting. You must be exhausted after your flight. A good cup of *chai* and a few *ladoos* will revive you."

Uh-oh. The sweet-stuffing tradition had begun. *Ladoos* were lentil-laden balls packed with *ghee*, Indian clarified butter designed to add a few fat rolls in that fleshy gap between the sari and the *choli*, the short top worn beneath. Mom's favorite was *besan ladoos* and I remembered their smooth, nutty texture melting in my mouth. Despite my vow to stay clear of the sweets, saliva pooled and I swallowed, hoping I could resist.

Exiting the terminal equated with walking into a furnace and I dabbed at the perspiration beading on my top lip as Anjali signaled to a battered Beamer. "My driver will have us home shortly."

I didn't care if her driver beamed me up to the moon, as long as the car had air-conditioning.

While Anjali maintained a steady stream of conversation on the way to her house, I developed a mild case of whiplash as my head snapped every which way, taking in the sights of downtown Mumbai.

Cars, diesel-streaming buses, motorbikes, bicycles, and auto-rickshaws battled with a swarming horde of people on the clogged roads in a frightening free-for-all where it was every man, woman, and rickshaw driver for themselves.

The subway on a bad day had nothing on this.

Anjali—immune to the near-death experiences occurring before our eyes—prattled on about *parathas*, my favorite whole-meal flatbread, and her Punjabi neighbors, while I gripped the closest door handle until my fingers ached. Our driver, Buddy (Anjali had a thing for Buddy Holly and thus dubbed her man-about-the-house Buddy, thanks to his Coke-bottle glasses), maintained a steady stream of Hindi abuse—at least I assumed it was abuse, judging by his volume and hand actions—while his other hand remained planted on the horn.

Pity I hadn't held onto those earplugs from the flight. Would've been handy to mute the Mumbai melodies. I squeezed my eyes shut for the hundredth time as a small child darted out after a mangy dog right in front of our car. On the upside, every time I reopened my eyes, something new captured my attention. Fresh flowers on street corners, roadside vendors frying snacks in giant woks, long, orderly lines at bus stops. Bustling markets and sprawling malls nestled between ancient monuments.

Amazing contrasts—boutiques and five-star restaurants alongside abject poverty, beggars sharing the sidewalks with immaculately coiffed women who belonged on the cover of *Elle*, smog-filled streets while the Arabian Sea stretched as far as the eye could see on the city's doorstep.

When Buddy slowed and turned into a tiny driveway squeezed between a row of faded whitewashed flats, I almost missed the frenetic Mumbai energy that held me enthralled already.

"We're home." Anjali clapped her hands. "Leave your luggage to Buddy. Time to eat."

As I followed Anjali into the blessed coolness of her house, my hands shaking from the adrenaline surging through my system, I had an idea. Maybe soaking *ladoos* in white rum and lime juice would counteract the calories?

My very own Mumbai Mojitos.

Take a bite, get happy.

Eat two, get ecstatic.

Eat a dozen, get catatonic and forget every stupid reason

why I'd traveled thousands of miles to pretend to be someone else.

Great, perpetuating this scheme had affected my sense of humor, along with my perspective.

Hoping my duty-free liquor had survived the road trip from hell, I perked up at the thought of my favorite drink (to be consumed on the sly as Rita reminded me a hundred times, in case I forgot I wasn't supposed to drink while impersonating her) and climbed the stairs behind Anjali, trying not to focus on her cracked heels or the silk sari straining over her ample ass.

"Hurry up, child. The *ayah* has outdone herself in preparing a welcome meal for you."

Wishing I had a housemaid-cum-cook back home, I fixed a polite smile on my face as Anjali launched into another nonstop monologue, this time about the joys of grinding spices on a stone over store-bought curry powders. While she chatted I surreptitiously loosened the top button on my jeans in preparation for my initiation into India's national pastime—after cricket, that is.

"I hope you enjoy your curries hot, Shari. Nothing like chili to put pep in your step." Anjali bustled me into a dining room featuring a table covered with enough food to feed the multitudes I'd seen teaming the streets earlier. "Eat up, child. Men like some flesh on their women. Perhaps that's your problem?"

With an ear-jarring cackle, she proceeded to show me exactly how attractive men must find her by heaping a plate with rice, Goan fish curry rich in spices and coconut milk, *baigan aloo* (eggplant and potato), *chana dahl* (lentils), *pappadums* (deep-fried, wafer-thin lentil flour accompaniments resembling giant crisps), and *raita* (a delicious yoghurt chutney).

Had she noticed I hadn't said more than two words since I arrived? If so, she didn't let on, happily maintaining a steady flow of conversation while making a sizeable dent in the food laid out before us. With constant urging, I managed to eat a reasonable portion of rice and curry, leaving room for the inevitable barrage of sweets, wondering if I could sneak up to my room for a fortifying rum.

However, like most of my dreams in this world, it wasn't to be.

"Excuse me, Missy." Buddy shuffled into the room, his dusty bare feet leaving faint footprints on the polished white tiles. "There's been an accident."

Rather than looking at Anjali, Buddy darted glances at me with frightened doe eyes.

"Spit it out, man. What's happened?" Anjali spoiled her attempt at playing the imperious master standing over her servant by stuffing another ball of rice into her mouth with her curry-covered fingers and smacking her lips.

Buddy stared at me, panic-stricken. "It's the missy's bottles. They broke. Leak everywhere."

"Bottles? What bottles?" Anjali paused mid-chew, her plucked eyebrows shooting skyward.

I rarely swore. In fact, the F-word made me cringe. However, with my stomach rebelling against the onslaught of food, my nerves shot by the drive here, and my secret duty-free mojito stash now in ruins, all I could think was *fuuuuuck.*

• • •

I wanted to sleep in the next morning but Anjali didn't believe in jet lag. She believed in breakfast at the crack of dawn.

"Eat more, my girl. *Idlis* will give you strength for the day ahead." She pushed the tray of steamed rice cakes toward me along with the *sambhar*, a lentil soup thick with vegetables.

Not wanting to appear impolite on my first morning here, I spooned another *idli* onto my plate and ladled a sparrow's serving of *sambhar* over it. "What's on for today?"

"I've planned a grand tour of Mumbai especially for you." She held up a hand, fingers extended. "First stop, the Gateway of India."

One finger bent.

"Second, a boat cruise on the harbor."

Another finger lowered.

"Third, Chhatrapati Shivaji Terminus. Then Mani Bhavan, at the home of Mahatma Ghandi."

She waved her pinkie and I hoped our last stop included shopping.

"And finally, we eat at my favorite restaurant."

The thought of more food turned the *idlis* to lead in my stomach, and I edged my plate away. She didn't notice, her face glowing with pride, like a kid who nailed a test. I didn't have the heart to tell her I was more interested in Mumbai's malls than cultural icons.

"Sounds good." I injected enthusiasm into my voice, but it wasn't enough to distract Anjali as she eyed my plate and untouched *idli* with a frown.

Thankfully, Buddy entered the dining room and Anjali clapped her hands. "Time to go."

Relieved, I followed her to the car, thanking Buddy for holding open my door as I slid onto the back seat. He shuffled his feet in embarrassment but I caught the flicker of a bashful smile before he slipped behind the steering wheel. He'd been mortified over the duty-free bottle breakage, but what could I do? Confess to a secret alcohol stash? I'd brushed over the incident last night, citing special clear coconut juice I'd brought from the States before hiding the broken glass and condemning labels deeply in the trash. That's all I needed, for some nosy neighbor to out Anjali for secretly swigging alcohol.

As Buddy tested his Angry Birds skills—people were like the game app birds, seemingly flinging themselves at our car—I swallowed a curse. Oblivious to my morbid fear of inadvertently killing one of the many pedestrians jamming the sidewalks and spilling onto the road, Anjali stared at my hands, where I clutched at the worn leather.

"That's a lovely ring." She pointed at the ruby. "From someone special?"

"No." I released my grip on the seat to twist the ring around, wishing I didn't love it so much. Definitely not from someone special.

She didn't probe, her curiosity snagged by my watch. The gold link and diamond TAG had been a gift to myself with my first paycheck at Tate's law firm, a splurge I'd justified at the time by saying I needed to look the part at an upmarket practice, when in reality I'd wanted to impress the boss who'd already made a pass at me during the first two weeks.

"That a gift, too?"

Jeez, who was she, the jewelry police?

"A gift to myself."

Needing a change of topic fast, I pointed out the window. "That's the third cinema we've passed in a few blocks."

She craned her neck for a better look. "Nothing unusual. We're the movie capital of India, so there's a multiplex cinema on every street."

She had to be exaggerating, but as Buddy weaved in and out of the road chaos, I spotted five more.

"Personally, I prefer cable." Anjali rummaged around in her giant handbag and pulled out a *TV Soap* magazine. "Hundreds of channels, better viewing."

She flicked it open to a double-page spread of buffed guys with bare chests and brooding expressions. Not bad, if you liked that fake chiseled look. By the twinkle in Anjali's eye as she shoved the magazine my way, she did. "Bill Spencer is my favorite."

Clueless, I shrugged.

Horrified, she stabbed at a photo of a dark-haired, dark-eyed Adonis with rippling pecs and a serious six-pack. "Don Diamont. You've never heard of him? *The Young and the Restless*? Dollar Bill Spencer in *Bold and the Beautiful*?"

"Uh, no, I'm more of a rom-com gal."

Shaking her head, she snapped the magazine shut and thrust it into her bag, casting me a disbelieving glare. "I'm thinking Amrita did you a favor sending you here."

I didn't want to ask, but there was something cutesy and lovable about Anjali, and I couldn't resist. "Why, Auntie?"

"So I can educate you."

I stifled a snort. "About soap operas?"

"About *men*." She rattled her bag for emphasis. "These are the men you must aspire to. Handsome, tall, broad shoulders, rich."

"Fictional," I muttered, earning a click of her tongue.

She crossed her arms, hugging the bag and magazine to her chest. "You'll see. Once you ditch Anu's son, we can concentrate on finding you another boy."

I refrained from adding, "I want a *man*." No point encouraging her.

Buddy swerved into a narrow parking space between a cart and an auto-rickshaw. I didn't know what was worse: the promise of Anjali's matchmaking me with a soap-idol lookalike or the ensured whiplash every time I sat in a car.

"Good, we're here." She gathered the folds of her sari like a queen as she stepped from the car. "Where every tourist to Mumbai starts exploring." She threw her arms wide. "The Gateway of India."

I might not be a cultural chick but I had to admit the huge archway on the water's edge was impressive. Roughly sixty feet, it had four turrets and intricate latticework carved into the yellow stone. "What's this made from?"

"Basalt stone, very strong." Anjali linked her elbow through mine and drew me down the steps behind the arch to the water's edge. "Come, we'll take a short cruise on a motor launch."

I eyed the small, bobbing boats dubiously, hoping the captains steered more sedately than the drivers on the roads.

Anjali didn't give me a chance to refuse, slipping a launch operator some rupees and hustling me into a boat before I could feign seasickness. The motor launch shot off at a great speed and I clung onto the seat. Good thing I'd skipped the manicure before I met the Ramas. It'd be shredded by the end of today.

Anjali hadn't prepped me for the upcoming Rama meeting. Not to worry. Rita had more than made up for it. "The Rama welcoming party should be interesting."

"Coming face to face with Rakesh might be interesting." Anjali screwed up her nose. "Meeting that witch Anu?" She muttered a stream of Hindi, her tone vitriolic.

Witch? Intrigued, I waited for a pause. "So you know Anu?"

"You could say that." She folded her arms, her expression thunderous.

O-kay. Untold saga alert. Surprising Rita hadn't mentioned any history between her aunt and prospective mother-in-law. "Is there a problem between you—"

"Look." Anjali nudged me with her elbow and gestured toward the arch. Nice change of topic.

I conceded for now. "You were right—the view from here is fantastic."

The corners of her eyes crinkled with pride, as if she'd constructed the archway by hand. "It was built to commemorate the first-ever visit by a British monarch, King George V and Queen Mary in 1911."

"Interesting." She was distracting me with a tour guide spiel. I'd play along, lulling her into a false sense of security before resuming my interrogation. I pointed at a beautiful white-turreted, pink-domed building behind the arch. "What's that?"

"The Taj Mahal Palace." She touched the tip of her nose and raised it. "Very posh hotel."

"Maybe Rakesh will take me there?"

"Probably, if he's anything like his bragging mother." Anjali snorted. "I wouldn't know, I haven't been invited to the house yet to meet him, despite being the aunt of his betrothed." She made a disgusted clicking sound with her tongue. "Bet that's Anu's doing, too."

Fascinated by her obvious dislike for Rakesh's mom, I probed further.

"Hope she won't have to chaperone." I subtly sided with Anjali, hoping she'd elaborate.

Her lips thinned. "Don't worry about Anu. I'll deal with her; you take care of breaking the betrothal."

I scrutinized her, mulling her blatant antagonism. Why would a woman who'd been raised to accept arranged marriages be hell-bent on ruining one?

"Why are you helping Rita break her arrangement?"

Startled, Anjali shifted and the boat tipped alarmingly before righting. "Amrita is like a daughter to me. She deserves to choose her happiness."

Deep.

"Not all of us are so lucky." Anjali shrugged, the sadness tightening her mouth, making me wish I hadn't probed.

"What about Senthil? What's he like?" I hoped switching from marriage back to the Ramas would divert her attention.

"Very fine musician." Her lips clamped into a thin, unimpressed line before she turned away.

Guess discussing the Ramas hit a sore spot.

I pointed at a nearby island. "Is that temple significant?"

While Anjali prattled on about nearby Elephanta Island where the Temple Cave of Lord Shiva could be found, I pondered her revelations. She knew next to nothing about Rakesh, admired Senthil's musical skills, and despised Anu. It shouldn't have mattered, but her dislike for Rakesh's mom made me uneasy. If Anjali had another agenda, one I knew nothing about, it could jeopardize our entire scheme. Like I wasn't anxious enough.

I focused on the Mumbai skyline, captured by the complexity of this cosmopolitan city. I'd been here a day and barely scratched the surface, but from what I'd seen on Anjali's grand tour so far I was starting to get a feel for the place.

"You're awfully quiet," Anjali said as the boat docked and I helped her step onto land.

"Just taking it all in." The sights, and the mysterious disclosures.

She patted my arm. "Don't worry about meeting the Ramas. If Rakesh is anything like his father, you'll be fine."

"What's Senthil like?"

"Nice enough." She shrugged, her blasé response belied by a quick look-away.

"Shame I'll be dealing more with Anu and not him."

Anjali frowned. "Be careful with her. She's astute and devious." She made a slitting sign across her throat. "Cunning as a rat. Dangerous when confronted."

Uh-oh. The last thing I needed: a perceptive psycho. My nervousness morphed into full-blown terror.

Before I could discover more, Buddy pulled up and we piled back into the car, his presence effectively ending further communication about the Rama plot. When Anjali started rummaging in her bag, I braced for another hottie fix-up. Instead, she pulled out a snack bag. "*Sev?*"

"No thanks." The refusal was barely out of my mouth before she popped the fine, crunchy, deep-fried strands of chickpea dough into hers. By the time she finished the bag we'd arrived at our next stop, the biggest train station I'd ever seen.

I should stop pestering her and drop the subject of the Ramas, but the tidbits she'd revealed had only served to rattle me and I needed reassurance.

As we left the car, I tapped her on the shoulder. "Auntie, I'm a little concerned."

"About?"

"Meeting the Ramas." How to phrase this without getting her riled? "If Anu's so shrewd, won't she see through me?" And worse, reenact some of that throat-slitting action Anjali had mimed.

"We won't fail." Anjali squared her shoulders, ready for battle. "If she tries to intimidate you or harass you, she'll have me to deal with, the sneaky snake. She's a ghastly, horrid—"

"This place is still functional, Auntie?" I'd had enough of Anjali's adjectives. I got it. She hated Anu's guts and further questioning would only contribute to her blood pressure skyrocketing if the ugly puce staining her cheeks and sweat beads rolling down her forehead were any indication. Besides, the more wound up she got, the more I wondered what the hell I'd become embroiled in. If Anu discovered my treachery... I suppressed a shudder.

Anjali took a deep breath and exhaled, hopefully purging her angst. "Yes. Very busy place and the second UNESCO World Heritage site." She dabbed at the corners of her mouth and dusted off her hands. "Chhatrapati Shivaji Terminus was formerly known as Victoria Terminal."

My very own walking, talking encyclopedia. Goody.

"It's amazing," I said, unsure where to look first as we

bid farewell to a patient Buddy again and joined the throng surging toward the station.

Grand Central in NYC might be impressive but this place was something else entirely. A staggering feat of architecture, the station had countless archways and spires and domes and clocks that were an astounding combination of neo-Gothic, early Victorian, and traditional Indian.

As we entered, Anjali pointed to a platform. "Over one thousand trains pass through here daily. Efficient, yes?"

I nodded. "How many passengers?"

"About three million." She said it so casually, I could've mistaken it for 3,000.

"Wow, this place is incredible."

We strolled through the station, admiring the architecture, the wood carvings, brass railings, ornamental iron, and precise detail engraved into every stone.

As we neared the entrance, Anjali touched an archway with reverence. "So sad, the smog and acid rain is damaging this beauty."

I had to agree.

"Next stop, my favorite restaurant." Anjali rubbed her hands together in glee while my stomach rolled over in revolt.

I didn't dare ask why we'd skipped seeing Ghandi's home. I knew. She'd been so rattled by my less-than-subtle harping about Anu, she needed to comfort eat. Besides, getting into a car here was living dangerously. Getting between Anjali and her apparent love of food? I wasn't that brave. "Restaurant?"

"No tour is complete without a stop at Chowpatty Beach."

A beach? Good, maybe I could walk off the inevitable

gormandizing.

We made small-talk as Buddy commandeered the streets, dodging buses belching diesel fume and carts and people, so many people. Interestingly, my death grip on the seat had loosened considerably by the time we reached the beach. I must've been growing accustomed to the chaos.

Anjali gestured toward the shore. "Now we eat."

We abandoned Buddy and headed for the sand, the lack of restaurants confusing me.

Reading my mind, Anjali pointed to a row of street vendors lining the beach. "The best *bhel-puri* ever."

I'd never tried the renowned *chaat*, fast-food. With Anjali dragging me toward the nearest stall, it looked like I was about to.

She ordered and I watched, fascinated, as the young guy manning the stall dexterously laid out a neat row of *papadi* (small, crisp fried *puris*—flatbreads) and filled them with a mix of puffed rice, *sev*, onions, potatoes, green chilies, and an array of chutneys.

I may not have been hungry but the tantalizing aromas of tamarind, mango, and coriander made my mouth water.

"My treat." I paid the vendor, who gawked at Anjali as she popped three *bhel-puris* in her mouth in quick succession.

I laughed, loving her exuberance for food, more accustomed to it—even after a day—than the vendor.

"What's so funny?" she mumbled, eyeing the remaining three.

"I'm just happy to be here." I took one and shoved the other two in her direction.

"You sure?"

I nodded. "Positive."

She didn't wait, tossing the *bhel puris* in her mouth and sighing with pleasure.

That good, huh? I nibbled at mine, the instant sweet/sour/spicy explosion on my tastebuds making me want to demolish it as fast as Anjali. Maybe I shouldn't have been so quick to pass on the others…

Anjali grinned at what I assumed was my orgasmic expression. "We'll come back here one evening. You'll be amazed."

"By more food?"

She gestured toward the sand. "By everything. The beach is transformed with ferry and pony rides, balloon sellers, astrologers, contortionists, snake charmers, monkey-trainers, masseurs." She snapped her fingers. "You name it, this place has it. Very entertaining to people-watch."

Glancing at the smallish crowd, most of them dozing in the shade of trees, I couldn't imagine the carnival atmosphere she described. Would be well worth another visit.

Yeah, for the *bhel-puri,* too.

"Sounds great. What about tonight?"

She shook her head. "No can do. *Glee* finale."

I stifled a grin at her addiction to TV, along with food.

She rubbed her belly and winced—no great surprise considering what she'd stuffed in there. "Time to head home and rest."

Good. My mind spun with all I'd seen, and I couldn't wait to fill Rita in on the gossip.

Plus I needed to steel my nerves to meet the Ramas. My rapidly dwindling confidence had taken a hit following Anjali's disclosures about Anu.

This could get messy.

Looking for contemporary romance with a sexy fantasy twist? Check out RADIANT DESIRE by Inara Scott!

The object of every man's fantasy just lost her wings…

Kaia Verde is one of the four Faerie Handmaids of Zafira, Queen of the Fey. To redress an ancient wrong done to Zafira by a human king, the Handmaids make sport of mortal men, seducing and humiliating them. When Kaia sets out to seduce Garrett Jameson, but ends up being the one surrendering to pleasure, Zafira is furious. Kaia's punishment is simple: make Garrett fall in love with her by the summer solstice, then break his heart, or face eternity without her wings—or her soul. To make the task harder, Zafira tells Kaia she cannot use her faerie magic or charm to lure Garrett into her bed.

…and now she's losing her heart…

Kaia thinks her task will be relatively easy—as a faerie, she understands lust, and can love be much different? But once she is living among the humans, Kaia discovers the race she once disparaged is far more complex and beautiful than she imagined. She learns before she can break Garrett's heart, she must find a way to heal it. And eventually, discovers that losing her wings may be a far easier price to pay than losing her heart.